Lessons Learned

Sydney Logan

Dedication

To my parents,
who taught me it was okay to ask questions
and have an opinion, even if it wasn't the
most popular one. I love you.

1 Samuel 16:7

"Tolerance implies no lack of commitment to one's own beliefs. Rather it condemns the oppression or persecution of others."

John F. Kennedy

Table of Contents

Acknowledgements

To T.M. Franklin, who designed the beautiful cover for this second edition. Thank you for your friendship.

To Wyndy Dee, my lead editor, who told me she cried while reading my manuscript. For a new author with little confidence, it was exactly what I needed to hear. You continue to be a guiding light in my writing career. Thank you.

To Kathie Spitz, who has always been my biggest cheerleader and most importantly, my friend. You held my hand from start to finish, and I am beyond grateful.

To Shaina Hanson, who has stood by my side since the very beginning of this writing journey. Thank you for being my friend.

To Krista Richmond, thank you for reading every word of this manuscript and offering valuable advice.

To Rebekah Moss, who designed the first book trailer. Thank you for sharing your talents.

Thank you to the readers and book bloggers who embraced this book from the very beginning. Your continued support means the world to me.

To my sister, Jodie — See? No scrunchies. :)

And finally, to my husband. You are my very own "Lucas." I love you.

Prologue

Voices roar through the high school cafeteria as students navigate their way to the tables. The cliques are easily spotted: the jocks, the geeks, the beauty queens, the slackers.

Where will he sit today?

Despite the fact he's a handsome and impeccably dressed young man, he fades into the background. Knowing it's pointless, the girls don't bother to look his way, and the guys deliberately avoid his eyes.

He grips his tray tightly and heads toward the corner table with the rest of the outcasts. They nod hello, but that's the end of any real attempt at conversation. It's an unspoken rule of sorts. This is their refuge—a tiny bit of sanctuary in the hell that is public high school—and they're content to sit in peace.

He takes a seat, and I can see the exhaustion on his face. It's not a weariness that comes from too many sleepless nights. This is a bone-tired fatigue no seventeen-year-old kid should ever feel.

He's giving in.

Giving up.

In my peripheral vision, I see a senior stalk into the cafeteria. He's tall, with deep brown eyes and jet-black hair that won't stay in place. He's good looking, popular, and a little conceited, thanks to his father's wealth and status.

He has a reputation to uphold.

Rumors to squash.

A score to settle.

He pulls the silver gun out of his jacket pocket. Amid the chaos, no one notices.

I notice.

I try to run, but I'm frozen in place.

I try to scream, but there's no sound.

The first shot rings out, and suddenly, everyone's on the cold tile.

Tears, prayers, screams.

Another shot, and for some reason, I'm the only one who can't move. Who can't scream. Who can't do anything but watch as the young man's body slumps over his tray.

Finally, I find my voice and scream his name.

Chapter One

The piercing chime of my phone jerked me awake. Disoriented and shaking, I grabbed my cell and struggled to focus on the screen.

Congratulations, Sarah. You slept a whole three hours.

Falling asleep had been difficult. My restlessness could easily be blamed on yesterday's long drive or spending the night in a new place, but I hadn't slept well in months, so my fitful sleep wasn't all that surprising.

However, I could do without the nightmares.

It was nearly three in the morning when I'd finally arrived in Sycamore Falls. Exhausted from the drive, I'd collapsed on the couch, but sleeping proved impossible. It was just too quiet. I'd grown accustomed to noisy neighbors and blasting car horns.

A change of scenery could be exactly what I need, my

therapist had told me.

Sycamore Falls was definitely a change in scenery.

Stiff and sore from the uncomfortable couch, I groaned as I struggled to sit up. My body trembled when my bare feet hit the hardwood floor. I'd forgotten how cold this house could be, even in the summer, but anything with long sleeves would be in a box, and all the boxes were arranged in a chaotic mess in my living room.

Maybe some sunshine will warm me up.

I wrapped my blanket around me and circled the maze of boxes before shuffling toward the kitchen. It was neat and tidy as ever, with its faded yellow wallpaper. Grandma Grace had always loved wildflowers, and I smiled as I gazed at the collection of daisy canisters lining the wall next to the sink. Mom had been a terrible cook, so grandma had taken it upon herself to teach me. Baking was my favorite, and we'd spent countless nights in this kitchen with my apron covered in flour. Grandma had been fine with making a mess—as long as I cleaned it up—and that freedom had led to many honest discussions throughout the years.

"Sycamore Falls has its issues," Grandma had told me one autumn day while teaching me how to make fried apple pies. "We're too sheltered from the rest of the world. Sometimes that's a good thing. Sometimes it isn't. The world can be a scary place. It's good to know you have a safe place to come home to when the world gets a little crazy. You're one of the lucky ones, Sarah. You will always have a home here. Remember that."

I remember.

I opened the front door and was instantly greeted with cool morning air. Eager to see the house in the daylight, I gingerly walked down the steps and onto the sidewalk. Thankfully, Mr. Johnson had hired someone to mow the grass before I arrived, which allowed me to mark one thing off my to-do list.

As I gazed up at the house, I could see my list would be

long.

Growing up, I'd thought my grandmother's home was the most beautiful in Sycamore Falls. Majestic and blue with its white shutters and wrap-around porch, it was the place I'd always felt the most comfortable and safe.

Time hadn't been kind to the house, and that was my fault. Mr. Johnson had done his best, but a house needs tender loving care, and its last two years without an occupant had been rough on the place. The chipped siding needed a coat of paint, the flowerbeds resembled a jungle, and some of the shingles needed to be replaced, but none of that mattered.

I felt a small sense of satisfaction and breathed a sigh of relief.

I was safe.

I was home.

"Tell me you're joking. There can't be only fifteen hundred people in that town."

The dilapidated city sign proudly displaying the town's population passed my window in a blur.

"I didn't say fifteen hundred. I said fourteen hundred ninety-nine."

I felt a little guilty. After all, some poor soul was going to have to change the sign. Then again, with a town boasting the highest unemployment rate in the state, someone could probably use the work.

"I still don't understand why you moved back," Monica said. "You've never wanted to return to your hometown."

"I want to teach in a small town."

"Sarah, there are small towns just outside of Memphis."

"I want to teach here."

Monica's voice became a whisper. "Because it's safe?"

"Because it's home."

It was a simple answer and so much easier than the

truth.

After promising to call tomorrow, I tossed my cell onto the passenger seat and gazed at the highway. Monica was my best friend, but she couldn't understand my turmoil. Granted, she'd stood by my side through it all, but she wasn't the one consumed with memories and needing a fresh start.

She couldn't possibly understand.

Breathing deeply, I flexed my fingers around the steering wheel and tried to concentrate on the scenery. The two-lane highway leading into town was surrounded by nothing but countryside and brimming with wildflowers. As I crept closer to the city limits, the mountain range became visible, standing tall and proud and unbelievably green.

I reached for the radio dial and pressed a button in search of the local station. I grinned when John Cooper's gravelly voice filled the air. The man had to be in his sixties by now, and his tired tone reflected those years. Coop had been on the air every weekday afternoon since I'd been a kid. He hadn't been very popular with the teens because he'd played oldies instead of anything remotely current. When his raspy voice introduced a George Jones song, I smiled.

It was just further proof that very little changed in Sycamore Falls.

"Sarah Bray, is that you?"

It was only the eighth time I'd heard those words in the past hour, but who was counting?

Sighing softly, I closed the freezer door and dropped the ice cream into my grocery cart. When I turned around, I was greeted with the pearly white smile of Shellie Stevens.

"It *is* you!" Shellie clapped her hands, reminding me of

the regional basketball game when she had fallen from the top of the cheerleading pyramid, landing face first onto the gymnasium floor. I vividly recalled the blood and her horrified expression when she realized her two front teeth had been broken.

But that was a long time ago, and it would probably be impolite to mention it now.

"Hi, Shellie. How are you?"

"I heard you were back in town. Teaching at the high school, I hear."

"Yes, I am."

"I'm the cheerleading coach." She smoothed her hair with her palm. It was still long and blond and straight out of the bottle.

"Are you a teacher, too?"

"Nope, I'm a dental hygienist over in Winslow."

How ironic.

"You don't have to teach to be a coach," she explained. In small towns, it was sometimes hard to find good coaches. It was even harder to keep them here.

I smiled. "Well, I'm sure you're a wonderful cheer coach."

"You'll make the second new teacher this school year. One just recently moved here from New York to take Mr. Franklin's place," Shellie said as she followed me down the produce aisle.

Charles Franklin had been my American history teacher my sophomore year. His was the only class besides English I'd truly enjoyed.

"Did he retire?"

"He suffered a stroke and passed away in March."

"Oh, I'm sorry to hear that."

"We miss him." Then, her face brightened. "But wait until you see the new teacher. He's single and so handsome. Rumor has it he was in the middle of some big scandal up North and moved to the mountains to make a fresh start. Kind of like you, actually."

The people in Sycamore Falls probably knew as much about his "scandal" as they knew about mine, but that wouldn't stop them from gossiping. I wondered if the poor guy had any idea what he was getting himself into by moving to a small town.

After exchanging phone numbers, Shellie headed for the checkout while I grabbed what I needed and dodged other friendly faces. It was useless. Pastor Martin caught me in the deli and invited me to church. Lee Ann Patterson, a former classmate, asked if we could meet for dinner one night this week, and Imogene Jordan found me near the bread aisle. She brought tears to my eyes by telling me I was beautiful—just like my mother.

By the time I made it to the cashier, I was an emotional mess.

"You're Grace's granddaughter. Sarah, I believe."

"That's right. How are you, Mrs. Thomas?"

"Oh, you remember me," she said with a smile. My grandmother and Catherine Thomas used to sit together at church every Sunday morning. The woman had to be eighty years old by now. "Are you all settled in?"

"Getting there. I still have some unpacking to do."

She began to scan my items, and I briefly panicked when I realized I didn't have enough cash. I'd so rarely carried it in Memphis.

"Are you all right?"

"I only have a debit card," I whispered, completely embarrassed and thankful no one was in line behind me.

"Oh, that's fine, dear. We accept credit or debit," Catherine explained, pointing to the little machine attached to her register. "We just have the one phone line, though."

I jumped when she yelled at the manager to get off the phone so she could swipe a card. Just then, a teenage boy appeared out of nowhere and bagged my groceries.

"Grace would be so happy you've come home." Mrs. Thomas handed me the receipt to sign. "She always hoped you would, you know."

Emotion bubbled inside of me as I scribbled my name. "No, I didn't know."

"Oh yes, Grace always said a young girl needs to spread her wings, but a young woman needs roots, as well. That's why she left the house to you in her will. She knew you'd be back someday. She was such a sweet, sweet lady."

I thanked her and followed the young man and my groceries to my car.

"Are you the new teacher?"

Smiling, I pressed the remote to open the trunk. "I'm one of them, yes. Are you in high school?"

"Yeah, I'm Matt. I'll be a senior this year." He was grinning proudly, like all seniors tend to do. Carefully, he placed my groceries in the car. "So, what will you teach?"

"English literature."

"To seniors?"

"Yes."

He closed my trunk and smiled. "That's cool. You're a lot prettier than Mrs. Perry. Maybe I'll take English lit after all."

"I'm afraid you don't have a choice. It's required."

He frowned. That was something else about seniors. They hated to be reminded about graduation requirements.

"Enjoy the rest of your summer vacation," I said with a grin. Matt waved, but he was still sulking as I climbed into my car and drove away.

After dropping off the groceries at home, I drove across town to Mr. Johnson's Hardware Store. I was gazing in confusion at all the various paint samples when I heard a friendly voice.

"Sarah Bray, you're as pretty as a picture."

His hair was now completely gray, but his smile was still sweet.

"Hi, Mr. Johnson," I said, grinning at the man. Thanks

for taking care of the lawn. I hope you didn't mow it yourself."

He laughed. "I'm too old to mow, Sarah, but I was happy to find someone who could do it. Going to paint that old house of Grace's?"

"Well, I'm going to buy the paint. I'm hoping to hire someone to paint it for me. You wouldn't happen to know—"

"I know just the person!" Mr. Johnson smiled broadly. "I'll be right back."

Well, that was easy. Of course, I shouldn't have been surprised. Mr. Johnson knew everyone in Sycamore Falls.

I turned my attention back to the wall and thumbed through the shaded cards. There were literally forty shades of blue, and I groaned in frustration.

"I know. They all look the same to me, too."

The accent was warm and soft and undeniably Northern. When I turned around, I was staring into a pair of beautiful crystal-blue eyes.

"Wow," I whispered. I scanned the paint swatches, wondering if such a shade of blue would look good on the exterior of my house.

"Mr. Johnson said you might need help selecting paint."

"It's impossible," I muttered. "I just wanted to buy some blue paint. Why is this so complicated?"

The handsome man stepped closer to my side. "It isn't, really. Just pick what you like."

I like crystal-blue. Luckily, I didn't say those words aloud.

"I need to paint my grandmother's old house—well, my house now."

"Mr. Johnson says you've just moved back to Sycamore Falls."

I sighed. The prodigal daughter returning home from the big, bad city was sure to make the local tongues wag.

"Why are you making that face?"

"What are they saying about me?" Nervously, I glanced

at the men over my shoulder. Mr. Johnson and two other customers were huddled around the cash register and watching us intently with gigantic smirks on their faces.

He shrugged. "Not much. Just that your name is Sarah Bray and you're a teacher. Your parents died when you were sixteen and your grandmother raised you until you went away to college. You taught for a while in Memphis, and now you're living in your grandmother's old house. You'll be teaching at the high school when classes start in two weeks."

I laughed.

"Not much, huh? That's pretty much my life story."

He smiled. "Not really. I don't know *why* you left Memphis. I'm Lucas Miller, by the way."

"It's nice to meet you." I managed to tear my eyes away from his long enough to focus on the samples. "So, Lucas Miller, which shade of blue do you recommend for the exterior of a house?"

Lucas motioned to the adjacent aisle, and I groaned when I saw yet another vibrant wall of colors.

"For starters, you need to be looking at *exterior* paint." He was failing miserably at hiding his smirk.

"There's a difference?"

This time he laughed loudly. "Have you ever painted a house?"

"No."

"Do you plan on painting this house yourself?"

"I was actually hoping to hire someone to do it, which is probably a good thing considering I can't even pick out the paint."

"You could hire me."

"You're a painter?"

"No, but I have some experience in construction, and I have a few weeks off. I'm just working here to earn some extra money over the summer."

Lucas looked to be about my age, and I wondered what he actually did for a living. He knew my entire life story.

Would it be inappropriate for me to ask?

Probably so.

"You could paint it in two weeks?"

"I think so, if the weather cooperates."

"I couldn't pay you much."

"You could pay me with dinner."

Of course, Mr. Handyman would be a flirt. "You'd paint my entire house in exchange for dinner?"

"Well, Mr. Johnson says you must be a great cook because your grandmother taught you everything you know."

"Mr. Johnson knows entirely too much about my life."

"I think he probably knows everything about everyone," he said with a laugh. "So, am I hired?"

I eyed him skeptically. "Don't you even want to see the house first?"

"No need."

"Why not?"

Lucas grinned. "Who do you think mowed your lawn?"

"I really appreciate you doing that," I said with a laugh.

His face grew thoughtful. "The house needs a lot of work, Sarah."

"I know. I don't suppose you do landscaping, too?"

"I do a bit of everything," Lucas said, "although, landscaping might cost you *two* dinners."

Mr. Johnson and his buddies cackled at the register.

I wasn't interested in dating—even if he did have a chiseled chin and pretty blue eyes—but dinners in exchange for labor seemed like a sweet arrangement to me.

"It's a deal. When can you start?"

"Tomorrow," he replied, grinning brightly and shaking my hand.

Chapter Two

After choosing Rocky Mountain Sky Blue and thanking the conniving, yet helpful, Mr. Johnson, I drove over to my old high school to look around.

Walking the halls of Sycamore High as a teacher instead of a student was a little surreal. Never in my wildest dreams did I ever believe I'd return to my former school, but here I was, standing in the doorway of Room 108—the very room in which I'd discovered my hatred for Shakespeare and my love for Poe.

There were some subtle differences. There were more computers along the wall, and to my absolute joy, the ancient green chalkboard had been replaced with a dry-erase board. Otherwise, my old English classroom looked exactly the same.

It was oddly comforting.

Slowly, I walked over and took a seat behind the teacher's desk. In Mrs. Perry's mad dash into retirement, she'd forgotten her wooden nameplate. My fingers ghosted over the etched letters, and I smiled as I remembered my former teacher. She wore her pink lipstick a little too brightly, and her pantyhose always had runs, but she was passionate about books and loved her students.

"I thought I heard someone in here," a soft voice echoed from the door. I looked up to see a sweet, familiar face standing in my doorway.

"Aubrey," I said with a smile.

Aubrey Bryant and I had been best friends from the first day of kindergarten until I hit my rebellious teenage years and ignored everyone who'd ever meant anything to me. I had convinced myself that if I didn't care about anyone, then it wouldn't hurt so much if they abandoned me. In the process, I'd lost every friend I'd ever known, including Aubrey.

She took a seat in one of the student desks and offered me a sweet smile.

"I was just doing some work in my classroom. It's so good to have you home."

"Thank you," I said, hating how awkward this felt. "What do you teach?"

"Algebra and Geometry."

I wasn't surprised. If it hadn't been for Aubrey, I never would have made it through Ms. Kelly's math class during our freshman year.

"How are you?"

It was such a simple question, so I decided to be honest.

"Overwhelmed, I think. But it's a good overwhelmed. I just have so much to do before school starts."

"Me too." She grew quiet then, and I sensed what was coming. "Sarah, I heard about what happened in Memphis. I can't even imagine what that must have been like for you."

14

Not trusting myself to speak, I merely nodded.

"We were all so worried. You see something like that on the news and you just can't believe it's real."

"It's real," I whispered, my voice breaking. "It was very, very real."

Suddenly, she was kneeling at my side, whispering soothingly. We hadn't spoken to each other in over eight years, and yet here she was, promising me things were going to be all right now.

I wanted so desperately to believe her.

We shared a hug, and she pulled a chair close to mine as she began telling me about her life. Not surprisingly, she'd married Tommy Bryant, former star quarterback and her high school sweetheart. They had a three-year-old, and Tommy taught P.E. and coached the football team.

"I'm so glad you're here," Taking my hand, she led me over to the supplies closet to show me what few materials Mrs. Perry had left behind. "We have a really wonderful school and plenty of great kids who want to learn. Their goals are pretty much like ours had been when we were their age—to graduate and get the hell out of Sycamore Falls."

I couldn't help but smile. Some things never changed.

"And yet, here we are."

"Here we are," Aubrey laughed quietly. "It's strange how things work out, isn't it? I mean, Tommy and I wanted to get as far away from this place as possible, but we're still in Sycamore Falls, happy and content."

Either Mrs. Perry didn't use many supplies or she took them with her, because the closet was practically empty, except for some old textbooks that I was sure we'd used back when I was in school.

"We did," Aubrey replied when I mentioned it. "Mrs. Perry hated new textbooks. The newest editions are probably stuffed in a closet somewhere."

I dropped into one of the desks and took a good look around. The walls used to be white, but the room was definitely in need of a fresh coat of paint.

"It's a little dreary, isn't it?" Aubrey murmured, reading my mind.

"Just a little, yeah."

"You know," she said with a wicked grin, "I bet Rocky Mountain Sky Blue would look great in here."

My eyes widened in disbelief. Aubrey laughed loudly, and the sound filled the empty room.

"Oh, Sarah, don't look so surprised! Did you forget how quickly gossip spreads in Sycamore Falls?"

"No, but that was *literally* an hour ago. How did you hear?"

"Tommy and Lucas are best friends. His classroom is right next to yours, actually."

I was confused.

"But you said Tommy teaches gym."

"I'm not talking about Tommy," Aubrey said. "Lucas will be teaching American History right beside you."

Suddenly, I remembered Shellie's description of the new history teacher.

Single. Handsome. Northern.

"Funny, he didn't mention that."

She grinned brightly. "Lucas moved here from New York about four months ago. At first, everyone was a little suspicious. After all, who would willingly move away from Manhattan to live *here*?"

I nodded. It was a fair question.

"But he was the only applicant for Mr. Franklin's job," she continued. "He needed a job until the new school year started, so Mr. Johnson hired him part-time down at the hardware store. He's even helped Tommy a bit with summer football practice. The community has really grown to love him."

"Lucas seems very nice."

"He is," Aubrey replied with a nod. "Still, you have to wonder what brought him here. He says he just needed a change, but *something* must have happened."

Ah, yes, the supposed scandal.

"Maybe he just wanted to teach in a small town."

"That's what he told Tommy," Aubrey nodded, but I could tell by the tone of her voice she wasn't convinced.

Suddenly, her eyes brightened. "He's a really sweet guy, Sarah, and he's single!"

And so it begins.

"No, Aubrey."

"Are you single?"

"Yes, and I intend to stay that way."

"But why?"

I narrowed my eyes. "Are you actually pouting?"

"Maybe," she admitted with a giggle.

I rolled my eyes. Aubrey had always loved playing matchmaker.

"He's super nice, Sarah."

"I'm sure he's wonderful. I hope he's equally as wonderful at painting my house because he starts tomorrow."

She grinned. "I know. He told Tommy."

"And Tommy told you." I shook my head and smiled. "You know, despite the annoying gossip mill, it's still comforting to be home."

Aubrey's face softened.

"Will you tell me about it someday?"

"Maybe someday."

Taking a deep breath, I asked the question that had been weighing heavily on my mind since returning to Sycamore Falls. "Aubrey, do you think I'm a coward for coming home?"

She smiled sympathetically and reached for my hand.

"After what you've been through, I don't think anyone would have blamed you if you'd completely left the profession. Trust me. No one here thinks you're a coward."

Tommy had football practice at five, so Aubrey had to get home to the baby. While walking each other to our cars, she invited me over for dinner, and I promised to come one night this week.

Aubrey opened her car door before turning to me. She pulled me into a hug and whispered, "I'm so glad you're home. I've missed you."

I squeezed her tightly.

"I've missed you, too."

On my way home, I took a detour down Main Street to see if anything had changed. There were three new fast food places, and the medical clinic appeared to have had a renovation. Benji's Diner was still open for business, and the old men still congregated in rocking chairs on the restaurant's porch, offering a friendly wave to anyone who happened to pass by.

That's the great thing about the country. People are friendly and welcoming, and they actually smile at you, even if they don't know your name.

It was such a stark contrast to the city.

Attending college in Memphis had been like moving to another planet. I'd shared a dorm with Monica, a beautiful African American girl who had clawed her way out of the ghetto with dreams of becoming a college professor. Despite the fact we had nothing in common except for a few education classes, we had become best friends.

I had embraced my life in Memphis, dating a little and making new friends. Listening to jazz on Beale Street became my favorite weekend activity. That's where I'd met Ryan, a music major from Little Rock who loved to play the saxophone. We dated until my demons—both past and present—became too much for him to handle.

Once I arrived back at the house, I quickly unloaded the paint supplies before heading to the living room to begin the miserable process of unpacking. The thick burgundy curtains made the room a little dim, so I reached for a lamp.

A thousand memories flooded me as the room was illuminated in a soft yellow haze.

Running my hands along the faded white walls, I paused briefly when my fingers came into contact with the old framed photographs. My grandmother had loved taking pictures, and I'd always been her favorite subject.

I'd been such a happy child; the girl in the frame was proof. Dangling upside down from a tree with my brown pigtails and cute dimples, it was hard to fathom that this brave kid used to be me.

Once upon a time, I had been fearless.

I suppose youth has a strange way of making you foolishly courageous.

At the end of the row of photographs was my favorite picture of my parents. Mom was in her simple white dress and dad was wearing his best Sunday suit as they smiled into each other's eyes on their wedding day. I'd spent my childhood gazing at the picture, desperate to grow up and find a love just like theirs—full of mutual respect and complete adoration for one another.

I still believed their marriage was a fairy tale.

With a heavy heart and tears prickling my eyes, I trailed my finger along the glass frame, wiping away the dust.

I missed them.

The rest of the day was spent cleaning and unpacking. I had two weeks until school started, which was good, because it would take me that long to get the house organized. As I carried a box upstairs, I noticed the wooden banister was a little loose. I mentally added it to my repair list before opening the door to my old bedroom.

A new wave of memories washed over me, leaving me breathless.

My room was just as I'd left it.

The walls were faded green and an embarrassing display of everything I'd loved when I was a teenager. Sycamore High School pennants hung above the bed and a few basketball trophies lined the top of the bookshelf. A Kenny Chesney concert photograph was displayed on one wall while a Coldplay poster hung proudly on the other.

Clearly, I'd been a musically confused teenager, as one had absolutely nothing to do with the other.

While exploring the room, I spotted my dad's old record player. Growing up, I'd collected vinyl records like most girls collected Barbie dolls, and I'd begged Mr. Johnson to keep a supply of record needles on hand, just for me.

I glanced toward my closet and smiled.

Standing on tiptoe, I opened the door and pulled my record collection from the top shelf. Collapsing on the floor, I sighed longingly as I flipped through the album covers. I'd stolen many of the records from my dad's old collection, and seeing Creedence Clearwater Revival mixed in with Michael Jackson's *Thriller* proved my musical confusion spanned the decades.

Or maybe I just liked good music, regardless of the labels.

I needed a place to sleep, so I placed MJ on the turntable and spent the rest of the evening cleaning my old room. I stripped the bed, added fresh linens, and dusted every flat surface. When the old grandfather clock echoed from downstairs, I felt a distinct tiredness wash over me. It was almost a conditioned response. For two years of my life, that chime had signaled the end of the day.

It was such a comforting sound.

Later, while lying in bed, I thought about my first day back in my little hometown. The people in Sycamore Falls were just the same—sweet, friendly, and nosy. I'd expected all of those things. What I hadn't expected was the constant mention of my family and my emotional reaction to it.

Would it get any easier?

I hoped so.

I closed my eyes, and with Michael Jackson serenading

me, I fell into a dreamless sleep.

Chapter Three

With a weary groan, I glanced at the clock on my nightstand.

7:00 a.m.

What the hell?

Jumping out of bed, I rushed over to the window to see who was waking me up at such an ungodly hour. It was a beautiful mountain morning, but the scenery paled in comparison to the handsome man with the weed eater, plowing his way through my jungle of shrubs.

Far too eager to say hello, I took the quickest shower in history and threw on a vintage tee and capris before I headed to the kitchen. It wasn't long before bacon was sizzling on the stove. I had no idea what Lucas liked to drink, and I didn't own a coffee maker, so I poured two glasses of juice and hoped for the best.

As I stepped onto the porch, my body froze.

"Sarah, you look stunned."

I *was* stunned. You could actually see my grandmother's flowers now—all reds and purples and unbelievably pretty.

"I hope you don't mind," Lucas said, gauging my reaction as he slipped on his shirt. "Tommy suggested I start with the flowerbeds. His exact words were, 'You are bound to get snake bit in that yard of hers.' So, to avoid death by rattlesnake, I decided to do some landscaping."

I laughed. "Your accent needs a little work."

"Well, Tommy's accent is impossible to imitate," Lucas said, grinning at me as he climbed the porch steps. "Good morning, Sarah."

"Good morning. I brought you some orange juice."

He thanked me and quickly guzzled it down.

"I've started breakfast. Bacon and eggs okay?"

"Bacon and eggs sound great."

It was a little awkward, inviting him inside. After all, he was a stranger, but Tommy and Aubrey loved him, so I figured it was safe. I pointed toward the downstairs bathroom, and he went to wash up while I scrambled the eggs and popped bread into the toaster. I was just placing everything on the kitchen table when he returned.

"So you're not mad?"

The question surprised me. "Why would I be mad?"

Lucas took a seat at the table. "I wasn't exactly forthcoming with information yesterday. I probably should have told you I was teaching at the high school, too."

"I'm not mad," I replied, pouring him another glass of juice before sitting down. "I was just surprised. Why didn't you tell me?"

"You didn't ask."

"Well, that's because I'd known you for thirty seconds."

He bowed his head and looked appropriately ashamed. "If I clean out the gutters, will you forgive me?"

"Possibly," I smirked.

23

"You're all heart." He grinned at me and reached for another biscuit. I had to bite my lip to keep from laughing. Something told me Lucas was a true bachelor and hadn't had a home cooked meal in ages.

"Shellie and Aubrey told me you're from New York City."

He looked confused. "Who's Shellie?"

"Maybe she goes by Michelle now? We called her Shellie back in school."

"Oh, the cheerleading coach?" Lucas asked, grimacing slightly when I nodded. "She's uh . . . been really friendly."

I could just imagine. Shellie had always been a shameless flirt.

"Yes, I'm from New York City," he said, eager to change the subject. "I received my bachelor's degree from NYU, and I've been teaching history for the past five years."

"That's how long I've been teaching, too."

"So we're probably pretty close in age," Lucas hedged shyly.

"Probably so. I'm twenty-seven."

"Me too."

Lucas lifted the gallon of juice and poured each of us another glass. If there was a scandal, he certainly didn't seem eager to share it, which I could appreciate. My situation wasn't exactly a secret, but I still wasn't ready to talk about it.

He thanked me for breakfast, and I followed him back outside to find a ladder already propped against the house.

I cast a sideways glance at him.

"You already cleaned out the gutters, didn't you?"

He chuckled. "Possibly."

Rolling my eyes, I laughed and headed back inside, ready to clean up the mess we'd made. One thing was for sure—Lucas liked to eat, and I had a feeling I was going to have to make another trip to the grocery store very soon.

I spent the morning unpacking and cleaning the

downstairs. It was such a big house, especially when compared to my Memphis apartment, so the thought of keeping it organized was a little overwhelming. Grandma always kept the house neat as a pin, and now that I was an adult and it was my home, I could appreciate how difficult it must have been for her to keep it tidy, especially as she'd grown older.

I decided to start with my books, so I grabbed one of the massive boxes and carried it over to the barren shelf. There were a few things there—mainly family photo albums and some of my high school yearbooks—but it was the old family Bible that caught my attention.

Dropping down onto the floor, I crossed my legs and pulled the Bible from the shelf, placing it gently in my lap. Swallowing nervously, I slowly flipped through the pages until I found our family tree.

I still remember the day my grandma wrote my parents' names on the page. It had been a Wednesday. The funeral was over and the visitors had finally disappeared, leaving us alone in the house for the first time. I could still recall the stillness in the air and the finality of it all when she wrote their dates of death on the page. I could remember running up the stairs and slamming the door to my bedroom, where I buried my head beneath the pillow and grieved. After two days of tears, I'd finally emerged from my room, and my grandma gently took me by the hand and led me into the kitchen.

She didn't say a word; she just handed me an apron.

I quickly became a baking pro.

Reverently, I ran my fingers across their names, wondering what they'd think of the woman I'd become. Would they be proud? Would they be disappointed?

I had no idea.

My dad would be disappointed that I hadn't regularly attended church since my parents' funerals. Growing up, attending both services on Sunday had been mandatory, but after their deaths, my faith had been shaken to its core.

My father had always said 'God would never put more on us than we could bear,' but to a sixteen-year-old orphan, that particular bit of religious wisdom was hard to comprehend. Did God really believe I could survive without my parents? Was this truly God's plan for me?

And if so, did I want any part of it?

Grandma understood my internal struggle and hadn't forced me to attend services with her on Sundays. She and I spent many evenings baking in the kitchen or sitting on her front porch while I vented about everything from silly boys to high school Geometry. She never once made me feel like a heathen for asking questions or not attending church. My grandma truly understood my desire for answers and encouraged me to search for them.

In many ways, I was still searching for them.

Placing the Bible back on the shelf, I finished unpacking my books and then rearranged some of the living room furniture. Most of it really needed to be replaced, but it would have to do for now. I added a few picture frames to the end tables, and I had just finished dusting when the grandfather clock struck noon.

"Sarah?" Lucas yelled from the kitchen.

"In here!"

He appeared in the doorway, and I laughed when I saw his overalls were covered in dried paint.

"Did you get into a fight with the paintbrush?"

"We had a slight disagreement, yes." Lucas smiled, appraising the living room. "You've been working hard in here."

"It's getting there." It still needed a few things—some plants, maybe, and a new television—but with the boxes out of the way and the dust cleared, it actually looked cozy.

"It looks great." He grinned and pointed toward the old upright piano in the corner of the room. "Do you play?"

"I used to. Mom forced me to take lessons when I was a kid."

Both of us sat down along the bench. Sliding his fingers across the keys, he pushed a note, and the sound was jarring and discordant.

"That can't be right," he grumbled sourly.

I laughed. "It just needs tuning. I'm sure it hasn't been touched in years. Grandma couldn't play at all, but it'd been in the family forever."

"And you'd play for her because it made her happy."

I nodded and ghosted my hands along the keys.

"You miss her," Lucas whispered.

"Very much."

I played a few scales, but the piano was horribly out of tune. Cringing, I quickly placed the lid over the keys and offered him a smile.

"I bet you're hungry, aren't you?"

His sheepish chuckle was his only reply.

By the end of my first week in Sycamore Falls, I found that I loved my new routine. Lucas arrived like clockwork around seven each morning, and we'd share breakfast before he headed out to work on the house. I would spend my time unpacking, shopping, or playing hostess to the many neighbors who dropped by unexpectedly. Everyone had been so kind and always offered a gift to welcome me home—usually something edible. Catherine Thomas, the cashier from the grocery store, had stopped by with an apple pie, much to Lucas's delight. She'd sat with us at the kitchen table and sighed happily while he devoured three slices.

I couldn't be certain, but I was pretty sure that was how the rumors started.

I first noticed it when I went back to the hardware store to purchase more paint. I'd smiled patiently while Mr. Johnson told the old men around the counter Lucas was "spending an awful lot of time at Sarah's house." And yesterday, when I'd stopped by the grocery store, Catherine had eyed the items in my cart, reminding me Lucas preferred swiss cheese on his sandwiches.

It was inevitable, really. This was a small town and we were two single adults. When you combined those earth-shattering details with the fact he was painting my house, and our classrooms were side-by-side . . .

We really didn't stand a chance.

It was late in the afternoon, and I was curled up on the couch with one of the photo albums when Lucas appeared in the doorway, announcing it was starting to drizzle.

"There's a chance of rain tomorrow, too."

It was disheartening that the weather was suddenly being uncooperative. He couldn't paint in the rain, which meant we'd be even more behind schedule. It also meant he wouldn't have an excuse to come over, and I'd be cooking for myself.

This disappointed me more than it should have.

"I thought about asking Tommy to help, if you wouldn't mind."

"I don't mind at all."

The house was huge, and I'd worried all along it was too big a project for one person.

"I could paint some on Sunday, too."

"I don't know if you should risk it," I said teasingly. "You might get stoned in the town square for working on the Sabbath."

The color drained from his face, and I burst out laughing.

"I'm kidding! Just make sure you have all the supplies you need because nothing is open on Sundays around here."

"I've noticed," Lucas chuckled. He then nodded toward the photo album in my lap. "What are you looking at there?"

"Just some old family pictures."

I offered him a seat, and he leaned close while we examined the faded photographs, listening intently as I showed him my family history.

"Sarah, will you tell me about your parents?"

I sighed as I gazed at the picture of my mom and dad, one of the last photos taken before the accident.

"My mom's name was Carol." My finger ghosted across the print. "She was a Kindergarten teacher. My dad's name was Jason. He'd worked in the mines for most of his life, but when I came along, Mom convinced him it was just too dangerous, so he took a job with the local newspaper. The pay wasn't great, and he didn't enjoy working behind a desk, but my mother rested easier at night."

I continued to flip through the pages, pointing out special pictures of the three of us together.

"What happened to them?"

"Car accident," I whispered.

He said nothing, but I could feel his eyes on me as I focused on the photographs.

"I was spending the day with my grandma while they went into town to do some shopping. An eighteen-wheeler hit them head-on. The driver had fallen asleep."

I blinked back my tears and continued turning the pages.

"I'm sorry, Sarah."

Sniffling quietly, I nodded my thanks and pointed at a photo of my parents at Christmas.

"Your mom was really pretty. You look just like her."

I felt my blush creep across my face. "Thanks. Growing up, I looked more like my dad." I smiled down at a picture of me swimming in the river when I was about eight years old. "See? I have his dimples."

"You do." He laughed lightly, lifting his hand and slowly brushing it against my now flaming cheek. His piercing eyes locked with mine. "Those dimples were one of the first things I noticed about you."

His hand lingered there, and I felt my heartbeat quicken. Nervously, I flipped the page, and he dropped his hand, settling it once again in his lap.

"Is that your grandmother?"

I nodded. I loved this picture with the two of us smiling brightly into the camera. The little white church stood proudly in the background and a blanket of snow covered the mountains.

"This was our last Christmas together. She didn't force me to go to church every week, but I went on Easter and Christmas because I knew it made her happy to have me there."

"Church is very important here, it seems," Lucas said. "My family isn't particularly religious."

"I struggled with it, especially after the death of my parents," I admitted. "When you live in a small town like this, it's not always easy to question things. We aren't *encouraged* to question. We're supposed to have faith and believe there's a reason for everything. That concept was a little hard for a sixteen-year-old girl to grasp."

"What about for the twenty-seven-year-old girl? Is it any easier?"

Suddenly, my vision was filled with the cold, dead eyes of a teenage boy, and my hands began to tremble.

"No," I whispered weakly. "Sometimes, it's even harder."

Chapter Four

Despite the fact that it was late summer, there was a distinct chill in the air. Soon, the leaves would begin to change. Honestly, there were few things more beautiful than the crimson and gold which would soon be visible along the mountains. A little later, the leaves would fall, and what was once a beautiful mosaic of mountain color would turn into a brown, crunchy mess in my yard.

I couldn't wait. Raking leaves would just be another sign I was home.

Just like the meteorologist predicted, it rained on Saturday. The dreary weather gave me the chance to lie around the house in my fuzzy socks, curled up on the couch with a book and a cup of hot chocolate. It was peaceful and relaxing, but as the day lingered, I couldn't deny I felt a little lonely. I'd gotten rather used to having

Lucas around, and for the first time in a week, I was alone.

"You're being ridiculous," I muttered, tossing my book aside and heading toward the kitchen. I searched the pantry shelves for something quick and easy to fix for dinner. I'd just decided on mac and cheese when the phone rang.

"You're coming over to our house for dinner, and I'm not taking no for an answer."

"Hello to you, too," I laughed into the receiver. "Aubrey, seriously, I appreciate the offer, but I'm just going to make some mac and cheese and call it a night."

"Nonsense, I want you to meet the baby. Tommy is dying to say hello, and I know for a fact you're alone in that big old house. Now, grab a pen and jot down my address."

The red brick house was easy to find, especially with Aubrey standing on the porch, waving wildly.

"You're here!" Aubrey greeted me with a hug. "Don't kill me, okay?"

I was just about to ask why I'd want her dead, but then she led me into the brightly lit kitchen, and the mystery was solved.

"Hi," Lucas said, smiling in my direction. He was sitting at the table, bouncing a toddler on his knee, and for the very first time in my life, my biological clock went into a ticking frenzy.

"Hi," I managed to whisper.

"Sarah Bray!" Tommy shouted, grabbing me into a bone-crushing hug and lifting me in the air. In school, he'd always been the life of the party. It was nice to see that hadn't changed, even if he was cutting off my oxygen supply.

Tommy grinned at me and lowered me down to the floor. "Well, Lucas was right. You're still as good lookin' as ever. I don't know what it is about you country girls, but all of you just seem to get prettier with age."

"Your wife especially," I said with a laugh.

"Don't I know it!" Tommy proudly wrapped his arm around Aubrey's shoulder. "It's good to have you back, girl."

"Thanks, it's good to be back."

Aubrey headed toward the stove while her husband pushed me toward the empty chair next to Lucas. He seemed to be having a very animated conversation with the child in his lap.

"Who's your friend?"

The little boy grew silent, but his bright eyes watched my every move.

"This is Daniel," he said. "Can you show Sarah how old you are?"

Daniel held up three fingers.

"Wow, you're three?"

He nodded and shot me a toothy grin.

"He's a little shy around strangers," Aubrey said as she placed another glass on the table. "Trust me, it won't last. Lucas was a stranger an hour ago, and now look at them."

I couldn't look at them. Seeing Lucas with a baby in his arms was doing crazy things to my heart.

I was going to kill Aubrey.

Dinner was delicious, and the four of us chatted like we'd known each other forever. Of course, three of us had, but Lucas fit right in as if he'd always been a part of our circle.

As the conversation continued into the night, I marveled at the fact that these two people had welcomed me so easily back into their lives. We'd been the very best of friends growing up, and I'd tossed them aside. Nevertheless, here they were, looking at me with friendly eyes and forgiving smiles as they told Lucas a few of the many embarrassing stories from our childhood.

"The river was always freezing," Tommy said, chuckling lightly. He was trying to be quiet because Daniel was asleep in my arms. As Aubrey predicted, the little boy's shyness had disappeared. Sharing my mashed potatoes with him probably had a little something to do with his change of heart. After the dishes had been cleared and we settled around the kitchen table, the little guy had crawled right into my arms, and with some gentle rocking, he'd promptly passed out.

Aubrey grinned at me. "Sarah always loved the rope swing."

"It always scared the rest of the girls, but Sarah was fearless," Tommy said, draping his arm across the back of his wife's chair. "She'd just dangle from the rope and jump right in."

"Wasn't it dangerous?" Lucas asked me, clearly disturbed I'd so willingly fling myself into a river.

Tommy laughed. "Hell yeah, it was dangerous, but we were kids and thought we were invincible."

"But we weren't," I whispered, gazing down at the baby sleeping peacefully in my arms. We'd just been kids, without a care in the world and with no idea how fragile life could be. We took it for granted, as most kids do, and had no clue of the dangers that lurked outside our sheltered little world.

I looked up to find Lucas's eyes on me, all warm and soft. We shared a smile while Tommy and Aubrey continued telling their stories. They really didn't need our input. They were finishing each other's sentences, just like always.

"How's your arm?" Lucas asked softly.

"Numb," I mumbled, making him laugh.

"Oh, let me put him to bed," Aubrey offered, rising to her feet. "I have a feeling the boys are getting ready to desert us."

Tommy was already standing and looking forlornly

toward the living room.

"Football," Aubrey muttered, rolling her eyes. She lifted the baby into her arms. "We'll be right back."

"But it's the Colts . . ." Tommy's voice faded as he followed her down the hallway, leaving Lucas and I alone at the kitchen table.

"Isn't it a little early for football?" Granted, I wasn't a sports fanatic, but football was typically on television in the fall, and we were still in the middle of August.

"It's a preseason game."

"Oh." I nodded, as if this made perfect sense.

"Speaking of football, Tommy is going to bring some of his players over on Monday. He thinks with their help, we can probably get the house painted in a couple of days."

This was great news, although it definitely meant another trip to the store to restock the fridge. I didn't know much about football players, but I had a feeling they liked to eat.

"That's nice of them, but I think they just want the free food," I teased.

"I can't blame them. The food's great." Lucas grinned at me, leaning a little closer. "He also invited me to church tomorrow at Sycamore Baptist. Everything in this town is Sycamore something . . ."

I laughed.

"Yeah, we aren't really creative with the names. Are you going?"

He nodded thoughtfully. "I think so. Everyone has been so welcoming to me, and I've been invited many times. It seems like I should make an effort, you know?"

"I can understand that, yeah."

"What's it like?"

"Church? I wouldn't know. I haven't been inside Sycamore Baptist since my grandma's funeral, but I imagine it's the same. Very traditional, a lot of shouting . . ."

He looked puzzled. "Shouting?"

"It can get very . . . spirited." I smiled at him. "You'll see."

"You could come with me."

It wasn't the first church invitation I'd received, but it was the first time I actually felt guilty for saying no. Just because I'd found some peace with religion didn't mean I was ready to sit in a pew.

"I don't think I'm ready, Lucas."

Just then, Tommy and Aubrey reappeared, and I breathed a quiet sigh of relief. Lucas offered me a gentle smile before following Tommy into the living room, and I joined Aubrey over at the sink.

"Now, aren't you glad you came?" Aubrey asked with a mischievous grin.

"It was fun," I admitted, smiling as she handed me a hand towel. "Tommy hasn't changed a bit, and Daniel is adorable."

"Lucas is pretty adorable, too."

I shot her a glare.

"Come on, you can't tell me seeing him with a baby didn't make your heart beat just a little faster. I know it did, because there is nothing sexier than a man who is good with kids."

I said nothing, which was a mistake because, in my silence, she had her answer.

"I knew it," she sang triumphantly.

"Aubrey, this little matchmaking scheme of yours isn't going to work."

"It might work. You should have seen his face when you were holding Daniel."

"You're crazy."

"I know what I saw," Aubrey said, handing me a plate to rinse. "He couldn't take his eyes off you."

"I am not having this discussion with you."

"Why not?"

"Oh, I don't know," I snapped. "Maybe because I've

known the man for exactly one week?"

An uneasy silence settled between us while we finished the dishes.

"Okay, it's a little soon to be talking babies," she agreed.

"Thank you."

"But can I just say one thing?"

Defeated, I tossed the towel onto the counter and nodded for her to continue.

"Ten years ago, I lost my best friend."

My heart sank.

"Aubrey, I—"

Shaking her head, she said, "No, I don't want an apology. It's not necessary, and you're already forgiven. You've *always* been forgiven. The only reason I'm mentioning it now is because I don't want you to make the same mistake when you're trying so hard to make a fresh start. Don't be afraid to let people into your new life."

I blinked back my tears and pulled her into a hug.

"I missed you, Aubrey."

"I missed you, too." Sniffling quietly, she pulled away and smiled brightly through her own tears. "But we aren't going to be sad anymore. You're home now. It's a new life, with a new job and a new house . . ."

"And new friends," I said softly just as Lucas appeared in the doorway.

"Aubrey, I'm headed home. Thanks for dinner."

"I should go, too." I gave her a hug and thanked her for having me before grabbing my coat from the kitchen table. "Next time, I'm cooking."

Aubrey smiled. "Deal."

As Lucas walked out onto the porch, she placed a container full of leftovers into my hand.

She winked. "For tomorrow. You know, just in case you have company after he gets out of church."

She always did have ears like a hawk.

"Aubrey, we're just—"

"I know, I know," she smiled at me and pushed me out the door. "You're just friends. Call me!"

She slammed the door in my face.

I shook my head in exasperation before turning around. Lucas was waiting at the bottom of the steps.

"Stop smiling."

"I'm not smiling." He chuckled, and I rolled my eyes as we walked to our cars. "Okay, I'm smiling a little. They weren't subtle at all, were they?"

"You *knew?*"

I was mortified.

"I didn't at first, but then you walked in." Lucas grinned and leaned against my car. "Not that I minded."

How awkward was this?

Lucas opened my door for me, and I gently placed the leftovers on the passenger seat before sliding in behind the wheel. Once he closed the door, I rolled down my window.

"Since she went to all the trouble to pack the leftovers, you're more than welcome to stop by after church if you'd like."

"I'd like that."

"And I'm really sorry about tonight." It was vital he understood that I had nothing to do with the matchmaking ambush.

Lucas leaned his elbows against my window, peering inside.

"I'm not," he whispered.

Even in the darkness, his eyes were shimmering blue and completely sincere.

I had no idea what to say, so I mumbled goodnight and quickly drove away, feeling a little excited and more confused than ever.

Chapter Five

"You should visit during your fall break," Monica said. "Memphis misses you."

I cradled my cell close to my ear while checking the leftovers in the oven. "There are more than half a million people in the city. I doubt I'm missed too much."

There was a brief moment of silence.

"I think Ryan misses you."

"Impressive. I could just *barely* detect the contempt in your voice when you said his name."

"You know he's never been my favorite person," she muttered, "but he does ask about you whenever I have the great misfortune of running into him."

I stiffened. I didn't want Ryan asking about me.

"What do you tell him?"

"I tell him you're unbelievably happy and he should

move on with his dull and boring life."

Harsh, but effective.

As she continued to ramble, I nervously glanced at the clock. It was just after twelve, and while you were never quite sure how long a Sunday morning sermon might last, chances were good the rumbling stomachs of the congregation would encourage the preacher to move it along.

"I'm sure Ryan is much happier without me," I said diplomatically. After all, I didn't have an excuse to be bitter. I left *him*. "He'll meet someone wonderful. Someone who can be everything he needs."

"He's dating someone. I saw them together at a club a few nights ago."

"That didn't take long." I didn't feel a bit of resentment, though. I'd put him through hell, and he deserved to be happy.

"You were too good for him, anyway."

I laughed. Monica was loyal to a fault.

"I'm just saying there's only one you. I miss my girl."

"I miss you, too, Moni."

Monica boldly stood by my side when I'd returned to Sycamore Falls two years ago to lay my grandma to rest. Being the only African American woman in the church—not to mention in the county—it had been impossible for my friend merely to fade into the background. To them, she was different, but Monica hadn't taken it personally. In my eulogy, I'd told the sweet people of my hometown that my grandmother was my hero because she'd encouraged me to view the world with open eyes and an open heart.

Monica was a true friend. For me, she'd driven the seven hours from Memphis and endured the curious glances and the hushed whispers of the people in my hometown. When I'd graduated with my teaching degree, she'd cautioned me about taking the job at the high school because it was a rough school with even rougher kids. I should have listened, but I'd been too wide-eyed and determined to make a difference in the world.

"So what are you doing today?"

I anxiously checked the clock.

"I'm having a friend over for lunch." It wasn't a complete lie. Lucas and I were friends. "What about you?"

Monica sighed tiredly. "I have papers to grade. Remind me never to teach summer session again."

I gasped as the sound of crunching gravel echoed from the driveway. Promising to call later next week, we said our goodbyes and I rushed to the stove, grabbing a mitt and pulling the steaming casserole out of the oven.

I'd been expecting it, but the knock on the door still made me jump.

"Come on in!"

Lucas walked through the door, dressed in a dark suit and tie, and I nearly dropped the dish onto the floor.

"Hi," I managed to squeak while carefully placing the food on the counter.

"Hey." His sigh was weary as he collapsed into the nearest chair.

"Are you okay?"

He looked bewildered.

"I thought church was supposed to be a calming place," Lucas murmured. "There was nothing calm about *that*."

I laughed loudly and grabbed some plates from the cabinet.

"Some Baptist churches are livelier than others, I think. I attended one with my friend Monica back in Memphis, and hers was a little calmer—or at least it was until the choir began to sing. I didn't mind that so much, though, because the music was fantastic."

"When we did go to church—which wasn't very often—we attended St. Teresa's," Lucas explained, loosening his tie. "Everything was very regimented and methodical. This was—"

"Loud?"

"*So* loud," he whispered, rubbing his fingertips along his temples. "Everyone was friendly, but I'm not sure I'll ever go back."

"One of the great things about living in America is you don't have to go back if you don't want to." I pointed toward the dish. "It's probably still too hot, but help yourself. I'll find something for your headache."

After four aspirin and three plates of turkey casserole, Lucas was feeling much better. He'd even found some positive things to say about the church service.

"The sermon was nice. It was all about loving your neighbor. The message was good. I just wasn't expecting the commotion that erupted."

"I remember those spirited commotions," I replied. "It comes from a sincere place. It's just how they worship. For most of them, it's the only way they know *how* to worship."

His face grew thoughtful as he considered that.

"More?" I nodded toward the nearly empty casserole. He groaned in appreciation and shook his head. "Okay, let's go into the living room. There's something I want to show you."

Following close behind me, I led him over to the piano. Once we were seated, I smiled at him and pressed my foot against the pedals.

I took a deep breath and began to play the opening bars to "Amazing Grace."

"You got it tuned!" Lucas smiled, his blue eyes shining.

I nodded and continued to play, and more than once, I heard him sigh softly.

"See, *that* was calming," Lucas said quietly when I finished. "They didn't play 'Amazing Grace' today."

"Maybe they'll play it next time. You'll never know unless you go back."

"I'll consider it, on one condition."

I knew what was coming.

"What's that?"

"You go with me."

We smiled at each other until I turned my attention back to the keys.

"I'll think about it."

We sat on the piano bench for the next hour, me playing softly while he talked about his family. His parents still lived in Manhattan and worked in real estate. Lucas's voice was warm as he talked about his parents, and how they'd instilled within him the desire to work hard while making the most of his opportunities. He was an only child, and it was clear he'd grown up with every imaginable luxury.

"Why would you leave all of it behind?" I wondered aloud. I felt him stiffen, and I immediately regretted my words. "I'm sorry. It's truly none of my business. I just can't imagine why someone like you would move to a place like this."

His eyes were wounded. "Someone like me? You mean someone with money? I'm not a snob, Sarah."

"That isn't what I meant at all," I said apologetically. "I meant someone with your opportunities. You could teach anywhere. Why would you want to teach here?"

This time, he turned his attention to the keyboard. He gently pressed one key at a time.

"The city can be a very unforgiving place. I needed some distance. I needed to teach where the students might actually appreciate it."

"Sycamore Falls is certainly a far cry from the city."

"I won't lie; it's been quite a culture shock. There's no diversity here, and you really have to watch what you say. I told Mr. Johnson that I was a Democrat, and he looked at me like I'd spit on the American flag."

We both laughed.

"The people in this town are truly good. They are hard-working and loyal—"

"—and deeply conservative," Lucas finished.

"Conservative isn't necessarily a bad thing," I reminded him, "but there has to be a happy medium, I think. Having traditional values doesn't give anyone the right to be judgmental or hurtful."

He turned his face toward me and smiled.

"Agreed. So, if this place is so wonderful, why did you move to Memphis?"

"I had a scholarship," I explained, "but I was also an eighteen-year-old girl who wanted to see more than the Appalachian Mountains."

"I take it you didn't like what you saw?"

"What do you mean?"

"Well, you moved back," Lucas pointed out. "Something brought you home."

I gazed down at the white and black keys, needing to focus on anything else but him. I didn't want him to see the sadness in my eyes, because that would only lead to more questions.

"It was just time to come home."

The silence was deafening, and when I found the courage to look his way, I could see by the expression on his face that he understood.

"Well, for what it's worth, I'm glad you came home," Lucas said, nudging my shoulder with his. "It's nice to have a friend."

"It is." I smiled at him, relieved he'd so willingly let me off the hook.

"It will be especially nice when school starts. At least you're familiar with the place."

"Have you been inside the school at all?"

He nodded. "Twice so far. The first was when I was interviewed, and then later, to check out the classroom after I was hired."

We went outside to sit on the front porch, spending the rest of the afternoon talking about Sycamore High and comparing it to our previous schools. Sycamore's facilities were practically archaic, and while I realized state-of-the-art technology and million-dollar football stadiums were great, they didn't mean a thing when it came to providing a safe place for students to learn.

Lucas seemed to agree. "I taught in the inner city. Our students had everything. E-readers. Laptops. You name it. But they also had to walk through metal detectors to get past the armed guards at the front door."

"It's not enough," I whispered, my hands shaking slightly as memories of that horrible day flooded my mind. Suddenly, I could hear the sirens roaring in my ears and the terrified shouts of the students as they fled the cafeteria.

Bile rose in my throat, and I hastily jumped out of my rocking chair, holding onto the porch railing for support.

"Sarah?"

I closed my eyes and took long, steadying breaths. When I opened them again, Lucas was by my side.

"Are you okay?"

"I'm fine," I murmured unsteadily, gripping the wood a little tighter. "The casserole just isn't agreeing with me."

He slipped his arms around my shoulder. "Come on, let's get you inside."

Leaning against him, I let him lead me back toward the living room. I collapsed against the sofa, and Lucas kneeled on the floor at my side.

"Sarah, you're shaking. Are you cold?" He quickly pulled the afghan from the back of the couch and wrapped it around me.

"Will you . . . get my purse? It's by the stairs . . . and some water . . ."

He was gone and back in a flash. I desperately tried to control my breathing as I dug for my medication. My shaking hands made it nearly impossible to get the bottle open, but the lid finally cooperated. Placing the little white pill against my tongue, I took a long drink of water and swallowed it down.

"I think we should call a doctor."

"On a Sunday?" I laughed weakly as I leaned back, resting my head against the arm of the couch. I hated taking the medication. Absolutely despised it. But sometimes, it was necessary. "I'll be fine, really."

He sat down on the floor and gently swept my hair away from my face. The palm of his hand drifted across my forehead, and the sweet gesture made me smile. We stayed like that for a while—him caressing my face, and me struggling to bring my heart rate back to normal. The medication made me so tired, and I knew it wouldn't be long before I fell asleep.

The look on his face was heartbreaking.

"I'm fine, Lucas."

"You keep saying that." His voice was soft and soothing. "Say something else."

"What do you want me to say?"

"Tell me what you love about Sycamore Falls."

I snuggled deeper into the couch as his hand continued stroking my face.

"I love the seasons." The warmth of the blanket and his tender touch made it difficult to keep my eyes open as my body finally began to relax. "The county fair comes every August and summers are spent fishing or swimming in the river. Fall comes, and everything that was so green in the spring turns to red and yellow and just blankets the mountain. Winters can be brutal but spring always comes back, thawing us out and making everything green again."

It was a struggle, but I forced myself to open my eyes. His expression was soft and sweet as he gazed at me.

"I can't wait to see it," Lucas whispered. His fingertips traced my cheek, and I leaned into his touch.

"You'll love it, it's beautiful."

"You're beautiful."

It was a faint murmur, and it was last thing I heard before I drifted off to sleep.

The soft plinking of piano keys echoed in my ears, and

when I opened my eyes, the room was shrouded in darkness.

How long did I sleep?

I blinked rapidly, forcing my eyes to adjust to the dimness of the living room until they were able to focus on the man sitting at my piano.

"What time is it?"

Lucas turned around on the bench and smiled at me. "Just after eight. I didn't mean to wake you."

"You didn't." I pulled myself up, keeping the afghan wrapped protectively around me. "I shouldn't have slept so long."

Lucas rose to his feet and joined me on the couch. "Are you feeling better? Are you hungry? I could fix something."

"I'm okay." Several quiet moments passed before I finally stated the obvious. "You stayed."

"I stayed."

I was stunned. My ex-boyfriend had never stayed.

"Why?"

"Because you were sick, Sarah. I was worried about you."

"I wasn't sick, Lucas. Not physically, anyway."

"Then what was that?"

I stared into the darkness and pulled the afghan a little tighter around my body.

"I have panic attacks," I replied quietly. "It was a mild one, though. My therapist would be proud."

"You have a therapist?"

"In Memphis, yeah. I check in with her by phone at least once a week."

I had no idea why I was telling him this. Maybe it was because he'd witnessed it and I felt he deserved some sort of explanation. Maybe it was because he honestly looked concerned and was ready to call a doctor.

Or maybe, just maybe, it was because he'd stayed.

"Sarah, will you tell me what happened back in

Memphis?"

It wasn't a secret. Anyone could do a search on the Internet, and the story would be right there on the computer screen. There would even be pictures. The news coverage had been extensive, especially in the state, and it would be easy to find news story after news story describing the events of that day. What couldn't be found in those stories, however, was how my life had completely changed, and those were the details Lucas would want to know.

"Someday," I promised him with a whisper. "Will you tell me what happened in New York?"

His sigh was resigned and tinged with a hint of relief.

Maybe sharing war stories would help us both.

"Someday," he agreed.

Chapter Six

Monday morning arrived, bringing with it the warmth of the country sunshine and a busload full of football players who were far too energetic for seven in the morning.

"Good morning!" Tommy sprinted onto the porch as his team descended from the bus. The players were wearing their green hoodies with Sycamore Panthers stamped proudly in white on the back. "Guys, say hello to your new English teacher!"

A few of the players waved at me. From somewhere deep inside the huddle, there were even a few whistles, which Tommy promptly brought to a halt with the threat of gassers.

"What's a gasser?" I whispered.

"It's a conditioning drill where they have to run from sideline to sideline. They hate 'em. Some are even puking by the time they're finished."

My eyes widened. "That's . . . disturbing."

"That's discipline."

Tommy had just started barking out orders to his team when Lucas drove up with Aubrey following close behind in her car. Lucas offered me a wave as he ran over to Tommy and the buckets of paint, while Aubrey stepped onto the porch with gigantic aluminum pans in each hand.

"There are more in the car and it probably still won't be enough to feed this bunch," Aubrey said before turning toward the team. "Tommy! Tell those boys to take off those new hoodies before they get paint all over them!"

The coach yelled out instructions while Aubrey and I made our way into the kitchen. Minutes later, some of the guys—now wearing their Panthers T-shirts—brought in the rest of the food, and we tried to make room for it in the refrigerator.

"Where's the baby?"

"With my folks. We knew he'd just want to stay outside with his daddy all morning, and Tommy needs to focus on his boys. I just pray they don't turn your house into a Kindergarten art project."

"I have faith." Besides, it couldn't look any worse than it did now.

"Speaking of faith, what did Lucas think about our church?"

I carefully contemplated my words while leading her toward the living room.

"He thought it was very high-spirited," I said, curling my legs beneath me as we collapsed onto the couch.

"You mean he thought we were loud."

I laughed. "A little bit. He liked the sermon, though, and he said everyone was very welcoming."

"Everyone was so happy to see him there. You should come."

"Maybe."

I didn't mention his invitation to go to church. Instead,

we started talking about school, and how we'd be sitting in classrooms at this time next Monday.

"Don't get me wrong. I love teaching," Aubrey said. "I just really wish I could stay home with Daniel. The first football game is next week, which means I won't see much of Tommy except at school. Pray your future husband hates sports because being a coach's wife can be the pits."

I smirked. "I'll keep that in mind."

We spent the rest of the morning talking about the faculty, many of whom had been teaching at Sycamore High when we were students. We'd occasionally hear Tommy growling out orders, and his team would grunt some sort of response, making us both laugh.

"He's very motivational, isn't he?"

Aubrey grinned. "He can be, yeah."

Lunchtime arrived, and the team was happy to sit along the wrap-around porch while devouring their ham and cheese sandwiches. Tommy took the time to introduce me to his players. I recognized the quarterback as the bag boy from the grocery store, and he ran right up to me, pulling me into a hug.

"You remember me, right?"

"Of course. How are you, Matt?"

"I'm good. Hey, we have to get you guys Panthers sweatshirts. The first game's Friday night, you know." He smiled at Lucas. "You have to bring her with you, Mr. Miller."

"I'll see what I can do," Lucas laughed, and I rolled my eyes. Even the kids were trying to play matchmaker.

It wasn't long until the sandwiches were devoured and everyone was back to work. I felt a little guilty that everyone was working on my house except me, so after cleaning up the lunch mess, I told Aubrey I was going to change clothes and grab a paintbrush.

"I think I'll go get the baby," she said. "I only have a week left with him before I go back to work."

We hugged, and I thanked her for feeding the crew

before I rushed upstairs to dig through my closet. After changing into a sweater and a tattered pair of jeans, I pulled my hair into a ponytail before making my way out onto the sidewalk.

"Wait!" Lucas yelled, running toward me and placing his hands on my shoulder. "This requires a slow reveal so you'll get the full effect. Close your eyes."

Giggling, I did as I was told, and he gently pivoted me toward the house.

"Ready?" His mouth was close to my ear.

"I'm ready."

I opened my eyes, and I gasped.

"I think Rocky Mountain Sky Blue was definitely the right choice," he whispered.

"It's nearly finished!"

I couldn't believe it.

Lucas laughed. "Not quite. This is just the front, and it'll need a second coat."

"I'd like to help. I mean, I've never really painted a house, but—"

"I could teach you," Lucas offered. "The guys have set up a scaffold on the back. We could start there, if you'd like."

I smiled. "Okay."

"I'm making a mess."

Lucas had been so patient, even when I accidentally dumped a gallon of the paint and he'd had to mix more. "You're doing fine. Just remember to roll it from side-to-side."

I sighed heavily and tried to keep a steady hand as the paint roller moved across the siding. He was standing beside me on the scaffold, using a brush to smooth out the places where I'd applied too much. We talked while we worked, but he never mentioned yesterday's panic attack, and I was thankful.

"So," Lucas said, dipping his brush into the bucket. "What do you think about Friday night's game? Should we go?"

The roller became slightly unsteady in my hand, but I was careful to keep my voice casual. "We could go. The new kids on the block should probably stick together when it comes to school functions."

"You're not exactly *new*," Lucas reminded me with a grin. "But yeah, we should do that."

"Okay."

It's not a date. It's a school function.

This would have to be my mantra for the rest of the week.

"Sarah, you've got—" Lucas motioned toward my face.

"What?" Blindly, I swiped at my nose, which caused him to laugh even harder.

"Your roller is dripping!"

I looked down to find my fingers covered in Rocky Mountain Sky Blue. I groaned in frustration as he handed me a towel.

"Stop laughing at me!"

This only made him laugh harder, so I grabbed his brush out of his hand and gently swiped his cheek, creating a lovely streak of blue from his ear to his chin.

I couldn't stop laughing. "Now we match!"

His laughing subsided just long enough for him to take a step closer and slowly lift his hand, carefully touching the tip of my nose with his finger.

"*Now* we match." Our laughter faded as he took another step closer. His eyes flickered to my mouth, and I held my breath when he leaned closer.

Suddenly, Tommy's voice rang out, causing us to jump away from each other. "There you are! What are you guys doing back here?"

Lucas mumbled something about avoiding interfering people, and I bit my lip to keep from laughing as I dipped the brush back into the bucket.

"You two have more paint on your faces than you do on the house!"

"All my fault." I was more than happy to take the blame.

Tommy looked at Lucas and then back to me before exploding with laughter.

"Don't you have something to do?" Lucas shouted down at him, clearly annoyed.

Tommy just smirked.

"Actually, we have practice in an hour, so the guys are cleaning up. We'll be back tomorrow, bright and early."

"Thanks, Tommy."

Lucas gathered our supplies while I carefully climbed down the scaffold. When I reached the ground, I looked up to admire our handiwork.

"We really do have more on us than we have on the house."

"Told ya," Tommy said with a grin, "although I have a feelin' neither of you mind too much."

Tommy winked at me before running toward the front of the house. By the time Lucas and I walked around, the boys were already packed on the bus, waving excitedly with their heads stuck out the window.

"Thanks, guys!"

The team cheered wildly, causing the bus to shake before it finally rumbled away, disappearing in a thick cloud of dust.

Late that afternoon, I decided to take a drive around town. Not much had changed at all on Main Street, but there were a few new shops, including a sporting goods store with Sycamore Panthers sweatshirts displayed in the window.

I bought two.

I had to guess at his size, but Mabel, the elderly saleslady behind the counter, had apparently gotten a good look at Mr. Miller at church on Sunday, and she promised me a medium would fit just fine.

"He's a very nice young man," Mabel said as she handed me my receipt. Her eyes crinkled when she smiled, reminding me a little of my grandma.

"Yes, he is."

After promising to come again, I headed home. On the way, I decided to take a detour—taking a left at Jackson's Pond and continuing on the old dirt road that led to the river. I'd practically lived there when I was a kid, and as teenagers, we'd hike the trail and camp close to the waterfall. It was nearly twenty feet high and one of the most serene places I'd ever known.

I wanted to show it to someone who'd never seen it. Someone who needed a little serenity in his life.

Grabbing my cell phone, I was amazed to find I had a signal. I had never called Lucas, but we'd exchanged numbers the day we met at the hardware store. I quickly gave him directions, and half an hour later, we were standing together at the trailhead of Sycamore Falls.

"You do remember I'm a city boy," Lucas said quietly, his eyes wide as he looked toward the woods.

"I remember, but I really want you to see the waterfall. It's a short and easy hike, I promise."

He didn't look convinced but followed me anyway. The trail was flat but rocky, and when I stumbled, Lucas quickly grabbed onto my hand. He didn't let it go, not even when we reached the riverbank, and I pointed across the water.

"Wow," Lucas whispered.

The sight of the waterfall took my breath away. I hadn't seen it in years, and back then, I'd been just a kid, viewing it with innocent, adolescent eyes. I'd loved this place, but I didn't fully appreciate it.

Not until now.

"This is really beautiful, Sarah."

"I know."

We sat down on the sand, listening to the roar of the falls and watching as it flowed into the current below. The river was a little low, making the jagged boulders visible above the rushing water. Sycamore trees—still bright green and full of life—majestically surrounded the water. It wouldn't be long until the leaves traded their emerald shade for the pretty colors of autumn.

"I bet this place is gorgeous in the fall," Lucas said, reading my mind. "We'll have to come back when the leaves change."

I smiled.

Yes, we would.

The rest of the week was busy as our summer vacations came to an end. Painting the house continued until mid-week when Tommy and Lucas decided they would finish the trim work while the team began renovating the wrap-around porch. In the afternoons, the Panthers would head off to football practice while Lucas and I went to school to prepare for our first week of classes. Mr. Mullins, the principal, finally provided me with a curriculum, and I spent my evenings creating lesson plans. I also learned I would be teaching a Creative writing class, which excited me a little more than it probably should.

I was 'settling in,' as my neighbors called it, and I loved the routine of it all.

On Friday afternoon, I was sitting in the kitchen and answering an e-mail from Monica when Lucas appeared in the doorway.

"You need to come outside," he said with an excited grin on his face.

"Okay." I clicked send and closed my laptop. He was still grinning as he motioned for me to follow him out onto the porch.

"Close your eyes."

"Are you insane? I'll fall down the steps if I close my eyes."

Lucas slipped his fingers through mine. "I won't let you fall. Now, close them."

He gently pulled me along the porch and guided me down the front steps. When my feet reached the sidewalk, he released my hand and placed both palms on my shoulders.

"Turn around and open your eyes," Lucas murmured.

"You know, I'm getting a distinct feeling of déjà vu."

He laughed. "Just do it."

The sun was blinding, but it wasn't so bright that I couldn't see the lovely blue house with white shutters.

Just then, a thunderous cheer erupted from behind us, and I spun around to find the football team, along with Tommy and Aubrey, gathered around the bus. Everyone looked so proud, and I had no idea I was crying until I felt a tear trickle down my cheek.

"What do you think?" Lucas asked softly.

I took another long look at my beautiful house before smiling up at him.

"I think I'm finally home."

Chapter Seven

"I'm Miss Bray, and welcome to English literature."

I'd practiced my intro in my head for weeks now, but as I stood before my first period class and actually said the words aloud, I realized just how inconsequential they really were.

They didn't care.

They weren't impolite or unkind. A few had actually smiled in my direction while I passed out the syllabus. They were simply seniors. School was the last place they wanted to be and they were more than ready to get through their final year of high school. English literature was an unfortunate roadblock in their journey to graduation, so I was automatically perceived as the enemy.

Because I was nervous, I'd already decided to keep today's lecture to a minimum, so we discussed the syllabus and I highlighted a few projects I would be assigning throughout the year. There were a few questions—mostly from the football players who, surprisingly enough, sat in the first two rows—and I assigned a short writing exercise to fill up the rest of the class period.

"Just write me a short autobiography," I announced to the class as they shuffled through their backpacks in search of pen and paper. Some muttered they couldn't believe they had to work on the first day of school, but I ignored them while I walked up and down the aisles of desks.

"You look especially lovely today, Miss Bray."

I grinned down at Matt. "And you have especially lovely handwriting. I have to ask. Why are my first two rows filled with football players?"

"Coach requires it."

"Coach thinks we won't pay attention if we sit anywhere else," Patrick said. I couldn't remember which position he played. Running back, maybe. "How's that porch, Miss Bray?"

I smiled at him. "The porch is great. It needs some new rocking chairs, I think, but it's beautiful. You guys did a great job restoring it."

The bell rang, and one class flowed seamlessly to the next. By the time lunch rolled around, I was starving and ready to get off my feet. I collapsed into my chair just as Lucas walked inside the classroom.

"Still alive?"

"Barely. My feet are killing me."

He leaned against my desk. "Well, that's because you're forcing your toes into those god-awful heels." Looking down at my shoes, he allowed his eyes to linger just a bit longer than necessary.

Men.

"You love my shoes."

"Yes, I do." He pulled a chair closer to my desk and placed a sandwich bag on top of it. "It's from the cafeteria. I've been assured their peanut butter and jelly is the best."

Over lunch, we talked to each other about our mornings, and we agreed it was great Tommy required his football team to sit near the front of the class. Lucas's second period class had been the worst, which wasn't unexpected considering they were freshmen.

Lucas finished his sandwich and tossed the bag into my trashcan. "They try so hard to be cool. I've never taught freshmen, but I had no idea they could be so immature."

"At least they'll talk to you. I could barely get my seniors to say a word."

"Be thankful." He smirked.

Suddenly, his expression softened. "How are you doing, really?"

Even though he didn't know why, he had to know I'd be anxious about today.

"I'm good," I replied honestly. "I was nervous this morning, but it's been okay so far. What about you?"

"I'm good, too. At least the kids are respectful here. If my biggest problem is a bunch of loud-mouthed freshmen, then I'll consider this school year a success."

The bell rang, and we both groaned.

"I'd forgotten how quickly time flies during lunch."

"And your planning period!" We both laughed as he rose from his seat. "Thanks for lunch. That was sweet of you."

"I'm a sweet guy," Lucas said with a heart-stopping grin. "Have a good rest of the day."

My fourth and final class of the day was more energetic and far more curious than the previous ones. I was happy to see two familiar faces as both Matt and Patrick dutifully took their seats in the front row. They probably needed an elective and assumed creative writing would be an easy course.

"You're originally from Sycamore Falls?" A student asked after I'd finished going over the syllabus.

"Yes, I am."

"And you came back?" Howie was another football player. "What would possess you to come back to this place?"

I smiled because, once upon a time, I'd been just like them. I had been so ready to leave this town behind and venture out into the world. It would have been hard for me to believe someone would actually escape and willingly return.

"Sycamore Falls isn't so bad," I said, knowing they'd disagree. The class didn't disappoint, and the debate continued until I finally told them to write their thoughts about their hometown in a two-hundred word essay due on Wednesday.

A redhead in the back promptly raised her hand. "Do we have to read these aloud?"

"I think that's a wonderful idea! Yes, please plan to read these aloud on Wednesday."

The groans were deafening.

After class was dismissed, I tiredly slumped into my chair. Kicking off my heels, I wiggled my toes and then breathed a sigh of relief.

I did it.

I had survived the first day of school, and I'd done it without a panic attack, a flashback, or one single tear.

I spent my afternoon sitting in my living room, listening to 80s monster ballads on my iPod, and grading my first period autobiographies. I was humming along with Bon Jovi when I heard a thunderous knock coming from the kitchen. Tossing my pen and papers aside, I raced toward the back door.

"Hey," I said, smiling at my unexpected visitor. He was wearing his Sycamore Panthers pullover. Mabel had been right. The medium really did fit him perfectly.

"Hey you. I've been knocking forever."

I laughed, pulling the buds from my ears. "Sorry, I was just grading papers."

"It's okay." He shuffled his feet nervously. "Would you sit on the porch with me?"

I smiled. He loved my porch almost as much as I did. Happy to leave my grading behind, I followed him outside, letting the screen door slam behind me.

"Don't get mad, but I bought you something."

He stepped aside, and there, hanging from the beams, was a beautiful porch swing rocking gently in the breeze.

"Oh . . ." I whispered in amazement.

"They were on clearance down at the hardware store," Lucas explained. "I know you talked about getting some new rocking chairs, but I saw this and thought maybe . . ."

I couldn't believe it. Growing up, I'd always wanted a swing, but Grandma didn't like them. She'd always preferred her old wicker rocking chairs.

"If it matters, you can just consider it a thank you for the pullover."

"Lucas, that sweatshirt was twenty bucks."

Laughing quietly, he sat down on the porch swing, pushing off gently with his legs. "Aubrey told me you'd probably fight me, which is why I installed it before I knocked on your door. I was afraid you'd hear the drill. Lucky for me, you had your iPod buds planted in your ears."

It was far too expensive of a gift, and I knew I shouldn't accept it. It was also the most amazing gift anyone had ever given me, and it was beautiful and looked perfect on my porch.

I was so torn.

"Just come sit with me, Sarah."

Unable to resist, I sat down beside him on the swing. He smiled at me, and together, we pushed. The creaking sound of the chains and wood was quite possibly the most tranquil sound I'd ever heard. Closing my eyes, I relaxed against the seat of the swing as we swayed.

"You love it," Lucas said softly.

"How can you tell?"

"You're smiling."

Sighing contently, my eyes fluttered open as I slid my hand along the smooth wood.

"Thank you," I finally whispered, "but you really shouldn't have. It's too much."

"Not if it makes you happy."

His bright blue eyes gazed into mine, and we shared a smile.

I *was* happy, and I knew, deep in my heart, that it had absolutely nothing to do with the porch swing.

"My hometown is the boringest place in the world," Howie announced while reading his oral presentation of the writing class. He received a few "amens" and I had to bite my tongue to keep from reminding him that 'boringest' wasn't a word. It was just the first assignment, and I'd told them I was grading on content and not grammar.

I had to bite hard.

Most of the essays had been much of the same—full of bad grammar and negative perceptions about their hometown. The sad fact was everything they'd stated in their presentations was true. Sycamore Falls wasn't culturally diverse and our movie theater did have three screens. The nearest big city was over an hour away, and Internet access was spotty in some areas of the county.

It was all true, and I told them as I walked around to the front of my desk.

"You're right. Sycamore Falls is very sheltered from the rest of the world."

Caleb, a quiet student in the third row raised his hand. "So, Miss Bray, if everything we've said is true, why did you come back?"

At that moment, twenty pairs of curious, expectant eyes turned my way. This class was just too intelligent and inquisitive. It wouldn't take long before one of them asked their parents, or searched the web, and that's when I'd be asked the questions I really didn't want to answer.

"Because, sometimes, you need sheltering," I replied softly.

Thankfully, the bell rang, and the students groaned with disappointment when I dismissed them for the day. I had just sat down at my desk when I heard a quiet voice echo from the front row.

"Miss Bray?"

I looked up to find Matt staring at me, his deep brown eyes sad and distant.

"Yes, Matt?"

"Do you think it's possible we're *too* sheltered from the rest of the world?"

I smiled softly and closed my lesson planner.

"I thought the exact thing when I was your age."

"But not now?"

I sighed and leaned back against my chair. "This might surprise you, but Sycamore Falls isn't nearly as sheltered as it used to be."

"Maybe not materialistically," Matt said with a shrug, "but what about socially? Did you hear about the all-district punter from Nashville whose parents wanted to move here to work at the clinic? His dad is a pediatrician. They even bought a house in town. They were here for one week, Miss Bray. *One week.*"

"Why just a week?"

"Because Sycamore Falls didn't roll out the welcoming mat for a black family," Matt said quietly.

I wasn't surprised. A quick glance around my classroom proved nothing had changed when it came to diversity in Sycamore Falls.

"People form opinions, and it can be hard to get them to change their minds. Unfortunately, it happens everywhere." I offered him a sad smile. "You know, Matt, you could have written about this in today's assignment. This would have been a fantastic class discussion."

He chuckled, but it wasn't a humorous laugh.

"Right," he mumbled. "Don't you know, Miss Bray? Teenagers are the most opinionated of all, especially if you don't conform to the norm. You can't be different. Not if you want to be accepted, anyway."

Matt slumped in his desk, and I couldn't help but wonder what was really bothering him. As the quarterback of the football team, the boy was worshipped at Sycamore High. Girls flocked to him and he was obviously the most popular guy on the team.

"Are you saying you're different, Matt?"

His expression turned somber.

"I'm the high school quarterback who's dating the captain of the cheerleading squad. I am the biggest walking stereotype, and I play my role every single day."

I was so confused, but I didn't get the chance to dig deeper. Aubrey suddenly appeared in my doorway, asking if I was ready to go. With the first football game in two days, Tommy was spending extra time on the field, leaving Aubrey alone most nights. I'd invited her and the baby over for dinner and an 80s movie marathon.

"I'm going to be late for practice," Matt muttered, grabbing his jacket and books. "See you later, Miss Bray." He muttered a polite hello to Aubrey and ran out the door.

"That looked serious. What's up with him?"

"I wish I knew," I said, gathering today's papers and stuffing them into my bag.

"No grading tonight! We have a date with Ferris Bueller, remember?"

I grinned. "Yes, I remember, but if I don't get them graded before Friday, I might not get to go to the football game, and we know what a tragedy that would be."

"Oh, you're going to the football game." Aubrey grabbed me by the hand and led me out the classroom door. "If you think I'm spending another football season sitting in those stands by myself, you've seriously lost your mind."

I couldn't help but grin. "Were you always this bossy? I really don't remember this side of you at all."

Aubrey ignored my question and hooked her arm through mine as we walked down the hallway. "Besides, we have to talk about boys."

"No, we don't."

"Really? Because there's a new swing hanging from your front porch that would suggest otherwise."

Sighing in defeat, I linked my arm through hers and accepted my fate.

Chapter Eight

"I've never seen so much green."

It was true. Our side of the stadium was packed with fans wearing their Sycamore green hoodies for the first football game of the year. The visitors' stands weren't nearly as full, and I wondered if it was the long drive or the bitter cold that had kept them away.

"Who are we playing?" I scanned the other side of the field, trying to remember which of the surrounding schools wore blue and white.

"No idea," Lucas grinned, "but they look really cold in their blue T-shirts."

The weather was always unpredictable in the mountains, even in late summer. One day, you could wake up to sunny skies and seventy-degree temperatures. The next morning, you'd be digging in your closet for a jacket because fall arrived early, causing the temperatures to plunge overnight.

"I bet poor Mabel had to make a batch of hoodies and sweatshirts just for tonight's game."

Lucas leaned close. "Are you okay? The crowd isn't too much?"

The crowd was noisy and loud, but I was okay so far.

"I'm good," I replied. Shivering, I glanced toward the concession stand. Maybe something warm to drink would help.

"Why don't I go see if they're selling hot chocolate or something?" Lucas offered.

"It's scary how well you can read my mind."

He grinned. "It's a gift."

Aubrey finally arrived and dropped down onto the bleacher next to me. Thankfully, she waited until Lucas was out of earshot to begin the interrogation.

"I love that the two of you are wearing matching hoodies. It's incredibly cute."

I rolled my eyes. "You know, if you take a look around, you'll see we match just about everyone on this side of the stadium."

"And it's your first date!"

"It's not a date. We are two new faculty members sitting together at a football game."

"Hmm." She wasn't at all convinced, but she let me off the hook and scanned the crowd. "Look at this place! I think the whole town is here tonight.

The bright, excited faces of our students reminded me of the football games we'd attended in high school. Our small group of friends would spend our Friday nights in the student section—all decked out in our Panther green—screaming wildly for Tommy and his team. There was always a bonfire afterward, and a few parties out near the river, which were illegal for any of us to attend. Of course, that hadn't stopped us—just like it wouldn't stop any of our students tonight.

It's amazing how high school never really changes.

The game began just as Lucas reappeared with three steaming cups of hot chocolate. We thanked him and settled in—with me sandwiched in the middle and being pressed against Lucas's side.

"You know Matt, of course," Aubrey said, pointing toward the field at number sixteen. Matt had his own cheering section, and the girls would explode with squeals each time he completed a pass or even turned his head in their direction. Aubrey spent the first half of the game pointing out the players and their positions. The crowd was deafening, and by halftime, we were leading by three touchdowns while my body was trembling from the cold.

"You're freezing," Lucas whispered in my ear.

I somehow resisted the urge to lean against the warmth of his body. We were surrounded by our students and their snooping parents, not to mention my infuriating, and less-than-subtle, best friend who was practically shoving me into his lap.

"Football games are great for cuddling under blankets," Aubrey offered helpfully. Lucas chuckled, and I shot her a glare. I had just returned my attention to the field and the cheerleaders' halftime dance when I felt a tap on my shoulder.

"Sarah Bray?"

I turned to find myself staring into the eyes of a middle-aged woman. She was wearing a Sycamore jersey with number sixteen printed in big white letters on the front.

"Yes?"

"I thought so. I'm Debbie Stuart. I went to high school with your mother."

I tried to force a smile. I wasn't opposed to talking about my mom. I was just proud I'd held it together through this first week of school. I'd hate to lose my composure during a high school football game while surrounded by hundreds of screaming fans.

"It's nice to meet you, Mrs. Stuart."

"My son is in your class. Matthew has never really enjoyed anything but football, but now he loves English."

"Oh, you're Matt's mother?" I asked, and she nodded proudly. "He's a wonderful young man and very hard-working."

"Thank you. His father and I are hoping all of his hard work leads to a football scholarship." Her grin faded slightly as her eyes raked across my face. "You have your mother's eyes. They were such a pretty shade. We always joked she was a true Sycamore Panther because her eyes were as green as our basketball uniforms. Did you know your mother played basketball?"

"Yes, she played point guard."

So had I. I'd been too short to play anything else.

She smiled fondly. "That's right. Lord, she loved your father. And you. I know she'd be proud of you, especially after everything that happened at your last school."

I could feel Lucas's eyes on me as I tried to hold it together.

"The entire community prayed for you," Debbie continued, oblivious to my anxiety. "The world is such a scary place, isn't it? To believe someone would bring a gun into a school."

Suddenly, the stands erupted with cheers and everyone rose to their feet, clapping wildly.

"They fumbled the kickoff!" Aubrey screeched excitedly.

I nodded slightly and tried to control my breathing, but it was all too much—the memories, the noise, and the lights.

Tension spiked, causing my body to shake uncontrollably.

Before I even knew what was happening, Lucas was pulling me by the hand and leading me down the bleachers. People passed me in a blur as he led me behind the concession stand. Despite the cold, I pressed my back against the concrete of the building, struggling to catch my breath. Lucas leaned close, wrapping his arms around me. I was freezing and far too emotional to resist, and I melted against him as I began to weep.

"It's okay," he whispered against my hair. "You're okay, sweetheart."

Having his arms around me while I cried was the strangest feeling. Ryan, my ex, had never been able to handle my unexpected emotional outbursts. I'd grown accustomed to hearing the door slam and crying myself to sleep once the anxiety finally diminished.

Ryan had never held me during a panic attack.

Not once.

My tears subsiding, I lifted my head until I found his eyes in the darkness. Lucas was gazing down at me, his eyes filled with worry.

"I don't know why you're my friend," I muttered shakily. "I'm a complete and utter mess."

Smiling softly, Lucas gently stroked my cheek, wiping away my tears.

"You're a beautiful mess."

It wasn't the first time he'd told me I was beautiful, but the words surprised me just the same.

Feeling slightly calmer, I buried my face against his chest once again. Sighing softly, his arms tightened around me. The whistles and cheers were a distant echo as we held onto one another in the darkness.

"Better?"

I nodded.

"Let me take you home," Lucas whispered against my ear.

I lifted my head toward his. "I can drive."

He looked skeptical.

"It's the weekend. I can't just leave my car at the stadium."

Lucas nodded. "Okay, but I'm following you home."

"Okay."

Taking my hand, Lucas led us out of the shadows.

"This porch swing is amazing," Aubrey said.

The freezing temperatures of last night gave way to a beautiful Saturday afternoon. Lucas had called at dawn, checking to make sure I was all right. He now had a small piece of my story, thanks to Matt's mom, and her reference to the gun. He didn't mention it, though, and I convinced him I was fine despite the fact my night had been restless. I'd finally given in around three and had taken my medication. After that, I did manage to sleep, but I had crazy nightmares. They'd seemed so real at the time, but I could hardly remember them in the daylight. I'd napped throughout the morning until Aubrey called, and I invited her over for lunch to apologize for abandoning her last night.

"I was just worried about you, but then I got excited." Aubrey grinned mischievously.

"I suppose hoping the two of you deserted me to go find a back road and a back seat was just wishful thinking?"

"Very wishful," I replied quietly, careful not to disturb the sleeping child in my arms. Daniel had been full of energy during lunch, but once we were outside, the rhythmic rocking of the swing had lulled him right to sleep. It surprised me how much I loved holding him.

"You need one."

Confused, I looked up. "One what?"

Aubrey nodded toward her son, and I rolled my eyes.

"Oh yeah, a baby is exactly what I need right now."

We grew quiet then, each of us lost in our thoughts. I knew she was curious about last night, and I felt compelled to offer her some sort of explanation.

"Aubrey, I had a panic attack last night."

She tilted her head. "Really? Is that why you left?"

I nodded. My fingers lingered in Daniel's hair, twisting the curly strands framing his peaceful face.

"Debbie didn't mean to upset you."

"I know she didn't. It's inevitable. I've moved back to my hometown. People are going to mention my parents. It's just something I have to get used to, you know?"

"Is that why you stayed away from Sycamore Falls? To avoid the memories?"

I sighed. "Memphis was such a clean slate. No one knew anything about my past or my family unless I wanted them to know. Random strangers didn't just walk up to me, ask about my parents' accident, or how I was handling it all. It was much easier to move on with my life."

"But you weren't moving on," Aubrey murmured. "You were avoiding dealing with the pain."

"That's what my therapist says, too, but in Memphis, I was at least able to function somewhat normally. I had a decent job and good friends, and I had a boyfriend who loved me as long as I kept my emotions in check."

Her forehead creased. "He should have loved you even when you couldn't hold it together."

"Maybe that's why he's my *ex*-boyfriend."

Her face grew thoughtful.

"Lucas took care of you last night."

"Yes, and it wasn't the first time."

Aubrey listened intently while I told her about the first panic attack I'd had in front of him.

"And he stayed, which is something Ryan had never done for me."

"I'm glad you have him, Sarah."

"Me too. He's a good friend."

Smiling, she cleared her throat. "So, have you been to the falls lately?"

I sighed. I was seriously beginning to think men gossiped worse than women.

"Lucas has a big mouth."

"It's not really his fault. Tommy just can't keep a

secret."

"It's not a *secret*, necessarily. It's just another reminder that nothing in this small town is sacred."

She smiled.

"Tommy says you are absolutely all he talks about. He really cares about you, Sarah."

"I care about him, too."

"But?"

"But I'm an emotional mess, and I'm just not sure a serious relationship would be the wisest decision right now."

"I disagree. I think focusing on something positive and good is exactly what you need. Besides, Lucas has his own demons. Maybe the two of you can help each other."

Daniel began to wiggle in my arms, and I snuggled him close to my chest, burying my nose in his hair. He always smelled so good, and I wondered if that was true of all babies or if it was just him.

"Lucas hasn't told me much about what happened in New York."

"He hasn't told Tommy a lot, either. You know, if you're interested, we could do some digging. The Internet is a glorious thing."

I was already shaking my head. "No way."

"Don't tell me you aren't tempted, Sarah."

"You know, Lucas could very easily do his own digging—and I guarantee my demons would be much easier to find—but he hasn't. He's respecting my privacy. Are you saying I shouldn't do the same for him?"

"Of course not," she replied. "I'm just saying it'd be tempting, that's all. *Something* brought him here."

"He'll tell me when he's ready."

After Daniel awoke from his nap, the three of us spent the rest of the afternoon baking and watching cartoons until they finally headed home for dinner, leaving me with my jumbled thoughts and dozens of cookies.

I boxed them up, deciding my creative writing class

needed a little taste of Grandma Grace.

"I was just like you when I was a senior."

Eager hands reached into the box of cookies while I walked up and down the aisles.

"I could not wait to leave Sycamore Falls. My grandma was the one to suggest I find a college in the city. In her mind, the only way I could truly understand the world was to live in it. She and my grandfather had lived in Atlanta for a brief period of time, and it was then, and only then, did they truly appreciate living in a small town like Sycamore Falls."

"How could anyone appreciate living here?" Carrie asked.

I could tell the rest of the class was wondering the same thing. They were just too busy devouring my cookies to question anything I was saying at the moment.

"It was confusing to me, too," I replied, settling onto the edge of my desk. "I was so desperate to leave it all behind I barely glanced in the rear view mirror as I drove out of town."

"But you came back," Matt pointed out, and the class shook their heads. It still amazed them I'd actually chosen to return.

"You know, Miss Bray, maybe you just moved to the wrong city," Howie suggested.

"I mean, going from Sycamore Falls to Memphis must have been a shock to the system. Maybe you should've picked a medium-sized town."

"Maybe so, but Memphis offered me a full scholarship."

The seniors murmured their agreement. When money is in question, you choose the school offering you the best deal.

"But that's a discussion for another day. I told you

about my grandma—and shared her cookies with you—because I want you to think about people who inspire you. People who accept you for who you really are. My grandma taught me so much more than just how to bake cookies. She taught me it was okay to ask questions and she encouraged me to spread my wings. I want to know who inspires you. Tell me all about the person in a 300-word essay, which we'll read aloud tomorrow."

They groaned, not necessarily because of the homework, but because none of them were particularly comfortable with public speaking. I softened the blow by letting them eat the rest of the cookies while they began to write, and it wasn't long until the bell rang. The class filed out, and I was just closing the lid on the leftovers when I heard a voice in the doorway.

"I thought I smelled your cookies."

I shook the container and lifted the lid. "I have a few left."

Lucas walked over to my desk, grabbed a cookie, and stuffed it into his mouth. He hummed in appreciation, and I laughed as I turned toward the board. I was just finishing writing tomorrow's assignment when I felt him close the distance between us. His chest brushed against my back, and my breath quickened. Placing the cap on the marker, I gently placed it on the tray before slowly turning around to face him.

"Hi," I whispered.

"Hi."

I glanced over his shoulder to make sure no one was watching. I could hear faint voices, but it was the end of the day and kids rarely lingered in the hallways.

"It's a beautiful afternoon," Lucas said softly. "I'd like to take you somewhere."

"You would?"

He nodded. "But you'll need to change. I don't think those heels will work on the trail to Sycamore Falls."

A slow smile crept across my face.

"You really loved it there, didn't you?"

"It's beautiful," Lucas said, his voice quiet and low. "It's also the perfect place to have a very important conversation."

My smile faltered.

"Lucas, I don't know if I'm ready—"

"You don't have to be ready," he said. "*I'm* ready. I want to tell you what brought me here. I want to tell you about New York."

My heartbeat sped.

"But why?"

"Because I can't expect you to share your darkest demons with me if I don't offer to do the same," he reasoned. "You don't have to be ready to tell me yours, but I'm ready to tell you mine—that is, if you want to hear them."

I took his hand in mine.
"I want to hear them."

Chapter Nine

Despite the sunshine, the air surrounding the falls was colder than our last visit. Fall was definitely just around the corner, and I couldn't wait to show Lucas how pretty the mountains could be in the autumn.

He'd been noticeably quiet on the walk to the falls, and I understood why. He was preparing to bare his soul to me, and I could appreciate how difficult that must be. I also knew, deep in my heart, it really didn't matter what he confessed to me today. Lucas was quickly becoming my best friend, and despite not knowing the reasons behind my breakdowns, he'd taken care of me each and every time I'd fallen apart in front of him. He'd never belittled me or made me feel ashamed for being weak, and he'd never once asked for more than I was ready to give.

Today, I would do the same for him.

When we finally reached the falls, Lucas led me toward a giant boulder near the trees. He handed me the blanket he'd been carrying, and I wrapped it around us. We sat side-by-side, gazing at the swelling river before us. The recent rains had caused the river to rise, and the current was swift today. A gust of wind made me shiver, and Lucas wrapped his arm around me, pulling me close to his side.

"It's always colder near the water," I said quietly.

"Yeah."

I gazed at his profile as he stared out across the river. He really was handsome. Had I ever told him so?

"Sarah, why are you staring at me?"

I laughed.

"I was just thinking you're very cute."

He grinned at me.

"I'm a grown man. I can't be *cute*."

"Fine, you're very handsome. Better?"

"Much." Lucas laughed quietly, pulling me closer.

Our laughter faded as he pressed his forehead against mine. His crystal-blue eyes were tortured as his voice dropped to a faint whisper. "What if you hate me?"

"I could never hate you."

"I didn't do anything wrong. I promise you."

"I believe you."

Taking a deep breath, he pulled away, and I immediately missed his warmth. We were still snuggled beneath the blanket, but we were barely touching. Something told me he needed some distance, at least during his confession.

"Her name was Marina."

Of course, this sad story would start with a woman. I hated her immediately.

"A girlfriend?"

"No." His eyes, now icy and hard, were fixed on the river. "She was my student."

My blood ran cold.

"Marina was seventeen but dressed like she was twenty-five," he continued quietly. "She was an Honors student whose parents expected her to get into Harvard. Since her only B was in American History, her parents asked if I would tutor her. She was a good student, and I wanted to help her raise her GPA, so I agreed."

Lucas rose to his feet, and I pulled the blanket tighter around me. Like a caged lion, he began to pace along the sand.

"I was tutoring two other students that same semester, so it wasn't as if she was special, but she thought she was. I had no idea she had a crush on me—not until the day she leaned across her desk and kissed me on the cheek."

My heart was now thundering in my chest. *He didn't kiss her back. I know he didn't.*

"I've gone over it so many times in my head. What did I do to give her the slightest hint I would think of her in such an inappropriate way? I swear I was nothing but professional. I never touched her—not even a pat on the back."

I nodded numbly. "What did you do when she kissed you?"

"I immediately left the classroom and went straight to my principal to report the incident. When the police questioned Marina, she happily admitted to kissing me. She then confessed she was pregnant, and she named me as the father."

I gasped softly as his voice broke. I had to resist my desire to console him. I wanted to hold him. I wanted to hug him. I wanted to tell him I believed him.

"New York City is this massive metropolis of over eight million people, but when a student accuses her teacher of statutory rape, the big city is suddenly a very small place. Word spread like wildfire, and I was placed on administrative leave within the hour. My parents were mortified, and my professional reputation was shot to hell."

"But you were innocent!"

My outburst pulled him out of his misery, and he turned toward me, offering me a sad smile.

"How do you know, Sarah?"

"Because I know you."

Lucas walked toward me, dropping to his knees on the sand and placing his hands over mine.

"Yes, I was innocent," he whispered. "The investigation was embarrassing and excruciatingly long. When my attorney pushed for an amniocentesis to determine paternity, Marina completely freaked out. Her lawyer tried to convince the court the procedure was just too risky to the baby, but the judge ordered it anyway. That's when Marina finally confessed the child's father was actually her twenty-two year old boyfriend. I was cleared of all charges—and there was a formal public apology—but the damage was done. It would always be a shadow over me—something I'd have to explain to any future employer."

I squeezed his hand reassuringly.

"It's the most terrible feeling—being accused of something you didn't do. It's especially horrible when it's something so humiliating. Even though I was found innocent and my job was reinstated, I just couldn't go back to the same school. I took a leave of absence and spiraled into a depression that scared the hell out of my parents. It was actually my mom who suggested moving out of the city."

"I understand," I replied. "I'm surprised you even stayed in the profession."

"I thought about leaving, but I still love teaching, in spite of everything. I know that doesn't make much sense."

It made perfect sense to me.

I grinned. "Sycamore Falls is definitely 'out of the city.' How did you find it?"

"My parents liked to vacation in the mountains," Lucas explained. "It was always so beautiful and serene, and I promised myself if I ever moved away from the city, I'd find my own place in the country. I got online and looked for job openings, and I found the history position at Sycamore High. I researched the area—"

"I bet that didn't take long . . ."

His eyes grew wide. "This place isn't even on Wikipedia!"

I laughed. "We should write an article for the website."

"We should," Lucas agreed with a smile, his fingers squeezing mine before he rose to his feet and sat down next to me. Smiling, I offered him the blanket, and he snuggled beneath it, wrapping his arm around my shoulder, and pulling me close. "So, for someone who wanted to make a new start, this seemed like the perfect place."

"Does it still seem that way?"

"At first, I wasn't sure. For one thing, I had to get used to driving. I had my license, of course, but in Manhattan, there isn't much of a need. I walked, took a cab, or used the subway, so driving everywhere has definitely been an adjustment. I'm getting better. Tommy's been teaching me."

"He gave me lessons when I was sixteen," I laughed. "He said if I could drive his truck, I could drive anything."

Lucas chuckled. "Everyone has been so friendly and the town is beautiful, but after a few weeks, I just wasn't sure I could be this detached from the world. I grew up with museums and culture, and here it's just . . ."

"I know. It's very sheltered."

"Which isn't necessarily a bad thing, but I have suffered a bit of culture shock," Lucas said, "but to answer your question—yes, I think this was the perfect place to make a fresh start."

"I'm glad, but don't you worry about rumors?"

"Principal Mullins knows everything. I was very honest about my past and my reasons for moving to Sycamore Falls. I can't worry about gossip because there is absolutely nothing I can do to control it. I just have to trust the administration will support me if it becomes an issue."

"The principal loves you, and so do the students and faculty."

Lucas sighed. "I hope so because I really love teaching here. The kids are respectful, which is something you don't always find in the city. I've made great friends, and I've met you."

His eyes burned with sincerity as he stroked my cheek.

"I won't lie. Meeting you has been the very best thing that's happened to me since moving to Sycamore Falls. I knew I had to tell you about New York. You have no idea how much I've agonized over it, trying to find the right time to tell you, and not even knowing if you'd believe me."

"Of course, I believe you, Lucas."

He looked relieved. "I'm glad, because yours is the only opinion that really matters to me."

"Thank you for telling me." Suddenly, I felt very guilty because he'd shared something so personal with me, and I just wasn't ready to do the same.

"Hey," he whispered, brushing his thumb across my chin. "I didn't tell you about my past so you'd feel compelled to tell me about yours."

I laughed nervously. "You know, this mind reading thing is really kind of sexy."

Lucas grinned, but then his eyes flashed with determination as he held me a little tighter.

"Do you know how much I care about you?"

It was impossible not to know. It was also impossible to let myself completely acknowledge it, because that would mean opening my wounded heart to someone who deserved far better than the emotional mess I'd become.

"I care about you, too," I whispered sincerely.

Suddenly, Lucas was lifting me and settling me sideways against his lap. Instinctively, I wrapped my arms around his neck, and he pulled the blanket tighter around us. He'd seen me at my worst, and I'd wept in the man's arms, but somehow, this was far more intimate than either of those nights.

"Sarah," he whispered, nuzzling my cheek with his nose. "I don't think you understand."

The look on his face melted my heart, but I couldn't let him say it.

"Don't," I whispered, placing my palm against his cheek.

"*Now* who's the mind reader?"

I smiled softly.

"Why won't you let me?"

"Because it's too soon. You can't really mean it, not until you know everything there is to know about me."

"That's not true at all. I could say it right now and I would absolutely mean it," Lucas replied. "I know I don't have all of the details—and God knows I've wanted to ask—but I know you'll tell me when you're ready. I also know nothing you tell me will change the way I feel."

He didn't understand, and it wasn't his fault. Instead of trying to make him understand, I decided to make a joke.

"You can't really know how you feel about me, Lucas. I mean, we haven't even kissed. What if it's terrible?"

Immediately, I knew it was the wrong thing to say. I was sitting on his lap and wrapped around him like a vine. Our faces were so close that I could see the little flecks of gray in his blue eyes, and I had chosen *this* moment to throw down the gauntlet.

A slow smile crept across his face, and reading his mind wasn't at all necessary, because I knew.

Challenge accepted.

I was still unprepared for the moment his lips touched mine. Not because the kiss was hot and passionate, but because it was romantic and tender, and it was exactly the kind of kiss I'd always wanted to share with someone at the waterfall. My arms tightened around his neck as he stroked my back, and I was so overwhelmed I was practically trembling when we finally pulled away. He rubbed his nose against mine before brushing his lips against my cheek. Sighing softly, I buried my face against his neck.

"You were right," Lucas whispered in my ear. "That was absolutely terrible."

"Truly awful," I agreed with a giggle.

We stayed like that—wrapped in a blanket and snuggled in each other's arms—until the sky turned to dusk.

The second week of school passed quickly, despite the fact my mind was constantly preoccupied with thoughts of Lucas and our first kiss. In that moment, our entire relationship drifted into this sea of murky water where everything was cloudy and confusing.

It was especially confusing because he hadn't touched me since the day at the falls.

In many ways, I was relieved. Lucas wasn't pushing me to give more than I was capable of giving, and I couldn't deny I was thankful. But there was another part of me—the lonely and selfish side of my heart—that was disappointed because he was keeping his distance.

To the casual observer, nothing had changed in my life. My classes were going great and I was making it through the day. Lucas and I still shared lunch each day while keeping our usual professional distance. If it wasn't for the heated glances he'd sometimes cast my way, I'd wonder if I hadn't dreamed our entire afternoon at Sycamore Falls.

It was a long week.

When Friday arrived, I was convinced there must be a full moon because the kids were out of control. Rumors were rampant about a fight in the lunchroom between two football players, and the entire student body was afraid the players would have to sit out tonight's game as punishment. Apparently, we were playing Winslow, and they were our biggest rivals. By the time my fourth period class rolled around, I knew getting them to write anything would be a struggle. However, for a class who hated public speaking, they were more than willing to voice their opinions about the fight.

"Did you see Matt's eye? It'll be black tomorrow."

"Patrick's arm is probably broken."

I glanced at their empty desks. That certainly explained why both boys were absent from my class.

"I think they were fighting over me," Carrie said.

I noticed a few of the girls rolling their eyes. She might be the head cheerleader and the quarterback's girlfriend, but Carrie was far from the most popular girl in school.

Howie smirked in her direction. "I'm pretty sure your name wasn't mentioned."

Carrie shot him an icy glare.

"Oh, and how would you know?"

"Because I was standing right there?"

"Okay, okay!" The last thing I needed was to break up my own fight. Instead of assigning a writing prompt, I gave the class permission to write about anything that was on their minds. I knew I'd be reading twenty first-hand accounts of the fight, but I was desperate to make this last half hour of class pass as quickly and painlessly as possible.

"Have a good weekend," I announced when the bell rang.

The students turned in their papers, and I sighed with relief when the room was finally empty.

Instead of taking it home with me, I decided to take some time to read their essays. Carrie's was fairly self-centered. She was confident the boys were fighting over her because Patrick had dared to say hello to her in the hallway just this morning. However, it was Howie's paper that really gave me some insight.

"Hey you," Lucas said as he peeked his head inside the door. "Working late?"

"Not really. I just wanted to read a few of these essays. The entire class wrote about the fight."

Lucas smirked and took a seat in one of the student desks. "Very clever, Miss Bray."

"It was honestly the only way to calm them down."

He nodded. "I just spoke to Tommy. He's benching them both for tonight, which is the right decision, of course, but I could tell he was disappointed."

"Well, Matt's the quarterback. It's not good for the team when your star player gets into a lunchroom brawl."

I couldn't deny I was impressed with Tommy. In a town where football is like a religion, it took a lot of nerve to bench those boys, especially tonight.

"So, are you going to the game?"

I laughed. "I think last week's game was enough for a while, don't you?"

"It is an away game," Lucas offered helpfully, "so maybe we won't be crucified for skipping this one."

"You don't want to go?"

"No, I'd rather have dinner with you."

It wasn't the response I was expecting at all. Was he asking me out?

"We could go to the diner, if you'd prefer. It will probably be deserted because of the game."

"I could cook," I offered quickly. I really did want to spend some time with him. It had been a long week, and I'd missed him.

Lucas smiled. "I was hoping you'd say that."

Chapter Ten

"You're adding too many chocolate chips."

After a simple dinner of spaghetti and meatballs, Lucas decided he wanted to learn how to bake.

"Maybe I like a lot of chocolate chips," Lucas said.

With a grin, I rolled my eyes and handed him the cookie sheet. I watched, worried, as he scooped too much dough onto the pan.

"Stop criticizing my baking skills and tell me more about your grandmother."

I adjusted the temperature on the oven and offered him a mitt. "What do you want to know?"

"I don't know." Lucas motioned toward the pan, and I nodded in approval at his attempt to scoop smaller lumps of dough. It was still too much, but he was trying. "I'm obviously desecrating her kitchen, so I feel like I should know a little more about her."

"I know one thing. She would say you're still using way too much dough." I laughed and grabbed the spoon out of his hands. I dropped small mounds onto the cookie sheet while he placed the first pan in the oven. When he returned to the island, I jumped slightly when he placed his hands on each side of my waist. Resting his chin on my shoulder, he watched quietly while I finished scooping the rest of the dough onto the tray.

"I really missed you this week," Lucas whispered, holding me a little tighter against his chest.

Warmth flowed through me, and I placed the spoon on the pan as I snuggled against him.

"You've seen me every day," I reminded him.

"You know what I mean."

I nodded. "I missed you, too."

"Yeah?"

"Yeah."

I felt him nuzzle the side of my neck, and I closed my eyes in contentment.

"I should set the timer," I murmured.

Lucas sighed, but he didn't argue when I pulled away. After adjusting the controls on the oven, I led him toward the living room.

"Do you want to watch a movie or something?"

"Sure."

I handed him the remote, and after flipping through the channels, he finally settled on *Ferris Bueller's Day Off*.

"I love this movie," he said with a grin.

Slipping his arm around my shoulder, he pulled me close to his side as we snuggled and watched my favorite movie. Ten minutes later, the timer went off, and Lucas offered to take the cookies out and put the next batch in. When he returned, he grabbed the blanket off the back of the couch and wrapped it around us. He kissed the top of my hair, and I had just snuggled into the crook of his arm when he began to recite the entire scene between Mr.

Rooney and Ferris's mom.

"*Nine* times," Lucas murmured, his voice perfectly matching the principal's tone.

"You cannot be this perfect," I mumbled.

"Sorry?"

I frowned. "I mean it. There must be a flaw somewhere. Anywhere."

His forehead creased—a sure sign he was deep in concentration and trying to decide if I was even remotely serious.

"You think I'm perfect because I can quote my favorite 80s movie?"

My heart stopped.

"*Ferris Bueller* is your favorite 80s movie?"

Lucas nodded.

"I'm pretty sure I'm going to have to kiss you now."

His eyes brightened. "Because I love *Ferris Bueller*?"

Scrambling onto his lap, I wrapped my arms around his neck. His hands settled against my hips, holding me close as I brushed my nose against his.

"Do you have a problem with that?" I whispered.

"None whatsoever."

I kissed him lightly, and he groaned, pulling me closer. Gentle fingers trailed along my spine as we kissed, and when I felt his lips part, and his tongue slide along mine, I knew the innocent kisses we'd shared at the falls were nothing but a sweet, distant memory.

"I really missed you this week," he whispered when we came up for air.

"You didn't have to stay away."

I trailed my lips against his neck, and he roughly whispered my name. Far too soon, the oven timer sounded again, and I regretfully pulled away. Breathless and panting, he leaned his forehead against mine.

"Don't go," he pleaded.

"The cookies . . ."

"I couldn't care less about the cookies."

His blue eyes were desperate and pleading, and with a quiet groan, I brushed my lips against his once more.

After tossing the burned cookies and finishing the movie, Lucas offered to help me read some of the essays from my creative writing class. We were still snuggled up on the couch with the blanket around us, but this time, we were actually working instead of making out like teenagers.

"Wow, your students use really descriptive language."

I laughed. "Isn't it amazing how they all had a front row seat to this fight?"

I knew their stories were truly creative and most of what we were reading was a complete fabrication taken straight from the teenage rumor mill.

"Howie's essay is interesting," he noted.

"I thought so, too."

Howie was convinced the fight had absolutely nothing to do with a girl and more to do with the fact that Patrick knew entirely too much about Matt's personal life. Howie had been careful to keep his thoughts vague, but I couldn't help but recall my last conversation with Matt.

"What are you thinking?"

"I was just remembering something Matt told me last week," I said. "I get the feeling he's not entirely comfortable with his life, and I'm not sure why."

"Well, he is a senior," Lucas reminded me. "Maybe it's just a bit of teenage rebellion?"

I dropped the essay onto my lap and rubbed my tired eyes. "I don't think so. I think it goes a little deeper."

"And I think you're tired."

I smiled sheepishly, unable to deny it.

After packing up the leftover cookies, I handed him the container before following him out onto the front porch.

"What are your plans for tomorrow?"

I shrugged. "I don't really have any. I need to finish

some grading and do some lesson plans for next week."

"Me too."

He reached for my hand and our fingers entwined. "Would you want to go to church with me on Sunday?"

I grinned. "Are you giving it another chance?"

"I thought I would, yeah."

I squeezed his hand. "Okay, I'll go with you."

"Really?"

"The roof may cave in," I warned him.

"Not a chance." Leaning down, he brushed his lips softly against mine. "Thanks for dinner."

"You're welcome."

Another kiss, and this time, I was pretty sure I felt my toes curl.

"And the cookies."

"Anytime," I whispered.

After promising to pick me up on Sunday morning, he kissed me one last time before we said goodnight. I locked the door behind me, grabbed my cell, and it was only when I glanced at the screen did I notice today's date.

September 8.

I'd been so consumed with school and Lucas that I hadn't realized that Saturday was the anniversary of my parents' death.

And just like that, I had plans for tomorrow.

The cemetery was just as I remembered, although I couldn't imagine graveyards really changed much through the years. Silk flowers surrounded stones of granite, and I was disheartened to find some graves were in better condition than others.

It didn't take long to find our family plot, and I was relieved to see the four gravesites were well maintained. I had no idea who was taking care of them, but I was grateful.

My eyes ghosted along my grandfather's headstone. He'd died when I was young, so we'd never really had the chance to become close. I could recall some Christmases with him, but honestly, it was all a big blur. My most vivid childhood memories were with my parents, and of course, with my grandmother.

"Hey guys," I said, sitting cross-legged in the grass. Wildflowers were scattered in shades of yellow and purple along the ground. "I know it's been a long time. I have absolutely no excuse, so I won't even try."

Thankfully, the cemetery appeared to be empty, giving me the privacy I needed to talk to my family without feeling self-conscious about it.

"I've moved back to Sycamore Falls. I'm living in Grandma's house. It has a new porch and it's the prettiest shade of blue now." I took a deep breath. "I'm teaching English at the high school. Aubrey and I have reconnected. She married Tommy, like we always knew she would. They have the sweetest baby boy. They teach, too."

I drifted my fingers along the stem of a dandelion growing wild in the grass.

"And there's Lucas." Carefully, I pulled the dandelion from the ground. "He's really wonderful. So patient and kind. I'm just not sure I can be what he needs. I'm afraid I'm too wounded."

A single tear fell down my cheek, and I hastily brushed it away.

"He really cares about me, and I really care about him, too, but even that scares me because everyone I love eventually leaves me . . . or I leave them. Sometimes, I wonder if maybe I can't truly be healed. Maybe the wounds are just too deep and raw."

A swift wind brushed across my cheek, and the dandelion seeds floated through the breeze.

"I miss all of you." Leaning closer to the stones, I reverently traced the letters of their names.

Minutes later, the sky began to darken, and I rose to my feet, gently brushing the grass off my jeans before making my way to the car. I'd just opened the door as the first raindrops began to fall.

It was the longest I'd ever spent at the cemetery, and I couldn't believe how exhausted I felt. Baring your soul was draining, but in some strange way, it felt cathartic.

Maybe I'd come back someday.

"For God hath not given us the spirit of fear; but of power, and of love, and of a sound mind," Pastor Martin quoted from the New Testament.

That scripture was profound. I couldn't help but think it might be even more effective if the preacher wasn't screaming it from the pulpit.

Lucas squeezed my hand, and I tried to relax.

It had been so long since I'd stepped inside this church—or any church for that matter—but everyone welcomed me with open arms and smiling faces. Aubrey and Tommy ushered us to their pew, and Daniel had immediately climbed into my lap. He was such a good baby, somehow sleeping through the commotion that surrounded us. Throughout the service, the congregation had given testimonies, and after each, the choir would sing. It was joyous, spirited, and loud, and Daniel had snored peacefully through it all.

I'd been naturally apprehensive about today, but the music was good, the sermon wasn't too terrible, and Lucas was by my side. Pastor Martin was a definite improvement from the preacher from my childhood who coerced youngsters into being "saved" with threats of eternal damnation and lakes of fire. I never understood the concept of using fear to convert the masses when, at the same time, you were trying to convince them they were serving a loving God.

Very confusing stuff for a kid.

As an adult, it was still puzzling, but at least you were capable of making your own decision about such things.

The preacher asked us to turn to a page in our hymnal, and the entire congregation stood to sing "Amazing Grace" before we were dismissed.

"Why don't the two of you come back to the house?" Aubrey asked, reaching for Daniel. He buried his face against her shoulder and continued to snore. "Tommy could fire up the grill. It might be our last chance until spring."

"Whatever Sarah would like to do is fine with me," Lucas replied.

Tommy then pulled him aside to say hello to our principal.

Aubrey sighed. "Is he really that perfect?"

"Yes, and it's maddening."

She giggled. "I think it's wonderful."

I watched while Principal Mullins introduced Lucas to some of the men surrounding their pew.

"Is that area still reserved for the deacons?"

"Yes, and our principal is one of the most vocal," she replied sourly. "You know the amendment in the constitution about the separation of church and state?

I nodded.

She leaned close, her voice now a mere whisper.

"Principal Mullins doesn't believe in it."

"What does that mean?"

But she didn't have the chance to answer because we were suddenly surrounded by smiling faces—none of which I recognized, but who seemed to know all about me. I smiled politely and breathed a sigh of relief when they finally walked away.

"So, you'll come back to the house?"

"Sure. What can we bring?"

"Just yourselves. Tommy will be so excited. He's been begging to grill for weeks. And the great thing is, we'll have their undivided attention because the Colts don't play this afternoon."

Across the room, Tommy was still in deep conversation with one of the deacons. Lucas's eyes, however, were fixed on me.

Naturally, Aubrey noticed.

"It looks like someone's attention is already undivided," she whispered in my ear.

"Something's changed."

I sipped my lemonade and watched from the deck while Lucas and Tommy chased Daniel around the big backyard. The power nap in church had done wonders for the toddler's energy level, and he'd been a holy terror since we'd arrived at their house. Daniel ran from the swing set to the slide, over to me and his mom, and then back to his sandbox in the grass.

"Don't ignore me, Sarah."

"You are so bossy, and I have no idea what you're talking about."

"You were never a good liar. More lemonade?"

I laughed as she refilled my glass. She was still the perfect hostess despite the insults.

"Fine, a few things have changed," I admitted.

"Such as?"

"He told me about New York." I offered no other details because it wasn't my story to tell. "And we . . . might have kissed."

She actually squealed, causing the boys to look in our direction.

"Just kissed?"

"No, Aubrey, I ripped his clothes off and did very naughty things to him on my living room couch."

Her smile was wicked and bright. "That's my girl!"

I rolled my eyes.

"Are you insane? Yes, we just kissed."

Daniel was in the sandbox once again, and Lucas and Tommy were sitting in the nearby grass, talking in hushed tones. I wondered if maybe they were having this very same conversation. The thought made me laugh out loud, causing Lucas to lift his head and smile at me.

"Sarah, he's in love with you. You know that, don't you?"

I shook my head. "He can't be."

"Why can't he be?"

"Because he's known me for about a month?"

Aubrey shrugged. "Sometimes, all it takes is a month. People always made fun of us when I told them it was love at first sight for Tommy and me, but the joke is on them. We're still together after all these years."

"You make it look so easy." Even I could hear the envy in my voice.

"It's not *easy*. I won't lie. Being married to a coach and raising a toddler puts a strain on a marriage, but we make it work."

I sighed softly. "He doesn't even know me, Aubrey."

"I have a feeling Lucas knows you better than anyone."

"You know what I mean."

"I do know what you mean. I also know what happened in Memphis isn't who you are, Sarah. It's something that *happened* to you. There's a difference."

We grew quiet while watching the boys. In no time at all, Daniel grew tired of the sandbox and was now begging his daddy to push him on the swing.

"Memphis wasn't your fault," Aubrey finally whispered.

"I didn't do enough to prevent it from happening. The signs were there, and I chose to ignore them."

"So you're supposed to be omniscient and perfect?"

"A young man might still be alive if I had been."

She sighed. "It was a horrible tragedy, absolutely, and I'm so sorry you went through that, but Sarah—"

"I know," I whispered. "It's time to move on."

Aubrey nodded in agreement.

"I only know the details from the news articles, but I know it wasn't your fault. Maybe sharing that part of your life with Lucas will help you come to terms with everything. Something tells me he'll be better than any therapist could ever be."

We spent the rest of the afternoon with them. Tommy grilled steaks and Aubrey baked the potatoes while Lucas and I played with Daniel in the sandbox. I felt a little guilty for not being in the kitchen, but Aubrey assured me that keeping her child entertained was more than enough help.

"Your conversation with Aubrey seemed pretty serious," Lucas remarked as he flipped his pail, forming a perfect mound of sand. Daniel's laugh was infectious while filling his own bucket, but when he turned it over and pulled it away, he was disappointed when his sand castle instantly crumbled.

"You have to take your time," Lucas encouraged him. "Pack the sand tight to form a strong foundation, and then be very careful when you lift the pail."

Daniel listened intently and followed the directions, clapping with glee when his next sand castle stood firmly in place. Satisfied with his masterpiece, Daniel jogged toward the swing.

"That's the thing about foundations," I whispered wistfully and trailed my fingers along the grains of sand. "When it's already weak, the slightest shift can make it fall apart."

Lucas's eyes ghosted over my face, and we both knew I wasn't really talking about the sand.

He took my hand and squeezed it reassuringly. "It might crumble, but it can always be restored. It might take some time—and a gentle touch—but it can be mended if it wants to be."

"What if it's too late? What if it's beyond repair?"

"I don't think anything is beyond repair. At least I hope not. Maybe it just takes a fresh start. A new beginning."

Both of our foundations were still shaky, but could we possibly be strong again?

"That's why I'm here," I said quietly.

His smile warmed my heart.

"Me too."

Chapter Eleven

It was dark by the time we headed home. We'd tried to leave earlier, but Daniel kept insisting we play "just one more minute."

It was hard to say no to those big brown eyes.

"How long have Tommy and Aubrey been together?" Lucas asked as he pointed the car toward town.

"Since seventh grade. Tommy invited her to a school dance, and they've been together ever since."

"They've never dated anyone else?"

"Not that I know of. We weren't particularly close our last two years of high school, but I can't imagine they've ever been apart. I've never met two people more perfect for each other." He looked confused.

"Why weren't you close the last two years of high school?"

"I wasn't close to anyone, but my grandma," I told

him. "After my parents died, I distanced myself from everybody. In my sixteen-year-old mind, if I didn't love anyone, then it wouldn't hurt me if they left me behind."

Lucas reached for my hand and continued to drive.

"Did you date a lot in high school?"

I smiled, grateful for the change in subject. "Not a lot, no. I had a couple of boyfriends, but there was only one that was even remotely serious. We'd tell my parents we were going to the movies, but we rarely made it there."

Lucas grinned at me. "Where did you go?"

"Parking, usually. We'd find some deserted back road and make out in . . ." my voice trailed off when I realized he'd turned down the dusty gravel road that led to Jude Taylor's farm, ". . . the back seat of his dad's old Chevy."

"A back road like this one?" Lucas's voice was deep and low as the car crept along the deserted road.

What is he doing?

"Umm . . . well, this one would be dangerous because it leads straight to Jude Taylor's house, and you're bound to get caught, but . . . uh . . . there's a side road up here on the left. It was a pretty popular parking spot when we were in high school."

He drove another mile before the promised road came into view. It was covered in gravel, and still headed straight back into the woods.

Out of sight.

Far out of sight.

Without a word, Lucas turned left.

He even used his signal light.

I would have laughed if I hadn't been so damn nervous.

"Lucas, have you ever done this?"

He brought the car to an abrupt stop just under a canopy of trees and turned off the ignition. The glow of the moon was our only light, and my body trembled with excitement when he unbuckled his seatbelt before reaching for mine.

"Nope," Lucas murmured, pulling my hand to his lips. I gasped softly as he gently kissed my palm. It was meant to be a sweet, innocent gesture, but it did nothing but ignite my blood.

In an instant, I was climbing over the back seat, pulling him along until our bodies were pressed against each other in the tight confines of his car.

"God, this was so much easier when I was sixteen."

Lucas silenced my giggle by crashing his mouth against mine. Our bodies entwined as we fumbled in the darkness, groping and kissing like a couple of teenagers. There was something about the night that made us bold, and our kisses became frantic. With trembling fingers, I hurriedly unbuttoned his shirt. Groaning roughly, his hand slipped beneath my blouse. I gasped excitedly when his hand ghosted along the lace of my bra.

"Sarah . . ." he whispered against my neck. Twisting my fingers in his hair, I pulled him closer, causing him to moan against my skin. My heart was thundering in my chest as he lifted his head toward mine. I gently caressed his handsome face while he gazed into my eyes, and I knew—deep in my soul—I was falling in love.

"What was his name?"

The strange question brought me back to reality.

"Whose?"

Lowering his head, Lucas gently kissed the corner of my mouth. "The boyfriend who used to take you parking in his dad's Chevy."

His lips brushed my jawline, and I sighed softly.

"Toby." His teeth found my earlobe, making me moan. "Toby . . . something."

"Did he make you feel like this?"

"No one has." Lucas's entire body shuddered as my hands slipped along his muscular shoulders, pushing his shirt away. My legs wrapped around his waist, and I arched into him, making him groan roughly. "Only you."

"Only me," Lucas whispered softly against my lips.

Our kisses became desperate once again until a sharp rapping on the window caused me to scream.

"This cannot be happening," Lucas mumbled miserably as I shielded my eyes from the brightness of the flashlight streaming through the glass. We hastily untangled ourselves and adjusted our clothes before rolling down the window.

Naturally, it was a deputy—grinning like an idiot.

Did small towns always have to be so predictable?

"Sarah Bray, is that you?"

I sighed heavily.

"For future reference, I want those words etched on my tombstone," I muttered to Lucas. "Yes, is there a problem, officer?"

He laughed, and it was the most annoying, grating sound I'd ever heard.

"You don't remember me, do you? We were lab partners in Biology our senior year," the policeman said, grinning down at me. "Hank Roberts? I asked you to the prom—repeatedly—but you kept sayin' no."

Hank Roberts. The boy who, on the day we were dissecting frogs, complained about the dullness of the scissors and proceeded to whip out his hunting knife.

This was completely embarrassing, but maybe he wouldn't take us to jail if I seemed somewhat apologetic.

"I'm really sorry about that, Hank."

Lucas coughed to cover his laugh.

"Far be it from me to interrupt when two consenting adults are having a little fun . . ." Hank's eyes finally traveled to Lucas, shooting him an angry look while shining the light in his face. "It *was* consensual, wasn't it?"

"Absolutely consensual," I assured him.

He nodded. "That's good, but this is private property now, so I'm going to have to ask you to leave. If Jude catches you two out here, he'll wanna press charges."

"We'll leave," I promised him.

"We're sorry, officer," Lucas apologized solemnly.

Hank chuckled. "Not a problem. Have a good night! Oh, and I'll expect to see the two of you at church on Sunday."

We waited until the lights of Hank's cruiser were completely out of sight before exploding with laughter.

"He'll see us at *church* on Sunday?"

I grinned. "I guess he thinks we have some repenting to do."

"Hmm." Lucas lowered his head and kissed me tenderly. "I'd have to disagree with him. I'm not sorry at all."

I gently caressed his face. "Neither am I."

"I am grateful he showed up when he did," Lucas said softly. "The first time we make love won't be in the back seat of my car." He grinned sheepishly and kissed me once more before climbing over to the front seat.

Stunned speechless, I quickly followed and fastened my seat belt. Lucas slipped his hand into mine, and without a word, he led us out of the woods and back out onto the highway.

September passed in a blinding blur of first semester assignments and settling into my new routine. Each day was pretty much the same—work, eat, friends, and sleep. Despite the monotony, I was at peace. There was a comfort in the familiarity of it all, and I found it was a calm that trickled into every facet of my new life in Sycamore Falls.

My panic attacks were less frequent these days, and I was thankful not to need the medication so much. My friendship with Aubrey was stronger than ever, and the town continued to welcome me home with open arms. To them, I wasn't the prodigal daughter returning home to escape her nightmare. I was just Sarah Bray—hometown girl, Jason and Carol's daughter, and Grace's granddaughter.

I was also Lucas's . . . *something.*

We'd yet to label it. It seemed a little soon to call myself his girlfriend; however, friends don't usually make out in the back seat of a car, so we found ourselves in a weird state of limbo that didn't seem to matter to either of us.

It bugged the hell out of Aubrey, though.

Naturally, there'd been a shift in our relationship since the night in the woods. We were more playful and flirty, except when we were at school where we were required to keep a respectable distance. Aubrey noticed the change between us—because Aubrey notices everything—but I just wasn't ready to share any of the details.

Today, we were looking at apartments.

"How did you even find this place?" I asked as we pulled into a gravel driveway. Apartments were a rarity in Sycamore Falls. Decent places were even more uncommon. This particular building had been recently renovated into one-bedroom units and looked clean and tidy from the outside.

Lucas shifted the car into park. "It was posted on the community board down at the hardware store."

"You don't like your house?"

"I do. It's just too big for me. This place is closer to school, and the rent is cheaper."

This apartment was also closer to my house, which made me ridiculously happy.

"Ready?"

He nodded, and we climbed out of the car. Lucas pointed toward the first door on the left. "Apartment number one."

I couldn't hide my smirk. "How original."

Lucas slipped the key into the lock and cautiously pushed the door open. Neither of us was brave enough to step inside.

I chanced a glance at him. "Nervous?"

"I just hope it isn't a dump."

Bravely, I took him by the hand and led us inside, closing the door behind us. The living room walls were stark white and smelled of fresh paint. The carpet was brown and looked brand new.

I couldn't deny I was pleasantly surprised.

"Not a dump at all," I assured him.

I heard his quiet sigh of relief as we made our way through the rest of the apartment. It was a quick look because the place was insanely small, but each room was neat and clean. All of the kitchen appliances were new and the bathroom fixtures shined.

"I think it's perfect," Lucas said when we returned to the living room.

"I think so, too."

With a smile, Lucas placed his hands along my hips and pulled me close.

"Do you know what makes it even more perfect?"

"What's that?"

"It's closer to your house."

I smiled and wrapped my arms around his neck.

"And closer to me is a good thing?"

"Closer to you is a very good thing." Leaning down, he rubbed his nose against mine.

"I have to admit being close to you is sometimes a struggle, though."

"Why is it a struggle?"

Suddenly, my back was being pressed against the living room wall and his hands gripped my waist. His eyes were dark and intense as he slowly brushed my hair aside. He lowered his head, gently trailing his lips from my cheek to my ear.

"Because, sometimes, it's just not close enough," Lucas murmured.

I melted against him as his lips covered mine.

I found myself becoming more comfortable at school as I grew closer to my students. Creative writing was the best part of my school day, because the teenagers were opinionated and willing to talk about anything. I'd purposely chosen some controversial topics, and some of those discussions had become heated. I loved those days because I could remind my students that merely listening to others' opinions didn't mean we had to agree with them. In those moments, I felt like I was actually teaching them something worthwhile, and not just how to correct their comma splices.

High school is always full of drama, and this week had been no exception. According to the rumor mill, Matt and Carrie had broken up via text message. Obviously, the news that the star quarterback had dumped the captain of the cheerleading squad caused quite an uproar. Carrie was moping around like a zombie, while Matt seemed completely unaffected by it all, leading everyone to assume he had another girlfriend just waiting in the wings.

It was all very dramatic.

Matt's grades, however, were slipping. Because Tommy required a C average, the faculty was required to send him a weekly report on his football players. A quick glance at my grade book led me to ask Matt to stay behind at the end of today's English class.

"You wanted to see me, Miss Bray?"

Sitting on the edge of my desk, I smiled at my favorite senior as he slumped in his chair. Kids always know when a lecture is coming.

"How are you doing, Matt?"

He shrugged. "Can't complain."

"Coach tells me some college scouts are coming to the games to watch you play."

His face brightened. "A recruiter from Florida State is coming this Friday. And Tennessee and South Carolina are interested in me. I don't really care where I go to college. I just want out of this town."

"I understand. That's why I'm a little concerned about your grades."

His smile faded. "How bad?"

"Let's just say Coach is asking for progress reports, and I'm dragging my feet a little because someone is failing my English class."

Matt groaned hoarsely and buried his face in his hands.

"You're usually an A student, so I'm concerned. What's going on?"

He raised his head, and I could see the indecision on his face.

"You know about me and Carrie, right?"

Nice try, kid.

"I heard about that, yes," I replied patiently, "but I don't think that's what's affecting your grades. As a matter of fact, I've noticed you seem more relieved than heartbroken when it comes to your break-up, so I don't think we can blame your English grade on your love life."

"My love life . . ." Matt muttered tiredly. "Yeah, it's a mess. And you're right. I'm not at all broken-hearted about Carrie."

His expression turned somber. "I wasn't being fair to her, Miss Bray. She hates me now, but trust me, it's so much better this way. It was pretty selfish of me to keep up the charade for as long as I did. Remember what I told you? That I walk the halls of this school, and I play my role every single day?"

I nodded.

"I just got tired of playing, Miss Bray."

His voice was hollow and sad, and in that moment, he reminded me of another high school boy—an intelligent young man with blonde hair and piercing blue eyes who had played his own role each and every day. He'd lied to his parents. He'd lied to his girlfriend. For years, he'd even lied to himself. One day, he made the brave decision to stop lying, and soon after, his life came to a violent end.

My fault.

"Miss Bray, are you all right? You look a little sick."

"I'm fine, Matt." I blinked back my unshed tears and reached for my grade book. Flipping through the pages, I took a deep breath and tried to focus. "If you'll write your analysis on *Macbeth* and do your other two missing assignments—"

"I'll do it!"

"Good. Get them to me by Friday, and I'll hold on to Coach's progress reports until then."

"You're awesome, Miss Bray!" Matt exclaimed as he leapt out of his chair. "I promise. You'll have it Friday morning."

Matt sprinted out of the room, nearly knocking Lucas to the ground in the process. He mumbled an apology and thanked me again before racing down the hallway.

"You know, you *are* pretty awesome, Miss Bray."

I collapsed into my chair. I didn't feel awesome at all. I felt weary, exhausted, and on the verge of my first panic attack in weeks.

Lucas walked around my desk, and suddenly, his hands were on me. He began gently massaging my neck and shoulders, and I couldn't keep from moaning.

"You know, Miss Bray, that's not a very appropriate sound for the classroom."

I didn't care. I just closed my eyes and let him work his magic on my tense muscles.

"However," Lucas said softly, "I do know the perfect place where you'd be free to moan as loudly as you like."

My eyes snapped open.

His new apartment? The back seat of his car?

At this moment, I'd follow him anywhere.

Chapter Twelve

"You know, this wasn't exactly what I had in mind."

"What did you have in mind?"

Too embarrassed to answer, I simply bit my lip and followed him toward our boulder. It had become our little snuggling place whenever we visited the waterfall.

I draped the blanket around my shoulders. "It won't be long until the weather isn't so cooperative."

"Then we will just have to take advantage of it as long as we can." He sat down on our rock and gently pulled me into his lap. "Are you going to share that blanket?"

Grinning, I wrapped it around us while we snuggled close and looked across the water. In the distance, you could see the leaves already changing color at the highest peaks. It wouldn't be long until the entire mountainside was covered in red and gold.

"I was thinking about you last night," Lucas said.

"What were you thinking?"

"There are some very important things I don't know about you."

"Like?"

"Like . . . what's your favorite color?"

I laughed. "Are you serious?"

His handsome face split into a wide, expectant grin, and we spent the rest of the afternoon playing twenty questions, learning the most inconsequential things about each other's lives. Favorite colors. Foods. Books. As the game continued, we became bolder with our questions, and he wondered how it was possible that I was still single.

"I'm pretty high maintenance," I replied jokingly, although it was the truth. "There was this guy back in Memphis."

"The man must be an idiot if he let you go."

"Actually, I let him go."

"Why?"

I smirked. "You might not have noticed, but I'm an emotional girl."

"And he couldn't handle it?"

"I didn't want to be something that had to be handled," I replied as I looked toward the falls. "He wasn't a bad person; it wasn't his fault. I was already wounded when he met me, and then . . ."

Bowing my head, I sighed as he nuzzled my cheek with his nose.

"Let's just say it didn't get any better."

"Maybe he should have tried harder."

"Maybe it just wasn't meant to be," I said. "I'm not broken-hearted or disappointed, honestly. He'll be much happier without me, and I'll be much happier without him." I tilted my head and offered him a smile. "I *am* much happier without him."

He grinned.

"So, what about you? Did you leave someone behind

back in New York?"

Lucas shrugged. "I dated some, but there was never anyone I was serious about, much to my mother's dismay . . ." His voice trailed off, sentimental and soft.

"You miss your parents."

"I do. They were always my best friends, and they stood by my side when I went through the situation with Marina. It was a horrible time in my life, and they were right there. The fact that I allowed it to put distance between me and my family is my biggest regret of all, even if they did understand my need for a fresh start."

"They sound like really wonderful people."

I knew what it felt like to miss your family. It was a pain I wouldn't wish on my worst enemy.

"They are. It'll be so nice to see them at Thanksgiving."

My heart sank. I hadn't even begun to think about the holidays. Of course, he'd go home.

He would go home.

And I would be alone.

"Hey, what is it?" he whispered and pulled me closer.

I forced a smile. It wasn't as if I could expect him to desert his family for Thanksgiving just because I was alone.

"It's nothing, Lucas."

The sun began to set, so we folded up the blanket and headed back to the car. The drive home was quiet, mostly because I was too wrapped up in my own head to carry on a conversation. Lucas seemed to understand I needed some space, so he simply held my hand all the way home, rubbing little circles along my skin until he finally pulled into the driveway. Always the gentleman, he walked me to my door.

"Thank you for this afternoon," I whispered.

He turned toward me, and I couldn't stand to see the pain in his eyes.

"Sarah, what's wrong? What did I say?"

"You didn't say anything." Reaching for the door, I was determined not to cry in front of him. I'd done enough of that to last a lifetime.

"Sarah, wait—"

"I'll see you tomorrow."

Closing the door behind me, I pressed my forehead against the wood. Listening intently, I waited for the sound of the car's ignition.

It never came.

Of course, he wouldn't leave me.

Wiping away my tears, I walked toward the living room and over to the bookshelf. I quickly found the photo album I needed and carried it over to the couch. Taking a deep breath, I placed the album in my lap and began to thumb through the pictures.

Sixteen Thanksgiving dinners.

Sixteen Christmas mornings.

Sixteen years of holidays with my family.

I flipped through page after page of my family as we surrounded our Thanksgiving table. Endless photos of me when I was a child, opening presents on Christmas day. My parents and grandma were always in the background, looking healthy and happy, and completely full of life.

I closed the photo album and set it aside.

I couldn't look at it anymore.

I had no idea what was wrong with me. It wasn't like this would be my first holiday without my family, but it would be my first without them in Sycamore Falls. Lucas would be with his parents in New York, and Aubrey and Tommy probably had their own traditions at their house.

I would be alone.

I *am* alone.

I buried my face in my hands and wept. I hadn't felt alone in so long, and suddenly, the feeling was suffocating me as memories flooded my mind.

Visions of us chopping down the Christmas tree.

Sitting on my father's shoulders while I placed the angel on top.

Spying from the top of the stairs in the middle of the

night as my mom and dad propped my bicycle under the tree, shattering any hope that Santa Claus was real.

"Sarah . . ."

I could hear his voice, but I was too lost . . . too consumed by the darkness and the grief to find him. Suddenly, I was in his arms, warm and safe, and he cradled me close to his chest while he murmured softly in my ear.

I had no idea how long we stayed like that, but after a while, my tears finally began to subside.

"I'm a mess," I whispered, wiping my face with the back of my hand. Very gently, Lucas tilted my head toward his. His blue eyes were pained as he examined every inch of my face. Without a word, he tenderly kissed my eyelids.

"I hate to see you cry," he murmured.

"I'm sorry."

"No, Sarah, *I'm* sorry. I've sat on your porch this whole time, trying to figure out what I said to upset you."

"It wasn't you. We were just talking about Thanksgiving, and it made me miss my family. It really hit me that I would be alone in this big house for the holidays."

"But you don't have to be alone. I want to spend the holidays with you, but if it's too much—"

I was so confused.

"But you're going to New York . . ."

"I'm not going to New York. I just said it would be nice to see my parents at Thanksgiving," Lucas replied, gently wiping a stray tear away from my cheek. "I invited them here."

"Here?" I asked, sniffling quietly. "Your parents are coming here?"

Lucas smiled down at me. "Mom doesn't believe me when I tell her my apartment isn't a complete dump. Plus, they want to see where I'm teaching, and they're very, very eager to meet you."

"They know about me?"

"You're pretty much all I talk about when I call home."

Suddenly, I was terrified.

"Your mother's going to think I'm a basket case."

Lucas gently laced his fingers through mine. "She will love you. There's just one problem. My apartment is extremely small. I don't even have a kitchen table. If only I knew someone who had a big house and liked to cook . . ."

"If only," I said, giggling softly. "Lucas, I would love that. Where would they stay?"

"I don't know. Do you trust the motel in town?"

I wrinkled my nose.

"Not at all. I could fix up a room for them . . . that is, if you think they'd be comfortable here."

"That wouldn't be awkward for you?"

I shrugged. "I don't think so. I'd love to spend time with your parents."

Mesmerized, I watched as his fingers slid along mine.

"I didn't mean to make you sad, sweetheart."

The sentiment flowed through me and melted my heart.

"You didn't. It was just the thought of being without my family. Sometimes, I forget I'm really alone in this world."

Lucas gently stroked my cheek with the back of his hand. "But you're not. You're not alone, Sarah. I couldn't walk off your porch because I knew you were upset. I didn't even consider going to New York for Thanksgiving because I knew I'd miss you too much."

Tears swam in my eyes, and I bowed my head.

Gently, he lifted my face toward his, forcing me to look at him. His voice was soft and sincere.

"You're not alone in this world. I'm right here, and I'm trying so hard to love you. All I want to do is love you."

He kissed me and it was soft and sweet. My fingers tangled in his hair as I pulled him closer, and he groaned when my lips parted. Suddenly, I was lying beneath him, and I whimpered when his mouth blazed a trail along my neck.

"Let me love you," he whispered roughly, and I whimpered as his entire body pressed into mine. I arched against him, and he swallowed my moans with a burning kiss. Our hands roamed, and it was when I felt his hand slide along the button of my jeans that I had my moment of clarity. The two months of pent-up emotion were causing us to be reckless, and I knew one of us had to come to our senses.

Lucas must have realized it at the same time, because the urgency of our kisses was suddenly gone. With a quiet groan, he buried his face against my neck as we both struggled to catch our breath.

Slowly, he lifted his face toward mine and peppered soft kisses along my cheek.

"Let me love you, Sarah."

This time, it wasn't an urgent plea fueled by lust. It was tender and sincere and the sweetest words I'd ever heard.

"I don't know if I can," I whispered honestly. "I don't know how."

It was the truth. Ryan had tried, but I'd been too wounded and weak to let him love all of me. I hadn't given him the chance to love every insecurity and flaw.

Lucas, however, had seen them all.

And by some miracle, he still wanted me.

"I'll show you how," Lucas promised with a whisper.

We smiled, and I framed his face with the palm of my hands before his lips found mine once more.

"You know, it's still weeks until Halloween."

It was too early on Saturday morning, and Aubrey was dragging me through the aisles of Wal-Mart. The forty-five minute drive to Winslow had only taken thirty, thanks to my friend's total disregard for the speed limit.

"You've obviously never shopped for a Halloween costume for a toddler," Aubrey said while fervently hunting through the racks. Screaming kids were running wildly up and down the aisle as frazzled mothers tried to control them with the promise of a Happy Meal. "The good costumes are probably already gone! I've waited too long, but Tommy always had practice or a game or . . ."

I let her ramble while I continued to dodge children wearing angel halos and zombie masks. In the distance, I saw a small display of fall decorations, and I navigated my way through the kids to get a closer look. Beautiful red and gold place mats and tablecloths hung neatly in a row, and I ran my fingers along the fabric.

"Oh, those are pretty!"

I counted out enough place mats for each chair. "I'm buying them for Thanksgiving."

"Are you cooking? I never do, but I was going to invite you to my mom's for dinner."

"I appreciate the invitation, but I'm cooking for Lucas and his parents." I smiled. Aubrey arched a curious eyebrow, and I sighed. "Yes, Lucas's parents are coming for Thanksgiving."

"You're meeting his parents . . ."

"Yep."

"And you were going to tell me this when?"

"I'm telling you now."

I could feel Aubrey's eyes on me as I tossed the tablecloth and mats into the shopping cart.

"So, did you find what you wanted?"

Aubrey glanced down at the costumes in her hands. One was Buzz Lightyear and the other was a giant pumpkin. I had a feeling I knew which Daniel would prefer. "No. I can't decide because I've been momentarily stunned by the fact you're being introduced to the parents, and you seem completely nonchalant about it."

I was actually a complete nervous wreck, but I figured it was still October. Why panic now?

"Sarah Bray, don't ignore me—"

Her ringing cell phone interrupted her rant, and I

smiled sweetly and sniffed a nearby scented candle while she answered it.

"Is he all right? . . . No, I understand. We'll be right there." She quickly snapped her phone shut and tossed both costumes into the cart.

"Aubrey, what's wrong?"

Tugging me by the arm, she pulled away from the costumes and toward the registers. Her eyes were wide and brimming with tears. "We have to get back to town."

My heartbeat turned frantic. "Is it the baby?"

"No, it's Matt."

"Aubrey!" I practically shouted, grabbing onto her arm. "What's wrong with Matt?"

A tear trickled down her cheek.

"Someone's beat the hell out of him."

Chapter Thirteen

The clinic wasn't open every day—and it certainly wasn't open on Saturdays—but when the high school quarterback suffers an injury, it's amazing how quickly a doctor and his staff can be convinced to open their doors.

"I just don't understand," Aubrey said quietly while we waited for word from the doctor. Lucas was in the seat next to me while a few teammates kept vigil outside. "Why would Patrick do such a thing? *Again?*"

The details were sketchy, but from what we'd gathered, the team had gone to a party down near the river after last night's win over Bradley High. No one was sure what started the brawl between Matt and Patrick, but it ended with Matt being beaten to a bloody pulp. Some of his teammates had helped him home where his mom had done what she could to clean him up. Both the sheriff and the doctor were called at dawn.

Lucas sighed. "No one can blame it on a girl this time."

Gazing out the window, I noticed the small group of football players who'd congregated in the parking lot. Howie was there, and when he saw me looking, he offered me a sad smile and an unenthusiastic wave.

"There is some serious tension between those two boys, but I don't think it has anything to do with a girl," I replied.

Suddenly, Tommy appeared in the waiting room with Matt's parents by his side. Debbie was crying into her tissue with her husband whispering comforting words in her ear.

"Broken arm," Tommy announced grimly. "Doc says he's out for the season."

Debbie just cried harder, and I closed my eyes with a groan.

So much for those college scouts.

"That boy is going to pay for this!" Matt's dad bellowed loudly.

"He's been arrested," Aubrey offered softly.

Mr. Stuart snorted. "Arrested? He's Mike Wilson's kid. The boy has probably already made bail and sleeping soundly in his bed."

Mike Wilson was the only attorney in town.

Tommy glanced in my direction. "Sarah, he's asking for you."

"Matt?"

He nodded. "Just to warn you—he looks pretty beat up. Don't let it upset you."

Lucas placed his hand against my elbow. "Do you want me to come?"

"No, it's okay. I can handle it."

I think.

"Right this way," Dr. Jones said, motioning toward the door leading to the tiny examining rooms.

Taking a deep breath, I followed him down the narrow hallway and to the first room on the left. I was prepared, but I still gasped when I saw Matt's battered body lying on the bed. Bandages covered the entire right side of his face. He saw me and managed a smile.

"Hey." His voice was raspy and tired.

Dr. Jones excused himself before closing the door behind him. I slowly walked over to the bed and pulled a chair close to his side.

"The things you'll do to get out of reading *Macbeth*," I teased.

He laughed and then immediately grimaced in pain.

"Sorry," I whispered.

"It's okay, Miss Bray. Everything just hurts."

It broke my heart to look at him. He kept fidgeting uncomfortably, and his arm was in some temporary sling. I doubted they could put a cast on him at our clinic.

"Matt, what was the fight about? What can I do?"

He swallowed, and I wondered if he was dangerously close to tears.

"You like to help people, don't you, Miss Bray?"

Shrugging, I stared down at my hands in my lap.

"I like to try, yeah. Sometimes, it doesn't work."

"Like that kid in Memphis?" Matt whispered, and my eyes snapped to his. "Don't be mad, but I was curious. I had to know why someone who'd actually escaped this place would ever come back. Now, I know."

Tears pricked my eyes.

"Matt, I can't have this conversation with you."

He continued as if I hadn't said a word. "That guy . . . he was just trying to get through high school and start a new life somewhere, wasn't he? A life without judgment. A life without bullying. A life where you don't have to pretend to be someone you aren't. A place where you don't have to worry about someone beating the shit out of you because you're . . ."

Tears streaked down my cheek. "Matt, please—"

His eyes were squeezed shut. "I thought leaving Sycamore Falls was the answer to all of my problems, Miss

Bray. I thought if I could just get out of here . . . but it's not like that at all, is it? The whole world is full of crazy assholes who will always think it's fine to treat me like shit just because I'm . . ."

He choked back a sob, and suddenly, the only sound in the room was the strangled tears of an eighteen-year-old boy who had just made the biggest confession of his life.

He couldn't be . . .

The images and sounds of that day hit me like a wrecking ball.

Sirens.

Gunfire.

Blood.

So much blood.

My ears began to ring and my vision blurred, and I heard Matt scream for the doctor just moments before I hit the floor.

"More?"

I nodded and watched through teary eyes as Lucas refilled my glass. The alcohol was sweet and warmed my bones. It wasn't doing a thing for my pounding headache, though.

"Where did you find wine in this town?"

"I didn't. When I told my parents this county was dry, they insisted I bring a case with me."

"I love your parents. Please tell them to bring more when they come down for Thanksgiving."

Lucas smiled. "I need to find you something to eat."

He kissed my forehead, and I snuggled deeper into his couch and sipped my wine while he went to the kitchen to search for food. I wasn't particularly hungry, but maybe a little food would settle my stomach and keep me from passing out again.

After being deemed healthy by the doctor, Lucas had

brought me straight to his apartment. He didn't ask any questions, and I didn't offer any explanations. He'd simply led me toward his couch, wrapped me in a blanket, and held me close to his chest. I'd insisted on not taking any medication, and Lucas respected my wishes. I'd still napped on and off all afternoon, but my dreams were disturbing and ruined any chance I had of a restful sleep.

Lucas walked back into the room. "I made you a sandwich. I also got a text from Tommy while I was in the kitchen. Just like Mr. Stuart predicted, Patrick didn't spend a minute in jail."

"I didn't really expect him to."

He placed the plate in my lap. "Patrick's eighteen, so I was hoping. He was released into his father's custody. Tommy has dismissed him from the team, though."

"For Patrick, I bet that's worse than jail." I stared down at my peanut butter sandwich. It looked delicious, but the thoughts of eating completely turned my stomach.

"Please try to eat, baby."

I smiled. "Did you just call me *baby*?"

"Yes, I did," Lucas whispered as he stroked my cheek. "Why? Did you like that?"

I nodded. Actually, I liked it a lot. I liked it so much I forced myself to take a bite of his sandwich.

"Do you want to talk about it?"

The question was inevitable. I'd passed out at the clinic, and I'd been a sobbing mess all afternoon. "Not really, no."

"Do you *need* to talk about it?"

I did need to talk about it. I needed to tell him about Memphis and the shooting, and I probably needed to tell him about Matt.

I decided to test the waters. "Can I ask you something?"

"Sure—if you eat the other half of your sandwich."

I humored him and took a bite. Lucas handed me a glass of milk, and I frowned at the liquid in the glass.

"Did I drink all of the wine?"

Lucas smirked. "I'm cutting you off."

I sighed heavily.

"Okay," I said in between bites, "what is your opinion on homosexuality?"

His surprised expression would have made me laugh if this situation was the least bit humorous.

"That wasn't what I expected at all."

"Well?"

He gave me a puzzled look.

"Well, my general opinion is it's not really any of my business how someone lives his or her life. I don't necessarily *agree* with it, but I also don't want to see someone ridiculed or harassed because they're gay."

I nodded. "That's how I feel, too."

I took another bite of my sandwich in an attempt to avoid his eyes. I couldn't look at him. The man could read me like a book.

"Sarah, that's a pretty specific question."

I just continued chewing.

"Why did you ask?"

I didn't answer, and we sat in silence until my plate was empty. I carefully placed it on the coffee table before climbing into his lap. Wrapping the blanket around us, I buried my face against his neck as he held me close. I inhaled deeply, letting his sweet scent relax me.

"You're like a therapist or lawyer, right? Anything I tell you stays between us?"

"I'm not a therapist or a lawyer," Lucas whispered, "but I am the man who is absolutely crazy about you. So yes, anything you tell me stays between us."

I lifted my head to meet his eyes.

"You're crazy about me?"

"Absolutely insane."

I smiled. "I'm crazy about you, too."

He kissed me—a slow, sweet kiss that flowed through me. It was warm and tender, and when we finally pulled away, his eyes were bright and adoring.

"Absolutely insane for you." He nuzzled my cheek and held me close. Several minutes passed before I finally found the courage to say the words.

"Matt is gay."

His eyes widened in shock. "He told you so?"

"Not in so many words, no, but I think he will, and I think Patrick knows."

"And that's why Patrick keeps kicking his ass?"

I nodded.

"So, Patrick is either a homophobe . . ."

"Or he's the object of Matt's affection."

"Or both," Lucas said quietly. "Are you upset because he's gay?"

"No. It was just . . . déjà vu, I guess."

"Memphis?" he asked, and I nodded. "Do you want to tell me that story?"

"Yes, but not tonight. I'm afraid it doesn't have a happy ending."

He pulled me close to his chest. "You deserve so many happy endings. I wish I could erase every painful memory you have."

"I wish you could, too." I snuggled deeper into his arms. "When I'm with you, it's so easy to forget the world is a terrible place. I've never felt so safe or so . . ."

Embarrassed, I buried my face against his neck.

"Loved," Lucas murmured. "Do you feel loved, Sarah?"

I nodded against his skin. I did. I felt it every time he touched me. Every time he looked at me.

It terrified me.

It thrilled me.

"Let me say it," he pleaded softly.

I shook my head. "Not yet."

We held each other a while longer until Lucas sighed and kissed my hair.

"Stay with me tonight. I'll sleep on the couch. I just

want to take care of you. And then tomorrow morning, we'll go to church if you want. Or we'll stay right here, and I'll even cook breakfast. Just . . . stay with me."

I couldn't say no, and I really didn't want to.

"Okay."

Voices roar through the high school cafeteria while students navigate their way to the tables. The cliques are easily spotted: the jocks, the geeks, the beauty queens, the slackers . . .

Where will he sit today?

Despite the fact he's a handsome and impeccably dressed young man, he fades into the background. Knowing it's pointless, the girls don't bother to look his way, and the guys deliberately avoid his eyes.

He grips his tray tightly and heads toward the corner table with the rest of the outcasts. They nod hello, but that's the end of any real attempt at conversation. It's an unspoken rule of sorts. This is their refuge—a tiny bit of sanctuary in the hell that is public high school—and they're content to sit in peace.

He takes a seat, and I can see the exhaustion on his face. It's not a weariness that comes from too many sleepless nights. This is a bone-tired fatigue no seventeen-year-old kid should ever feel.

He's giving in.

Giving up.

In my peripheral vision, I see a senior stalk into the cafeteria. He's tall, with deep brown eyes and jet-black hair that won't stay in place. He's good looking, popular, and a little conceited, thanks to his father's wealth and status.

He has a reputation to uphold. Rumors to squash.

A score to settle.

He pulls the silver gun out of his jacket pocket. Amid the chaos, no one notices.

I notice.

I try to run, but I'm frozen in place.

I try to scream, but there's no sound.

The first shot rings out, and suddenly, everyone's on the cold tile.

Tears, prayers, screams.

Another shot, and for some reason, I'm the only one who can't move. Who can't scream. Who can't do anything but watch as the young man's body slumps over his tray.

Finally, I find my voice and scream his name.

My body jerked awake as the crash of thunder roared in my ears. Lightning flashed in the window, and I felt a momentary rush of panic when I couldn't remember where I was.

Then I heard Lucas's soft snoring coming from the living room, and I smiled despite my rapidly racing heart. The nightmares always frightened me, and I was out of practice. I hadn't had one since my first night in Sycamore Falls.

It wasn't a mystery why the nightmares were coming back now.

Smoothing my hand along the blanket, I sat up in his bed. It wasn't a big bed, but it was definitely big enough for two people and certainly big enough for us. He'd insisted on sleeping in the living room despite my protests.

My mind knew it was the right decision, but my heart was missing him. And, after the dream, I desperately needed to feel his arms around me.

I climbed out of bed and tiptoed toward the living room, and what I found made my heart race frantically once again. Lucas was sprawled across his tiny couch with his legs dangling off the sides. He didn't look comfortable at all, but his snores assured me he was sleeping peacefully.

The couch wasn't very big, but it *might* be big enough for two.

Very carefully, I settled myself against the cushion, and he murmured in his sleep when I slipped my arm around his waist. Instinctively, his arm draped my shoulder and he pulled me close to his chest. I snuggled against him and sighed contently.

"I missed you," he whispered. His voice was sleepy and soft.

"I missed you, too."

His hand cradled my face as he kissed the top of my head. I pressed my ear to his chest, and the sound of his heartbeat combined with his soft snores soothed me to sleep.

Chapter Fourteen

It was still raining when I awoke the next morning. The pitter-patter against the roof was loud, but it was a relaxing sound and only made me want to snuggle deeper into Lucas's arms.

I didn't want to go to church today.

I didn't want to move from this spot.

His fingers were gently dancing along my spine. It was the softest of touches, and the motion nearly lulled me back to sleep until a rumble of thunder caused both of us to jump. Lucas's arm tightened around me as I buried my face against his chest.

"Good morning."

I groaned tiredly, and he laughed.

"Not a morning person?"

"Not at all," I mumbled. I rested my head on his chest and gazed up at his handsome face. "Hi."

"Hi." He grinned down at me. "How did you sleep?"

"Not too bad. You?"

"Much better, once you joined me."

"You should have just come to bed. I *think* I could have kept my hands to myself."

Smiling, he pushed a strand of hair behind my ear. "I couldn't have."

Lucas pulled me up his body, his hands settling on my hips.

Touching my forehead to his, I sighed softly. "I probably have terrible morning breath."

"I don't care."

He placed a soft kiss along the corner of my mouth. My heart raced as his lips brushed mine, and when his tongue softly teased my bottom lip, morning breath was the very last thing on my mind. His hands slid down, gently cupping my bottom and pulling me tighter against him, and I moaned.

"I told you I couldn't have kept my hands to myself," Lucas said breathlessly.

I shifted against him, and he groaned hoarsely as my mouth covered his.

Lucas had been right.

The bed would have been a *bad* idea.

Thankfully, common sense prevailed, and after a few more not-so-innocent kisses, I offered to make breakfast while he took a shower. It was unbelievably tempting to stay tangled in each other's arms on this rainy Sunday morning, but we decided to go to church instead.

After all, Deputy Hank would be disappointed if we didn't make an appearance.

After a quick stop at the house to change, Lucas and I made our way to church. Deputy Hank smirked and nodded in our direction as we found a seat near the back. The entire congregation was buzzing, and it didn't take long to realize they were gossiping about the fight between Patrick and Matt.

In their usual front pew were Mr. and Mrs. Stuart, looking uncomfortable and completely exhausted. I wasn't surprised that Matt was nowhere to be seen. Patrick, however, was sitting directly across the Stuarts with his father by his side. His expression was cold and hard, and his eyes remained fixed on the preacher as he welcomed us.

"It is with a heavy heart I greet you this morning," Pastor Martin announced. "Our youth are conflicted. Friendships are being tested. Parents are struggling to understand. A community is striving to be supportive."

Members of the congregation looked appropriately shame-faced for gossiping.

Throughout the sermon, my eyes roamed along the pews. I noticed several members of the football team staring down at their laps with guilty expressions while the pastor preached from the book of Romans.

"Bless them which persecute you; bless, and curse not. Rejoice with them that do rejoice, and weep with them that weep. Be of the same mind one toward another. Mind not high things, but condescend to men of low estate. Be not wise in your own conceits. Recompense to no man evil for evil. Provide things honest in the sight of all men. If it be possible, as much as lieth in you, live peaceably with all men. Dearly beloved, avenge not yourselves, but rather give place unto wrath: for it is written, Vengeance is mine; I will repay, saith the Lord."

There were a few "amens" from the congregation, and Patrick's face was smug.

After the service, we declined Aubrey's invitation for lunch. I wasn't in the mood to be happy and sociable. I was, however, eager to pay a visit to Matt. Lucas seemed to understand, and he offered to drive me home.

"I can go with you," he offered again as he walked me to my door. The rain had finally ceased, and the sun was trying to peek out from behind the clouds.

"I really need to do this on my own, but I'll call you later? We could have an early dinner."

"Dinner sounds great." He smiled and kissed me softly. "Thanks for staying last night."

"Thanks for taking care of me."

"I love taking care of you."

We kissed goodbye, and I watched him drive away before heading inside to change into a pair of jeans. I had no idea what I was going to say to Matt. Maybe I wouldn't say anything at all.

I just wanted him to know I was on his side, and I would not let history repeat itself.

"I'm going to pretend to be surprised to see you," Matt said, grinning at me from his place on the couch. The swelling in his face had lessened a bit, but he was still covered in bandages. His arm was now in a cast, and he was surrounded by game controllers and pizza boxes.

"How are you feeling, Matt?"

"Doc gave me some kickass meds, so the pain isn't too bad."

Grabbing the remote, he turned off the television and offered me a seat on the couch. "How are *you*? You kind of scared the crap out of me when you passed out like that."

"Sorry," I mumbled. "Low blood sugar."

"Right."

We shared a smile.

"We missed you at church this morning, but I understand why you didn't go."

"I bet I was the topic of the sermon."

"Not *you*, necessarily, but he did talk about friendship and living in harmony. It was a good message."

I left out the line about leaving room for God's wrath. The kid had enough troubles.

We sat in silence for a few minutes. It wasn't uncomfortable, but I could tell he was trying to find the words to say what he needed to say.

"I'm gay," Matt finally whispered.

"I know."

He looked so relieved, as if he'd been dying to say the words for years. He probably had been.

"You're the first person I've ever told, Miss Bray."

"I'm glad you felt like you could share that with me."

His eyes searched my face. "But you don't approve."

"It doesn't matter if I approve. What matters to me is you're happy and safe."

"I'm neither of those things." With a grimace, Matt shifted on the couch. He was always fidgeting, and I wondered if he was simply nervous or if he was truly that uncomfortable. He was breathless by the time he got himself settled once again.

"You'd never know I worked out every day, huh? The simple act of lying on a couch wipes me out."

I smiled sympathetically. "You'll get your strength back."

"Yeah, but I won't get my throwing arm back," Matt replied, his voice full of sorrow. "It was my only chance of getting out of Sycamore Falls. A college scout won't even look at me now."

"You can still go to school. If you keep your grades up, you might even get an academic scholarship."

"I can't stay here," Matt whispered. "You know that, right? It won't be long until the whole town knows about me."

"Matt, I won't say a word."

Grimacing, he shifted his body once again. "I'm not worried about *you*. Patrick knows. By now, I bet the whole team knows."

I listened intently while Matt told me all about Friday night's party. Apparently, a group of guys from a neighboring county had joined them. The booze flowed, and when one of the guys asked Matt to dance, it didn't even dawn on him to say no.

"Drinking is so stupid. It makes you forget where you are and who you're trying to be. I danced with him, and when I walked him to his truck, we exchanged numbers. It was stupid and reckless, but I did it. He was cute, you know? But of course, we were followed, and Patrick saw it all. He's always suspected I was gay—I have no idea why—but seeing me dance with a guy just kind of confirmed it in his mind."

"Is that why you got into the fight at school?"

"It was part of the reason," Matt admitted. "Really, it was because Patrick really likes Carrie, and since he suspected I was gay, he felt I wasn't being fair to her. He called me a few names, and apparently, I fight better when I'm sober because I broke his arm that day."

Glancing down at his cast, he exhaled a noisy sigh. "Payback's a real bitch, Miss Bray."

I smiled sadly. "What about your folks? What are they saying about all of this?"

"Mom knows I'm gay, although she'd never admit it. A mom knows these things. Dad has no idea, and he will disown me. I *tried* not to be this way, Miss Bray. I tried. I dated girls. Kissed them. I even . . . well, you know."

I nodded while praying he didn't go into specifics.

"I tried so hard, but it's who I am, and I wish I could change it. I wish I could just meet a sweet girl and fall in love with her, but it's impossible. Nobody in this town is going to understand, and that's why I have to leave when I graduate. Even if it's just as rough out there. Even if I face the same prejudices. At least I won't have to face them in this town, where I have absolutely no chance at all."

Matt leaned back against the couch and closed his eyes. The speech had made him tired, and when his mom came into the living room to give him his next round of pain meds, I knew it was time to head home.

"Miss Bray," he whispered as I rose to my feet. "I think

you're the bravest person I know, and your secret is safe with me."

Debbie offered me a timid smile and placed his medicine on the table.

Matt was right. Mothers do know everything.

"Yours, too," I promised him.

Luckily, I was able to keep my promise because Lucas didn't ask a single question about my conversation with Matt. He just hugged me and made sure I was okay before taking it upon himself to cook dinner. He'd chosen to make homemade lasagna, and the only thing I was allowed to do was chop vegetables for the salad.

"My kitchen is never going to recover," I teased as my eyes swept across the room where utensils and cheese littered the countertops. Lucas just smirked and pointed me toward a chair. "It smells great, though."

"We'll see." He looked anxious as he scooped the portions onto our plates. That's when I decided, no matter how the lasagna tasted, I was going to promise it was the best I'd ever eaten.

Then I took a bite, and I was pleasantly surprised to find I wouldn't have to lie.

I moaned appreciatively. "It's so good, Lucas."

He smiled brightly and sighed with relief.

"So," he said between bites, "I've been thinking about that rope swing . . . you know, the one you always loved so much when you were a kid. Are you ever going to show it to me?"

"Would you like to see it?"

"Sure. Besides, we've yet to go swimming. We should do that before it gets too cold."

I grinned. My city boy wanted to swim in the river.

"Do you have swim trunks?"

"Do I need them?"

I could feel the heat creep across my face.

"The water can be pretty cold," I warned him, trying desperately to hide my excitement.

He chuckled nervously. "I just wondered if regular shorts would be okay."

"Oh," I muttered, completely embarrassed. "Sure, shorts are fine."

After dinner—and after my kitchen was back in order—I made a mad dash for my closet. I didn't have a bathing suit, so I grabbed an old T-shirt, a pair of shorts, and an extra change of clothes for after the swim. Rushing into the bathroom, I quickly changed and grabbed a couple of towels. I stuffed everything into a bag and slipped on a pair of flip-flops before rushing back down the stairs. Lucas was waiting at the landing, and I watched his eyes sweep over me as I walked down the stairs.

Suddenly, he frowned.

"You look disappointed."

He shrugged. "I am a little."

"Why?"

"I was just hoping you owned a bikini."

I rolled my eyes, and he laughed loudly before leaning down to kiss me.

"Are you sure this is the right place?" Lucas wondered aloud as we looked up at the gigantic sycamore tree standing proudly on the edge of the water. It was definitely the right tree, but there wasn't a rope in sight.

"I'm sure."

Lucas gazed over the hill and across the water. "We can still swim. To be honest, I wasn't excited about throwing myself off a suspended rope, anyway."

"Chicken," I muttered.

Swiftly, he lifted me into the air.

"Lucas!"

Wrapping my arms around his neck, I kicked and screamed while he laughed and bolted toward the water. Suddenly, I was airborne, and the last thing I heard before I hit the chilly water was Lucas's boyish laugh.

Splashing and sputtering, I kicked my way to the surface.

"It's freezing!" I yelled, wiping water out of my eyes. I'd forgotten how cold that first dip in the river could be! It always took my breath away until my body got used to the temperature.

"Whose idea was this?" Lucas shouted. His hair was dripping wet and he had the biggest smile on his face. He was also shirtless, and I was trying very hard not to stare.

"Yours!"

"Oh yeah." Lucas's arms found my waist, and my hands gripped his shoulders. "I'm pretty sure I just wanted to see you in a bikini, though."

Feeling brave, I let go of him just long enough to pull my T-shirt over my head. It wasn't like the soaked white cotton shirt was leaving much to the imagination anyway. Lucas inhaled sharply as I tossed it aside. Slipping my arms around his neck, I pulled myself closer to his chest. His wet skin brushed across mine, and I felt him shudder.

"I'm sorry about the bikini."

"Don't be," he murmured drawing me tighter against him. "Trust me. This is so much better."

I laced my fingers in his hair as he kissed me hard. Lucas lifted me into the air, holding me against his body and kissing me fervently. I whimpered when I felt his hips press into mine.

"Do you know how much I want you?" he whispered against my lips.

Without giving me the chance to answer, his mouth molded to mine. The freezing temperature of the river was forgotten as his hungry kisses warmed every inch of me. Whenever his lips weren't on mine, they were never far from my skin. He especially loved my neck, and when I felt his tongue lick the water droplets along my skin, I nearly came undone. My teeth found his earlobe, and I gently bit him, causing him to growl low in his chest.

"We have to stop," he whispered breathlessly.

My tongue licked the shell of his ear, and he trembled in my arms. Stopping was the very last thing on my mind.

"Sarah," he groaned softly. "Sweetheart, you're killing me."

"I'm sorry." Panting and shaking, I loosened my legs from around his waist. "I'm sorry . . ."

"Shh . . ." His voice was soft as I buried my face against his neck.

Very gently, he lifted me into his arms and carried me out of the water. Placing me on the sand, he reached for my bag and quickly pulled out a towel. I accepted it gratefully and began drying my shivering body. Finding a blanket in the bag, Lucas spread it out across the sand.

"I'm going to change out of my shorts," Lucas said softly. "Yours are still in the bag."

"Okay." Not daring to turn around, I just grabbed the bag and found my shorts. Was he watching? Did it really matter now? I slipped the wet shorts down my legs and quickly stepped into the dry ones.

"All done?"

"Yes."

As we settled ourselves on the blanket, Lucas placed his legs on each side me and pulled me against his chest. Taking another towel from the bag, he gently started to dry my hair.

"Lucas, I can do that."

"I want to."

After a few minutes, I heard him rustling in the bag once again. Very carefully, he pulled a dry shirt over my head, and I slipped my arms inside, letting the towel fall away. Holding me close, his nose drifted into my hair.

"I smell like the river."

"You smell like you," Lucas murmured sweetly. "It's

my favorite smell in the world."

Sighing softly, I relaxed against him as he held me close. The sun was beginning to set, and an orange hue reflected against the water. It was so tranquil and such a stark contrast to my emotions.

"I'm sorry, Lucas."

Gently, he brushed my damp hair aside and pressed a soft kiss against my neck.

"Do you hear me apologizing?"

"No."

"Do you know why?"

"Because you have nothing to apologize for."

"Neither do you."

"That was about two seconds away from becoming wildly out of hand. We've only been together a couple of months, and we're not ready. I know this, and yet, I made it worse by taking off my top."

I felt his quiet chuckle against my skin.

"Why are you laughing?"

Didn't he realize how embarrassed I was? I was never forward with men. Ever.

"You're apologizing for letting me see your—"

"Yes!"

He brushed another kiss against the side of my neck while trying to hide his laughter.

"You're a jerk," I muttered, but it wasn't long before I was laughing, too.

"Look at me," Lucas whispered. With a heavy sigh, I twisted around in his arms. Pulling me close to his chest, he nuzzled my nose. "I meant what I said in the water. I want you, Sarah. Very much."

"I want you, too, but—"

"It's too soon, I know." His eyes were warm and soft as he smiled at me. "I'm a man, and I am absolutely crazy about you, so there is this constant battle between my body and my brain when it comes to taking things slow with you."

Sighing softly, he gently kissed the tip of my nose. "But I'm also a patient man, and I am more than willing to wait."

"Really? You won't be disappointed?"

"I won't be disappointed," he said. "Just—and it pains me to say this—no more topless swims, okay? There's only so much temptation a man can take."

I laughed. "No more topless swims."

His gaze flickered to the dimming sky. "We should probably go before it's too dark to find the trail."

Taking my hand, he helped me to my feet and grabbed our bag.

"It's really too bad about the rope swing," he said as we climbed the hill back toward the trail. "Maybe we can hang another before next summer."

Next summer.

"I'd like that," I whispered.

"Me too."

Kissing my forehead, Lucas took me by the hand and led me out of the woods.

Chapter Fifteen

On Monday morning, the faculty lounge was buzzing with excitement as everyone gossiped in hushed tones about the brawl between Matt and Patrick. It was also the last week of school before Fall Break, and the few teachers who weren't talking about the fight were happily discussing their plans for the weeklong vacation. In a profession where the perks were few and the pay was inadequate, we teachers had to find joy in the simplest ways.

Fall Break was one of them.

I was just checking my mailbox when I heard my name.

"Hank said he caught them making out in the backseat of Lucas's car," the female voice whispered far too loudly. I recognized her as Mrs. Benson, one of the math teachers.

"You're kidding!" Another female voice—a little high pitched and nasal, which I knew immediately was Shellie Stevens.

Squaring my shoulders, I continued leafing through my mail—tossing the unimportant and keeping the rest—until I felt someone's eyes on me. Looking up, I found Shellie smiling brightly in my direction.

"Good morning, Shellie. Volunteering in the office today?"

"Yes, I am. How was your weekend?"

I forced a smile. "My weekend was fine, thanks. How's cheerleading?"

"Well, we've had some drama," she whispered—glancing behind her shoulder. *Now* she tries to be discreet? "My head cheerleader has just been traumatized by all of this."

"Well, Carrie's a bright girl. I'm sure she'll survive and come out stronger than ever."

"Yes, but she's my *leader*. The head cheerleader is supposed to appear strong and in control at all times. It affects the entire squad if she shows any sign of weakness. Those girls are like dominoes . . ."

It was difficult, but I somehow resisted the urge to roll my eyes.

"You have to remember Carrie is also a teenager." Honestly, I felt a little sorry for the young girl. As if being a high school senior wasn't tough enough, the last thing Carrie needed was an overbearing cheer coach pressuring her to stay strong for her squad. "She just needs some time. Don't you remember how it felt to be dumped in high school?"

Her face was a blank page.

"Of course you don't," I muttered under my breath.

"Anyway," Shellie grinned mischievously, and I knew what was coming. "Rumor has it you and Mr. Miller are spending an awful lot of time with each other."

I simply smiled and tossed a catalog into the nearby wastebasket.

"I bet the two of you have plans for Fall Break."

Suddenly, every female's head swiveled in Lucas's

direction as he walked into the faculty lounge.

"Good morning, ladies." He smiled at the two of us and reached into his mailbox, pulling out a mound of mail. His arm brushed mine, and I felt the blood rush to my face.

"Speak of the devil!" Shellie gushed excitedly. "We were just talking about you."

"Oh?" Lucas's eyes twinkled as he looked at me.

"Did you have a good weekend?"

"I had a fantastic weekend," he told her with a megawatt grin. "As a matter of fact, it was quite possibly the best weekend of my life."

Of course it was. Less than twenty-four hours ago, my naked chest had been pressed against his and my legs had been wrapped around his waist.

Shellie's eyes were wide and eager for information. "Really? What did you do?"

"I went swimming in the river."

Mortified and needing an escape, I turned my back toward them and poured myself a cup of coffee.

I hated coffee.

"Swimming? Isn't it a little cold for swimming?"

"I didn't notice the cold at all. The scenery was far too beautiful."

Call it intuition, but I had a feeling he wasn't talking about the trees.

"Well, that sounds . . . fun," Shellie muttered just as the first bell rang. "I'm volunteering today, so let me know if you need anything copied or stapled or . . ."

Is she flirting?

Pivoting on my heel, I narrowed my eyes in her direction.

"Thank you very much," Lucas said kindly.

Shellie tossed her blonde hair over her shoulder and flashed him a pearly-white smile before sashaying out of the faculty lounge.

Completely irritated and more than a little jealous, I

abruptly dumped my coffee into the sink and tossed the cup into the trash.

"Hey," Lucas whispered, his hand brushing against mine. It was just a slight touch and wouldn't be noticed by anyone, but it still sent a shiver up my spine.

I lifted my eyes to his, and he winked.

And just like that, my jealousy disappeared.

English class was tense.

I tried my best to get the students to focus on Macbeth's descent into madness, but honestly, it was like talking to brick walls. Every eye in the room was fixed on either Patrick or Matt—just waiting for one of them to pounce. Now that both young men had been kicked off the football team, they weren't sitting in their regular seats in the first two rows. Today, Matt was in the third row while Patrick was occupying a desk in the back corner of the classroom.

Howie volunteered to read aloud from Act 5, and when my eyes scanned the page, I immediately regretted opening the textbooks today.

"Out, out brief candle. Life's but a walking shadow, a poor player that struts and frets his hour upon the stage, and then is heard of no more. It is a tale told by an idiot, full of sound and fury, signifying nothing."

"What does that mean?" Howie asked after he finished the passage.

"What do you think it means?"

"I don't know." Howie glanced around the room, looking for help. "Life sucks?"

There were a few chuckles, and I smiled at his effort.

"Sometimes it does. Anything else?"

"Maybe it means he's playing a part," a deep voice echoed from the back.

Twenty pairs of eyes turned toward Patrick.

I glanced at Matt, whose eyes were glued to his English textbook.

Nineteen pairs of eyes.

"He's faking it," Patrick continued, his voice hard and cold. "Going through the motions. Pretending to be something he isn't in order to get ahead."

Every head swiveled back to me.

"That could certainly be one interpretation."

Suddenly, Patrick rose to his feet.

"*It is a tale told by an idiot, full of sound and fury . . .*" he said with conviction as he slammed his textbook shut. His eyes swept the room and settled on the back of Matt's head. ". . . *signifying nothing.*"

Thankfully, the bell rang, and Patrick grabbed his jacket and stalked out of the room. The textbook remained on his desk.

The room was deathly quiet, and I took a steadying breath before dismissing the rest of the class.

I could not *wait* to be finished with this play.

"Are you all right, Miss Bray?"

Matt was still sitting in his chair. His cast was prominently displayed with a few signatures in black marker along the plaster.

"I'm fine. How are you?"

He shrugged. "This is just day one. How many days are left in the school year?"

"Too many."

Matt nodded. "I can do this, Miss Bray."

He sounded so determined and optimistic, so I offered him a supportive smile.

"Hey, do you want to sign my cast? You'll be the only teacher . . ."

He pulled a marker out of his hoodie pocket, and I laughed while I proudly added my signature to his cast.

"Don't worry, Miss Bray. I can handle anything he dishes out. I'm not crazy. I know it's going to get rough."

A knot of fear formed in the pit of my stomach.

"Matt, if it gets too rough—"

Smiling, he stood and grabbed his textbook with his good arm.

"You'll be the first to know," he promised.

"Monica, I'd love for you to visit over Fall Break!"

Lucas glanced up from his pile of tests and grinned at me. My kitchen table was covered with exams that desperately needed to be graded before Friday. Lucas, at least, was being productive. I, on the other hand, had been on the phone with Monica for over an hour.

"Are you sure? You don't have plans?"

"I do now," I replied happily while checking the chicken baking in the oven. "Besides, there's someone I want you to meet."

"Oh?" Her voice was bright and curious. "An important someone?"

"He's pretty important, yeah."

Lucas didn't look up from his grading, but I could see his smile.

"You've met someone," she breathed softly.

Dropping my oven mitt onto the counter, I walked over to the kitchen table and climbed into his lap. He smiled up at me and immediately dropped his pen as he wrapped his arm around my waist. Lowering my head, I kissed him softly.

"Are you *kissing*?" Monica screeched in my ear, her voice a mixture of wild disbelief and extreme glee. Lucas chuckled and buried his face against my neck. "Put him on the phone right this instant."

Laughing, I offered him my cell.

"Hi, Monica," he said with the biggest grin on his face. "I'm Lucas Miller . . ." Unfortunately, she'd stopped screaming so I could only hear his side of the conversation. With his eyes never leaving mine, he trailed his fingers along my spine. "Yes, I was just kissing your best friend . . . yes, I have a job . . ." We both laughed, and then his face turned solemn as he pulled me closer to his chest. "Yes, I know she has. I will take care of her, I promise."

I smiled. Moni had always been protective of me.

"I look forward to meeting you, too," Lucas said softly before handing the phone back to me.

Leaning down, I kissed him once more before climbing off his lap and turning my attention back to the stove. Monica promised to call once she'd made arrangements, and we hung up just as the oven timer chimed.

"Should we eat at the island?" Lucas asked, pointing toward the stools. The kitchen table was still cluttered, although his pile of grading was now significantly shorter than mine.

"That sounds good."

We worked around each other—him finding plates and silverware while I finished heating the rolls—and it amazed me how easy it was to be all-domestic with someone I'd only known for a short period of time. So far, *everything* with Lucas had been effortless.

We ate in a comfortable silence as I tried to find trouble where there really was none, and even *that* was troubling to me.

"What are you thinking?"

Surprised, I looked up into his sweet eyes. "What makes you think I'm thinking about anything?"

"Because you haven't taken two bites of your dinner. You're not worried about Monica's visit, are you?"

"No, although the town didn't exactly welcome her with open arms the last time she was here."

"Why?"

"She's African American."

Lucas nodded in understanding.

"But you'll love her, and she'll love you," I assured him.

"So, what's wrong?"

I sighed softly and continued playing with my food.

"Nothing's wrong. Absolutely nothing is wrong, and it scares me to death."

His eyebrows furrowed in confusion. "Nothing is wrong, and that frightens you?"

"I'm not sane, Lucas. You'll figure this out soon enough, and then you'll run screaming."

He laughed quietly and dropped his fork against his plate.

"I seriously doubt that, Sarah." Taking my hand in his, he gently pressed a kiss to my wrist. "Aren't you happy?"

I trembled slightly as his lips ghosted along my skin.

"I'm happier than I've ever been." It was true. Being with Lucas had brought me a sense of peace I hadn't felt since I was a little girl.

"You know, it's okay to be happy."

"Is it?" I honestly had no idea.

Lucas stabbed a piece of chicken with his fork and lifted it to my lips. "It is. For example, you made me very happy this morning."

I took the bite and swallowed quickly. "What did I do this morning?"

"You were jealous of Shellie."

Frowning, I grabbed my own fork and forcefully gouged my food.

"She was gossiping about the two of us before you walked in. Apparently, Deputy Hank has a big mouth. The entire faculty knows about our little escapade in the back seat of your car, and she *still* flirted with you right in front of me."

"And that bothered you?"

"Of course it bothered me!"

Lucas was trying very hard to hide his laughter while I continued to massacre my dinner.

"I think we're done," Lucas said with a grin.

Pulling me by the hand, he led me into the living room and over toward the couch. Once he was seated, he promptly pulled me sideways onto his lap and nuzzled my neck. I sighed contently and trailed my fingers through his hair.

"You have no reason to be jealous," Lucas whispered against my ear, "and you have no reason to worry. Life is good, isn't it?"

"Life is *so* good, but that's when it usually falls apart on me."

"So, what's your plan? Look for drama where there isn't any, just so you'll be prepared in case something horrible happens?" I shrugged, and he sighed softly. "That's no way to live, sweetheart."

"I know, but old habits die hard."

He ghosted his lips along my jaw, and I shivered.

"It's time for new habits, Sarah. It's time to be content. We'll handle whatever . . . whenever it comes, but for now, can't we just be happy?"

"I want to *trust* being happy."

"Me, too." His eyes were shining and warm as they gazed into mine. Very tenderly, he brushed his hand across my cheek. "Maybe we can help each other with that."

Pressing my forehead against his, I sighed softly.

"Maybe we can."

Chapter Sixteen

"Have you ever been so glad to see three o'clock on a Friday?" Aubrey asked as we headed down the hallway. The teachers were actually racing the kids to get to the door. "This week has been absolutely insane."

She was right. School had been crazy. There's always a little excitement when vacation is on the horizon, but this week had been particularly wild. Thankfully, I'd kept control of my English class just long enough to finish *Macbeth*. To motivate my creative writing class, I'd bribed them with the promise of food, and I'd spent last night baking dozens of cupcakes.

It was a small price to pay for a little peace.

"You're bringing Daniel to my house for trick-or-treating, right?"

Halloween was still a week away, but I'd already stocked up on tons of candy. I'd never really been into

Halloween as a kid, but I couldn't wait to get dressed up and welcome my trick-or-treaters. Lucas promised to help. Monica didn't know it yet, but she'd be helping, too.

"Of course. Did I tell you he decided on Buzz Lightyear?"

"I'm not surprised," I said, laughing over the roar of buses thundering out of the parking lot and kids rushing toward their cars. My steps slowed as my gaze settled upon Matt's parking space. He and Howie were kneeling and looking carefully at Matt's truck tires.

Great.

"It's nice to see he still has one friend," Aubrey said softly.

"Yes, it is."

Now that he was no longer the most popular guy in school, Matt had become somewhat of a loner. Howie had proven to be a true friend, but I couldn't help but wonder how long it'd be until he, too, caved to the pressure. Matt was taking it all in stride, and in many ways, seemed relieved not to have to pretend to be something he wasn't anymore. Now, he could walk the halls without a gang surrounding him, and he could sit anywhere he wanted in class. Sure, there were rumors floating around about his new boyfriend, but this was high school, and there would always be gossip no matter who you were. Matt seemed to get that, and while I understood words could be hurtful, I also knew words were sometimes the least of your worries.

There had been some bullying—a freshman had keyed some vulgar language onto Matt's locker and a group of juniors had cornered him in the gym locker room—but no one had been physically hurt. I'd still been livid when I'd heard the reports, but Matt had made me promise to stay out of it. He assured me he'd let me know if things became too rough, but I didn't trust him to keep that promise.

"I wonder what's wrong."

I sighed wearily. "I don't know. Go on home to your baby. I'll check on them and give you a call later."

I walked over to Matt's truck, and both boys' heads snapped up when they saw me approach. A quick glance at the ground was all the explanation I needed.

The left front tire had been slashed.

"At least it's just the one," Matt said quietly. . "My dad is on his way."

"Yeah, but even one truck tire is expensive," Howie muttered.

I looked at Matt. "Have you reported this to Principal Mullins?"

Both boys laughed bitterly.

"Mullins won't do anything," Howie muttered.

"Then *I'll* report it."

Matt shook his head. "No, Miss Bray. Let me handle it, okay? I don't want you involved."

"I'm already involved."

His eyes were solemn and sad. "I know, and I don't want you to be. I can handle this, Miss Bray."

The crunching of gravel signaled the arrival of his parents. His dad jumped out of the vehicle to assess the damage while Matt's mom remained rooted in the passenger seat.

Her eyes found mine, and we shared a sad smile.

Voices roar through the lunch room as students navigate their way to the cafeteria tables. The cliques are easily spotted: the jocks, the geeks, the beauty queens, the slackers . . .

It's amazing how kids are kids—no matter where they live.

This cafeteria is smaller, and today, it's filled with green.

My eyes follow him as he makes his way through the crowd with his tray gripped tightly in his hands. Despite the fact that he's handsome and dressed in his Panthers green, he somehow fades into the background. The girls who once worshipped at his feet, and the guys who were once his teammates, pointedly avoid his eyes.

I can see it on his face when he finally finds an empty corner.

He's so tired.

It's not a weariness that comes from sleepless nights. This is a bone-tired exhaustion no eighteen-year-old kid should ever feel.

He's giving in.

Giving up.

In my peripheral vision, I see his former teammate stalk his way into the cafeteria. He pulls the silver gun out of his jacket pocket. Amid the chaos, no one notices.

I notice.

"Out, out brief candle," Patrick says. His voice is cold as ice as he recites Macbeth. "Life's but a walking shadow, a poor player that struts and frets his hour upon the stage, and then is heard of no more."

I try to run, but I'm frozen in place.

I try to scream, but there's no sound.

The first shot rings out, and suddenly, everyone's on the cold tile.

Tears, prayers, screams.

Another shot, and for some reason, I'm the only one who can't move. Who can't scream. Who can't do anything but watch as the young man's body slumps over his tray.

Finally, I find my voice, and I'm able to scream his name.

"Sarah! Sarah, wake up!"

With a jolt, my eyes flashed open.

I can't breathe.

Why can't I breathe?

"Deep breaths, baby," Lucas whispered soothingly as he held me close. Confused and frightened, I forced my breathing to try to match his while my heart thundered in my chest. Tears were still rolling down my face, and I hurriedly wiped them away.

"It was just a dream, sweetheart."

Just a dream.

It was just a dream.

Lucas held me close, rocking me gently as I struggled

to control my breathing. More than once, he offered to get my medication, but I'd been doing so well without them. I was stronger now, and I wanted to try to get through his episode without having to take a pill.

"What time is it?" The last thing I could remember was snuggling with Lucas on my couch and watching a movie on cable.

"Just past midnight."

"I fell asleep on you," I muttered, burying my face in the crook of his neck.

"You can always fall asleep on me." Sighing softly, he loosely trailed his fingers through my hair. I was beginning to relax, but his body was still tense. After too many quiet moments, I lifted my eyes toward his.

"What's wrong?"

Lucas closed his eyes, and when they opened again, they looked tortured and sad.

"Who is Josh?"

I gasped loudly. I hadn't heard his name in so long, and hearing it in this house and coming from Lucas's lips . . . it felt as if someone had kicked me in the stomach.

"How do you know about Josh?"

"You screamed his name when you were asleep." He swallowed nervously. "Was that *his* name?"

I was so confused. "Whose name?"

"Your ex."

Realization dawned, and I shook my head.

"No, no . . . my ex's name is Ryan."

"Oh."

Lucas frowned, looking as lost as I felt. I wanted to tell him it had just been a bad dream and hadn't meant anything, but I couldn't. For one thing, that would be a lie, and I refused to lie to him. Secondly, it probably wouldn't be the last nightmare I ever had, especially now that my past was colliding with my present in vivid detail and haunting my dreams.

"I'm sorry if I frightened you."

"Sarah, it was this blood-curdling scream," he whispered weakly. "It was the most painful sound I've ever heard. I kept shaking you . . ." Suddenly, his expression turned hard. "Did someone hurt you? Because if they did—"

"No one hurt me," I promised him. It wasn't a lie. Physically, I'd never been harmed. "Please, just try to forget . . ."

"I can't forget it, Sarah!"

I was speechless. Lucas had never raised his voice to me. Not once.

Frustrated, he let me go and climbed off the couch. Sitting up, I watched in stunned silence as he slipped on his shoes. Without either a word or a backward glance, he walked out of the living room.

The kitchen door slammed, and that's when I panicked.

Terrified that I'd finally pushed him away, I raced through the kitchen and out onto the front porch. The wood was cold against my bare feet, but I didn't care.

All I could see was the moon.

And him.

Taking a deep breath, I slowly walked toward the swing where he was sitting with his head bowed.

Sweet Lucas, who had been so patient with me since the moment we met. This incredible man, who'd never pushed for more than I was ready to give and who'd never asked for an explanation when I fell apart in his arms.

Had he finally had enough?

Kneeling onto the cold porch, I gently took his hands in mine. He lifted his head, and thanks to the moonlight, I could see his tormented eyes. Tenderly, I brushed his bangs away from his forehead and smiled sadly.

"I know I have no right to ask," I whispered, "but if you were to leave me, I don't know that I'd survive it."

Closing his eyes, he leaned forward and pressed his forehead against mine.

"You're going to freeze to death, Sarah."

"I don't care."

"I do."

He slowly rose to his feet and tugged me by the hand until I was standing by his side. Without a word, he lifted me into his arms and cradled me against his chest before walking back into the house. His eyes never left mine as he kicked the door closed behind us, and I clung to his neck while he carried me upstairs.

"Which room is yours?" Lucas asked when we reached the top.

I pointed toward my open door, and he stepped inside, gently sitting me on the edge of the bed.

"Where are your socks?"

"Top drawer."

He was only gone a moment, and when he returned, he kneeled on the floor and placed a fuzzy sock on each of my chilly feet. The gesture was so sweet, and my eyes brimmed with tears. Lucas noticed them, of course, and when a tear trickled down my cheek, his fingertips were there to gently wipe them away.

"You were so mad at me."

"I wasn't mad at you," Lucas said as his fingers laced through mine. "I just love you, Sarah. I love you so much, but I am so lost. I can't help you fight your demons if I don't know what they are."

Sighing deeply, he wrapped his arms around my waist and laid his head against my lap. Completely overwhelmed, fresh tears spilled down my cheeks as I ran my fingers through his hair.

I'd never met anyone like him. From the very beginning, he hadn't been afraid to show his feelings for me. He'd always been sweet and attentive and loving—far more loving than I deserved—considering how much of myself I'd been holding back. He'd shared his deepest sorrow with me, and I'd given him nothing in return, but a few panic attacks.

That ended tonight.

For the first time in forever, I felt brave.

"I love you, too."

Lucas lifted his head, and his surprised eyes gazed into mine. The fact that he was stunned speechless gave me the courage to continue.

"Joshua Ramsey was a student of mine in Memphis. He was shot and killed in the cafeteria, and it's my fault he's dead."

It wasn't the entire story, but it was a start.

Lucas stood and walked around the bed. I felt the blanket move behind me, and then I felt the mattress sink.

"Come here," he whispered, and relief flowed through me.

He isn't leaving me.

I unsnapped my jeans, letting them fall to the floor. He'd seen me in much less, after all, and I refused to sleep in denim. Leaving my shirt on, I climbed into bed, pulling the blanket close to my chin, and laying my head against the pillow. Our heads were close as we stared into each other's eyes for what seemed like forever.

"What are you thinking?"

Lifting his hand, Lucas gently caressed my face.

"I'm thinking there's far more to that story, and it's not your fault he's dead."

"How do you know?"

"Because I know *you*, Sarah."

It was the same thing I'd said to him when he told me about New York.

"I see how much you love your students," he continued softly. "I see how much you worry about Matt." His forehead creased. "There's a connection there, isn't there? Between Josh and Matt?"

I nodded.

"Was Josh gay?"

"Yes."

"And he confided in you—just like Matt confided in you."

"The situations are different, but yes."

"How are they different?"

Taking a deep breath, I rolled over onto my back and gazed at the ceiling.

"Josh Ramsey was a handsome and bright seventeen-year-old boy. His family came from money, but of course, everyone in that school had money. He wasn't an athlete. He wasn't popular. He certainly didn't have a girlfriend. He had *zero* friends. He was quiet and polite, and perfectly content to be an average student with average expectations. He wanted to fade into the background, and he was good at it."

My hands were shaking, prompting Lucas to reach over and lace my fingers through his.

"Go on," he encouraged.

I took a deep breath.

"Josh was in my AP writing class. He was a mediocre student at best in every other subject, but he loved to write. He confessed in one of his writing assignments that he really wanted to be a journalist and travel the world, and it was the first time he'd ever shown an interest in anything. I'd always jot down notes in the margin of their papers, and I encouraged him to talk to the guidance counselor about college. I knew he'd never get a scholarship with his grades, but I also knew tuition wouldn't be an issue for his family. I wasn't sure if he was really ready for college, but I thought maybe the counselor could point him in some direction—a technical school or something. Just something to keep him motivated."

Lucas nodded.

"As the school year progressed, his writings became more detailed and descriptive. Suddenly, he was sharing stuff about his parents and his siblings, and how he hated high school because he felt like such an outcast." I fought back my tears as Lucas squeezed my hand. "It was heartbreaking. I was young and idealistic and thought I could change the world. So, I encouraged him to make friends, and for a while, it actually worked. He wasn't suddenly Mr. Popularity, but I would see him eating with this one kid at lunch—a really popular kid—and it gave me hope that maybe he could enjoy the rest of his senior year . . ."

My voice began to break, and Lucas pulled me closer to his chest. I rested my ear against his chest and listened to his heartbeat, hoping the steady rhythm would calm me. "In one of his journals, he told me he had feelings for someone, and he was pretty sure they felt the same way. He asked for my advice, and I told him . . ." I swallowed convulsively and tried to keep from crying, ". . . I told him he should be honest. I told him he shouldn't be afraid to tell someone how he felt about them, because life is too short and . . . and you never know . . ."

Lucas pressed a kiss to my hair.

"Some time passed, and suddenly, I was hearing reports that Josh was being bullied. Someone had keyed his car—someone beat him up in the gym locker room—and it wasn't just at school. His family suddenly wanted to ship him off to military school, and they were forcing him to see a psychiatrist. They were trying to "de-program" him, he told me in his journal. I had no idea what he was talking about. I didn't ask. I *should* have asked."

Feeling suffocated, I pulled myself out of his arms and climbed out of my bed. In a daze, I walked over to my bay window and crawled inside. Lucas didn't follow me, and I was grateful. I closed my eyes and leaned my head against the wall.

"I did ask him to stay after class one afternoon," I said shakily. "We'd talked so much through his writings, but we'd never had a real conversation. That afternoon, he confessed to me he was gay, and the feelings he had were for a guy named Travis Morgan. Travis was a forward on the basketball team and was headed to Duke to play college ball. He was very aggressive on the basketball court and a hothead in general. His father was a surgeon and very distinguished in the community."

"And Travis wasn't gay," Lucas concluded.

I blinked back my tears.

"No, he wasn't gay. Josh confessed his feelings to Travis, and that's when the bullying started. The administration didn't try very hard to protect him. Dr. Morgan was a benefactor, and . . . well, Travis was very careful about keeping his hands clean, but the kid had a lot of friends. It finally got so bad that Josh's parents pulled him out of school. He wasn't allowed to keep in touch with me—the administration forbid it, as did his parents—but at least I knew he was safe from Travis's band of thugs."

I looked toward the bed to find Lucas sitting on the edge, watching me carefully. Yes, I was close to falling apart, but now that I was finally talking, I just wanted to finish it.

"Suddenly, it was the week before graduation, and we received an email from the principal telling us Josh was returning to school. He'd been placed on homebound, but he really wanted to take his final exams at school. He also wanted to attend graduation, which meant he'd need to participate in practice. Naturally, Travis wasn't pleased that Josh was getting to return to school, and when the underclassmen began to joke about Travis's boyfriend coming back . . ."

Wrapping my arms around myself, I began to rock back and forth, as my heartbeat sped. Lucas was suddenly there, folding me in his arms and carrying me back over to the bed. My breathing was shallow, and my head began to spin.

"You don't have to say anything else," Lucas whispered against my ear, but I knew that wasn't true. I had to tell him everything.

"Monday arrived, and I'd spent my morning giving finals. We had four separate lunch periods, and it was first lunch. I was just headed to the office when I spotted Josh in the lunch line. I hadn't seen him yet because AP writing was my last class of the day. I wanted to say hello, but I also didn't want to bring attention to the fact he was there, so I just stood along the wall and watched as he looked for a place to sit. His classmates ignored him, just as they'd always done, and he finally found an empty place in the back corner of the cafeteria."

My tears were uncontrollable now, and I buried my face against his shirt.

"I don't know what made me look toward the exit, but I did, and that's when I saw Travis."

I took a deep breath as the images of the day flooded my mind.

"Travis walked toward Josh's table. By this time, some of the kids had spotted him, but that didn't stop him from reaching into his pocket. Travis pulled out the gun and pointed it right at Josh . . ."

"Stop," Lucas begged hoarsely as he crushed me to his chest, but I couldn't stop. How could I possibly make him understand it was my fault unless he heard the entire story?

"I could live a thousand years, and I'll never forget the screams. And the blood . . . so much blood, and it was my fault. *I* told him to be honest. *I* told him to be real, and he listened to me. He listened to me, and now he's dead."

"Look at me," Lucas demanded, framing my face with his hands. I couldn't see him for the tears clouding my vision. "It was *not* your fault. It was a horrible, horrible situation, but it was *not* your fault, Sarah. You did not kill that boy. You did not place the gun in Travis's hand. It wasn't your fault, sweetheart."

It was the same speech I'd heard from so many people—Monica, my therapist, the police. Even Josh's mother. And there were times I'd actually believed maybe I wasn't responsible for Josh's death. But there were other times—dark, depressing moments that seemed to swallow me whole—when my mind tried to convince me otherwise. It had been a constant battle since May and was the driving force behind my return to Sycamore Falls. I'd needed distance from everything—the people, the city, the memories—it had all become too much, and I'd ached for the sanctuary of home.

I had no idea how long I cried—desperate, despondent tears—while I tried to purge my mind of the negative emotions that threatened to consume me. There were times when Lucas held me so tight I could barely breathe, but he never let go, and I didn't try to pull away. I was selfish, and I needed him, for as long as he'd have me.

Lucas's whispered in my ear, telling me how much he loved me and how I was the bravest person he'd ever known. He kissed every inch of my face, and after a while, my tears began to subside and my breathing slowly returned to normal.

Taking a deep, shaky breath, I finally opened my eyes.

He was still here.

Why was he still here?

"You didn't leave."

His eyes—those blue eyes I loved so much—were full of agony and pain as he searched my face. After a few minutes, Lucas finally smiled softly and traced my wet cheeks with his fingers.

"I could never leave, Sarah. I wouldn't survive it, either."

Tired and weary from my long confession, I collapsed against him. Holding me tightly, Lucas lowered us onto the bed and pulled the blanket around us.

"Try to sleep," Lucas coaxed.

"You'll stay?"

He kissed my forehead.

"I'll stay."

I was so tired, but I had to ask one more thing.

"Do you still love me?"

I felt his warm breath against my cheek. "You have no idea how much I love you."

It was exactly what I needed to hear, and I closed my

eyes.

Chapter Seventeen

I awoke the next day feeling lighter, as if a weight had suddenly been lifted from my heart. Lucas was wrapped around me like ivy with his head resting on my stomach. He must have gotten uncomfortable at some point, because his shirt and jeans were gone, leaving him in a pair of plaid boxers.

They were pretty sexy boxers.

I ran my fingers through his hair while he gently snored. It was getting longer, curling around the nape of his neck and along his ears. We'd definitely have to find him a barber before Thanksgiving. I didn't know his mother, but I had a sneaking suspicion she'd prefer her son to be a little more clean-cut.

Most mothers do, after all.

Anxiety bubbled in my stomach as I thought about their upcoming visit. What would they think of my hometown? What would they think of me?

Did it matter?

Not really.

Besides, I could only concentrate on one visitor at a time, and Monica would be arriving tomorrow.

Lucas's arm tightened around my waist as he began to stir. My fingers continued making an even bigger mess of his hair, and he hummed contently against the exposed skin of my stomach. He gently pulled the hem of my shirt a little higher, and I gasped when his lips brushed against my bare flesh.

"Waking up with you is officially my favorite thing in the world," Lucas whispered against my skin. "Good morning, Miss Bray."

"Good morning, Mr. Miller."

Lifting his sleepy eyes toward mine, I giggled as he crawled up my body, pressing me deeper into the mattress. His nose glided against mine, making me shiver.

"I love you, Sarah."

"I love you, too."

I pulled him closer and pressed his lips to mine. His quiet groan vibrated through me, and I giggled when his fingers slid along my ribcage. His eyes were shining with love for me, and I was thankful the giant cloud that had hovered above us last night was nowhere to be found.

Lucas laughed against my lips while his hand drifted higher—tickling and teasing—while he explored my hidden flesh. His tickles became torturous as his fingers crept higher, and I squealed loudly, causing us both to laugh breathlessly in between kisses.

Then his hand skimmed my breast, and our laughter faded.

Lowering his head, he tenderly nipped at my bottom lip as he caressed me through the fabric. Desire bloomed deep inside me, causing me to moan.

"Raise your arms," Lucas commanded softly and lifted my shirt over my head. It was quickly tossed aside, and his eyes devoured me. It wasn't the first time he'd seen me topless, but our time at the river had been fun and playful.

This was so much more, and while my first instinct was to feel shy and insecure under his burning gaze, the look in his ravenous eyes assured me I had no reason to be.

Lucas lowered his head, and my eyes fluttered closed as his mouth explored every inch of my flesh. Each brush of his lips was reverent, finding the places that made me sigh, and his tongue was adoring as he discovered the places that made me moan.

"So soft," he whispered, his voice aching and rough. Slowly, his fingertip blazed a trail from the column of my neck to the valley between my breasts, causing me to writhe with need. His touch was agonizingly tender, but my skin felt as if it was on fire.

Desperate to touch him, too, I raised myself onto my knees and slid my hands along his chest. Burying my face against his neck, he shuddered when I peppered wet kisses along the skin there. His head rolled back, and I kissed along his jaw line and down his throat as my hand swept across his abdomen. He groaned my name when my fingers drifted lower, and I felt his stomach muscles tighten when my hand lightly brushed along the waistband of his boxers.

Lucas's blazing eyes looked into mine, and I wondered if the desperate craving I saw there mirrored my own.

Suddenly, our movements stilled, and we gazed into each other's eyes.

"I love you," I whispered.

It seemed so inadequate, but he smiled like it was Christmas morning.

"I love you, Sarah."

As if those three little words granted permission, I slowly pushed his boxers down, letting my hands linger along his bottom. Breathing harsher, his hands settled along my hips, and his hazy eyes never left mine while he lowered my panties. With the barriers out of our way, the two of us sank against the mattress.

Lucas hovered above me, teasing my lips with soft

kisses as his chest pressed against mine. We were both trembling, but there was no uncertainty in his eyes and there wasn't a shred of doubt in my heart.

His hand slid along my thigh, and I gasped when he hitched my leg around his waist. I lifted the other, wrapping both around him and drawing him closer. Lucas gasped as he pressed his hips into mine, and I cried out when our bodies finally aligned.

"Open your eyes," he whispered. "I want to see those beautiful eyes, baby."

His voice was soft and coaxing, and I had no choice but to obey.

With a shuddering groan that ignited my blood, he began to move.

His hand gently stroked up and down my spine while we listened to the storm that raged just outside the bedroom window. Thunder roared overhead and lightning flashed in the window, but all I could focus on were his warm hands on my skin. I was sitting in his lap, and our blanket was wrapped around us like a cocoon.

"Sweetheart?" He drifted his hand through my hair, and I hummed softly, resting my forehead against his. "I owe you an apology."

I couldn't imagine why. This morning couldn't have been more perfect.

"I didn't even think about protection," Lucas whispered.

Oh.

"Neither did I. I guess we probably should have had that discussion at some point."

He laughed. "Probably. Do you want to have it now?"

"We can," I said, wrapping my arms around his neck. "I have to warn you, though. Mine will be the shortest story in history." He wasn't really paying attention anymore. His fingers were creeping up and down my spine, causing me to squirm in his lap.

"Lucas, are you trying to distract me?"

"You are very distracting," he whispered, burying his face against my neck. "You, sitting naked in my lap, is very, very distracting."

I bit back a groan as his teeth nibbled along my earlobe.

"So, why don't we have this embarrassingly short conversation, and then maybe we can distract each other."

Suddenly serious, he settled his hands along my back, pulling me closer. "Why would it be embarrassing?"

"Because I've slept with two guys, and you're one of them," I explained. "After I broke up with Ryan, I decided to get tested for every disease known to man. Everything was good, and I've been on the pill since I was sixteen. The end. Your turn."

A soft smile crossed his face.

"Just two? Really?"

Mortified, I nodded and buried my face against his chest.

"Hey, I'm glad it's just two," Lucas whispered gently against my ear. "Besides, my story isn't much different, although I was a little wild in college."

I lifted my head and frowned. "How wild?"

He rolled his eyes. "Not *that* wild. Just four total—well, five now. My last girlfriend had an affair with her boss, so I was tested. Everything was fine."

I breathed a sigh of relief.

"See, that wasn't so bad." Lucas kissed me softly.

With a sigh, I rested my forehead against his. "Thank you for last night, Lucas."

"Thank *you* for last night. Thank you for trusting me with your story. I just wish I could have been there to help you."

His eyes hardened, and I knew he was thinking about Ryan.

"Don't hate him. Nobody could help me, Lucas."

"I could have."

Smiling, I kissed him softly.

"Don't dwell, please," I said, cupping his cheek with my palm. "Last night was so emotional, but today . . . today has been—"

"Incredible," he murmured against my lips.

The blanket fell away from our bodies as he tumbled back onto the bed. Lacing my fingers through this, I lifted my body slightly before sinking back down, causing him to grab onto my hips and groan my name.

"Amazing," I whispered.

Sunday morning arrived, bringing with it more torrential thunderstorms. I was a little disappointed. I'd really wanted to show Monica the falls today, but maybe it was for the best.

I wasn't sure my body could handle a hike today. I wasn't entirely sure I could make it down the stairs.

It was the best kind of exhaustion.

Lucas snored in my ear, and I sighed happily. What a weekend we'd had together. I had bared my soul, and a heavy weight had lifted from my heart. He knew everything, and he was still here.

Lucas loved me, and I loved him.

My lips tingled as I remembered his heated kisses. After nearly two months of pent-up sexual frustration, making love for the first time had been a little frantic.

And the second, and the third . . .

Turning over in his arms, I gently traced his soft lips with my fingertip. Lucas scrunched his nose, making me giggle. His arm tightened around me as a sweet smile crossed his face. Leaning closer, I pressed soft kisses against his eyelids.

"Have I told you how much I love waking up with you?"

"You might have mentioned it," I whispered against his skin.

Lucas checked the alarm clock and groaned. "I think church is definitely out this morning."

I struggled to sit up, but he tightened his hold around my waist, making it impossible.

"Just one more hour," he mumbled, his voice a soft plea.

I groaned.

So tempting.

"We have to get out of this bed today. I need to make sure the guest room is ready for Monica, and then I have to get groceries for all of us . . ."

He smiled then. "Us?"

"Us."

"I love the sound of that," Lucas murmured before kissing me tenderly. "I love you."

"I love you, too."

"Do you know what else I'd love?"

"You'd love to take a shower with me?"

His sleepy eyes widened in surprise.

"I . . . was thinking . . . waffles," Lucas stuttered adorably, "but hell yes, I'd love to shower with you."

Kissing him quickly, I hopped out of bed and raced toward my bathroom. Our laughter echoed off the walls of the old house as he chased me down the hallway, and just like that, our amazing weekend became absolutely perfect.

"Well, you are adorable."

Monica had never been one to hand out idle praise, but she'd loved Lucas immediately, just like I knew she would.

The rain had made the long drive from Memphis even longer, but Monica had been in good spirits when she finally arrived. She'd only been here an hour, but the interrogation had begun straightaway. I'd offered to make dinner while silently praying she didn't completely scare him off. Monica never minced words, especially when my heart was involved.

She'd despised Ryan and had told him so frequently.

Lucas, the saint he was, had taken it all in stride, answering each and every question with a polite smile on his face. They sat around the kitchen table while he told her all about his parents and his growing up in New York. He even told her a little about the student who nearly destroyed his life, and I could tell Moni was impressed he'd be so open and honest with a complete stranger.

As for me, I'd spent the hour fixing dinner and glancing over my shoulder, just to make sure the man I loved wasn't running for the door.

"Yes, he's adorable." I placed a platter of burgers on the kitchen table. "Is the interrogation now complete? Could he possibly be allowed to eat his dinner?"

Surprised, Moni glanced at her watch.

"It's kind of late for dinner, isn't it? I mean, we're in the country. Don't you guys eat around five or six?"

"We had a late breakfast," Lucas replied before thanking me and placing a burger on each of our plates. Our waffles had actually turned into a late lunch thanks to the fantastic shower filled with wet kisses and soapy fondling.

Best shower ever.

Taking the seat next to him, I leaned over and kissed him softly on the cheek—a silent thank you for putting up with my nosy best friend. Lucas winked at me and offered me a heart-stopping smile before passing the plate to Monica.

"I've missed your cooking," Moni said with a groan as she took the first bite of her burger. "And *everyone* misses our Sunday night dinners."

Every Sunday night, our small circle of friends had congregated at my apartment. They each brought a side dish while I fixed the main course and dessert. Monica, a complete failure in the kitchen, always brought the wine.

"So, I know you work together, but how did the two of you meet?"

Lucas wiped his mouth with his napkin before answering. "We met at the hardware store."

"I was buying paint for Grandma's house."

He nodded. "I was sweeping the aisle, and just happened to look up to see this beautiful, damsel in distress—"

"I was *not* in distress . . ."

"—staring at a wall of paint samples." Lucas grinned at me. "You stood there forever, comparing the different shades of blue."

I laughed at the memory. "There was *a lot* of blue. Mr. Johnson finally had mercy on me."

"Mr. Johnson rarely moves away from the cash register. He had to help you because I was too chicken to do it myself."

My forehead creased with confusion. "You were? Why?"

"You were beautiful, and I was so intimidated."

Me? Intimidating?

I'd nearly forgotten Monica was even in the room, but I could feel her eyes on us, watching our exchange like a hawk. Lucas and I shared a smile before I turned my attention back to my friend.

"So, that's how we met," I said.

Monica grinned just as her cell vibrated on the table. She checked the screen, and her smile grew.

"Do you guys mind if I take this?"

Lucas rose to his feet. "Not at all. I should be heading home anyway."

They said their goodnights, and Monica headed to the living room while I offered to walk Lucas to his car.

"You don't have to go."

Taking my hand, he helped me down the steps. The storms had finally ended, but everything was still wet and smelled of rain.

"I think I should. You two haven't seen each other since August. I need to call my parents, anyway. Mom goes ballistic if I go more than three days without calling home."

Laughing softly, I wrapped my arms around his neck.

"I'll miss you."

"I'll miss you, too," Lucas murmured.

We kissed goodnight, and as I made my way back onto the porch, I heard the creaking of the swing. Monica was there, fiddling with her cell phone.

"Is there a reason I only have one bar of service?"

Laughing, I sat next to her. "You're in the mountains, Monica. Be thankful you have any service at all."

She sighed disapprovingly as I began to push.

"It's peaceful here," Monica murmured.

"It is."

I looked toward the mountainside. It was too dark to see them now, but the trees were littered with splashes of red, orange, and gold. The leaves were already beginning to fall, and it wouldn't be long before all was left was a mess to rake and plenty of bare trees.

"You're happy," Monica noted softly. "I didn't expect that."

I smiled.

"Don't get me wrong—I'm thrilled you seem so content. You just never spoke too highly of Sycamore Falls, so I didn't understand your desire to move back. I *completely* understood wanting to leave Memphis, but I never expected you to move back to your hometown."

"What's that expression? You don't know what you've got until it's gone?"

"Hmm."

We talked for a while about our careers. Monica was teaching four classes this semester, and the phone call she'd received was from a professor she'd been dating since August. Her big brown eyes sparkled while she spoke of him, and I smiled warmly. I'd never seen Monica in love, and it was a joy to see.

"You know, I don't think I've ever sat on a porch swing," she said.

"Isn't it amazing? It was a gift from Lucas."

"That boy's in love with you, Sarah."

I sighed happily.

"I know. I love him, too."

"Have you told him?"

"Yes."

Monica smiled. "Good for you. I like him a lot. He's good for you. He's good *to* you. That's something you've needed for a very long time."

"He's really wonderful. He's seen me at my absolute worst, and he still loves me."

Monica listened intently while I told her about the panic attacks that still plagued me from time to time, and how Lucas had helped me through them.

"How much have you told him about what happened in Memphis?"

"I've told him everything."

She seemed surprised. "Really? And how did he take it?"

"He's still here." It was still a little amazing to me—he'd so willingly accept me—flaws and all.

"I saw the way he was looking at you, Sarah. I don't think that man is going anywhere."

The rhythmic rocking of the swing was quickly lulling me to sleep. When I caught Monica stifling a yawn, I took it as a sign it was time for bed.

"I'm taking you hiking tomorrow," I told her as we walked back inside. I locked the door before leading her up the stairs. "You should bring your camera."

"You know, Memphis has trees," she teased as she opened the door to the spare bedroom.

"Not like these."

Rolling her eyes, Monica smiled and said goodnight.

Chapter Eighteen

"The trail is so wet," Monica grumbled as we hiked along the path leading to Sycamore Falls. "Did you even bring a first-aid kit? From what I can recall, there isn't a hospital for miles."

"Yes, I have a first-aid kit. Besides, if you'll shut up for a second, you'll notice we can already hear the falls. It's not like we're hiking up Mount Everest."

"Might as well be."

"Monica, we can still see the car."

She'd done nothing but complain since we'd left the house. Had she always been this negative?

"I've never understood the appeal of hiking, which is why I left my camera back at the house. Honestly, it's just woods and trees."

"Nature can be a beautiful thing," I said, pointing at a maple tree. Yesterday's rain was still glistening on the golden leaves, and I reached for the camera hanging around my neck. Adjusting the zoom, I started snapping pictures.

"Did you seriously just take a picture of a wet leaf?"

I shot her a glare. Had she always been this cranky? Monica had been my friend for nearly ten years. Surely, I would have noticed if she'd been this negative all the time. Had she really changed that much over the past few months? Or, had she always been this way, and I'd just been too blinded by my own negativity to notice?

Misery loves company, after all.

"Maybe we should just go back to the house."

"No, I really want to see the waterfall," she said, her voice soft and apologetic. "I'm sorry, Sarah. I'm just a city girl. If it isn't covered in concrete, I'm not sure how to walk on it, you know?"

Laughing lightly, I linked my arm through hers.

"It's just like with anything else. You take one step at a time and hope for the best."

Grinning at me, she kept quiet as I led her closer to the falls. We were surrounded by the beautiful colors of fall, but I didn't touch my camera. I'd come back later, and I'd bring a companion who would actually enjoy the scenery.

I thought of Lucas, and I smiled.

Going to sleep without him had been hard; waking up without him had been even harder. Unless we planned on living in sin, being apart was something we'd have to get used to.

Living in sin didn't sound so bad to me.

The idea made me laugh out loud.

"What's funny?"

"I was just envisioning the scandal if Lucas and I moved in together."

"Oh, I can just imagine," Monica muttered. "I remember the reaction when a black woman stood by your side at your grandmother's funeral."

I winced at the memory.

"No, it's okay. I get it. This is a small conservative town with zero minorities. I was going to stick out like a sore thumb, and I understood that. No one was rude to me. People smiled politely and then tried not to stare. Most failed, but it was fine."

I laughed, and she squeezed my arm affectionately.

"Besides, I wasn't here for them. I was here for *you*, and I'd do it again."

This was the Monica I remembered.

"Now, show me a waterfall before I stumble over this mountain and plummet to my death."

"You think *this* is a mountain? This is just a hill, Moni."

Her eyes widened in alarm as I took her by the arm, leading her through the trees and toward the rushing sound of the falls.

"*That* is a mountain.

The falls were surrounded by the same majestic sycamores, which always hugged the water, but today, they were a mosaic of autumn colors. Splashes of green, gold, crimson, and orange flooded the ridge while the waterfalls spilled into the river below. Thanks to the heavy rains, the river was raging as it cut a path through the mountainside.

"Holy crap."

I smiled and lifted the strap over my head.

"Would you like to borrow my camera?" I asked sweetly.

"How many trick-or-treaters does that make?" Lucas asked, looking up from his laptop. He'd been online most of the evening, claiming he was doing research for an upcoming lesson on the Civil War.

I suspected otherwise.

"Thirty-three!" Monica moaned, kicking the door closed. I'd put her in charge of handing out candy while I finished loading the dishwasher. She'd been greeting visitors for exactly ten minutes and had done nothing but gripe the entire time.

Actually, she'd done nothing but complain all week.

Thank goodness, it was her last night in Sycamore Falls.

I wasn't sure which one of us was happier about it.

We'd spent the week doing nothing—which was fine with me—but Monica wasn't used to so much downtime. In the city, there was plenty to keep you busy when school was out of session. In Sycamore Falls, not so much. I'd tried to keep her entertained, but Monica wasn't a reader and television bored her to tears.

We'd had *some* fun. Monica had met Aubrey and her family, and she'd gotten to know Lucas a little better. That was the real bright spot of our time together—Monica's absolute acceptance of him. It wasn't necessary, but her approval was nice and made our visit a little more enjoyable.

Someone knocked, and Monica glared at the door.

Lucas chuckled. "Thirty-four."

"You're going to scare the kids away," I said, snatching the candy out of her hands. Reaching into the bowl, I hastily pulled out a candy bar. "Here. Maybe chocolate will get you in the Halloween spirit."

Reaching for the door, I smiled brightly when I saw two giant zombies standing on my porch.

"You know, I think there might be an age limit on this trick-or-treating thing."

"Nope, we asked the sheriff," Howie said.

Matt was by his side, grinning brightly. "He made us promise to behave ourselves."

"Well, you guys look great."

Deciding this would be the perfect way to end my Halloween, I poured what was left of the candy into each of their bags. Hopefully, the sugar rush would subside by Monday morning when they were back in my class.

"Thirty-five," I announced after closing the door and

turning off the porch light. "That was Howie and Matt."

Monica's eyes never left her phone. "They had pretty deep voices for kids."

"They're seniors," Lucas explained.

Closing his laptop, he smiled up at me as I placed the empty bowl on the table. I climbed into his lap and wrapped my arms around his neck.

"You've been spending an awful lot of time on the Internet lately. I bet you're on some dating website, looking for the perfect woman."

Monica snorted.

"No need," Lucas said sweetly. "I've already found her."

I hummed and nuzzled his neck.

"Very smooth," Monica muttered. "I was just looking at the online edition of the *Sycamore Falls Tribune*. Does your newspaper really only come out once a week?"

Lucas laughed. "We don't have too many scandals."

"Well, you seem to have at least *one*." Monica scrolled through her phone. "Did you actually have a student dismissed from the football team because he's gay?"

I froze.

Lucas hurriedly reached for his laptop and began to type. "Where did you see that?"

"Sports section—in the comments."

My eyes quickly scanned the computer screen. With over fifty replies, the comment wasn't hard to spot.

Rumor has it our former star QB was tossed off the team because he couldn't keep his hands to himself in the locker room.

The comment was signed with a generic username.

"If that's true, I know a kickass attorney who'd love to get his hands on that case," Monica said.

This can't be happening.

"Patrick?" Lucas asked softly.

"I don't know."

"Who's Patrick?" Monica's voice was a full octave higher. It was the most excited I'd seen her all week. "Is he the boyfriend?"

"He is definitely *not* the boyfriend."

Lucas held me a little tighter and pressed a soft kiss to my cheek.

"I'll tell her," he offered softly, and I nodded.

With trembling fingers, I scrolled through the comments—some in support of Matt and some staunchly against—while Lucas explained the entire situation to Monica. I felt a little guilty for divulging Matt's story, but Monica lived eight hours away. Who was she going to tell?

"And he confessed this to you?" Monica asked.

"To Sarah."

I could feel her eyes on me as I tried to focus on the screen. Tears blurred my vision, making it impossible. I finally lifted my head, and her brown eyes were anxious and full of worry.

"What is it about you that makes tortured young men bare their souls?"

"It's not the same thing."

"Not yet."

"Watch it, Monica." Lucas's voice was dark and threatening as his arms tightened around me.

Monica's head swiveled in his direction.

"Don't tell me to watch it. You have no idea what she went through!"

"I have some idea."

"Really?" Monica cocked her head to the side. "Do you know how she cried for weeks after Josh was killed? Do you know her panic attacks were so severe that monster doses of anti-anxiety meds did nothing to calm her down? She didn't eat. She certainly didn't sleep. She finally ate a Twinkie after I threatened to hospitalize her."

To this day, the scent of a Twinkie made me vomit.

"That's enough," Lucas told her, his voice surprisingly

gentle when compared to the venom in his tone. Tears were trickling down my face as he held me close.

"Do you know what an asshole her ex-boyfriend was and how he 'just couldn't deal' with her emotional outbursts?" Monica's voice was a little softer now. "Ryan—the man who supposedly loved her? Who'd told her he wanted to marry her?"

"I'm not Ryan."

"You'd better not be."

"Stop it, Monica." My voice was loud and strong, despite my tears.

A deathly silence fell over the room, giving me the chance to wipe my eyes and catch my breath. With the sweetest of touches, Lucas brushed his thumb across my wet cheeks.

"I should go pack," Monica whispered.

Without another word, she grabbed her cell and headed up the staircase.

The morning air was cold against my skin, and I reached blindly for him, eager to feel the warmth of his arms around me. My eyes snapped open when I realized his side of the bed was empty.

Monica hadn't returned to the kitchen last night, but Lucas had still insisted on spending the night with me. He was so protective, and while it warmed my heart, it was also something I wasn't accustomed to. I'd fought my own battles for so long. Granted, I might fall apart *later*, once I was tucked safely back in the sanctuary of my apartment, but I'd always tried to defend myself.

I never imagined I'd need to defend myself against Monica.

I understood her concerns. She'd watched helplessly while I plunged into a deep depression of which I was still trying to claw myself out. Yes, I'd left some minor details out of my confession to Lucas, but it wasn't a chapter in my life I wished to revisit, and I knew the graphic details of my grief would only upset him.

There was still so much about that time I just couldn't recall. I don't remember Moni threatening to take me the hospital, but I do remember the Twinkie. I remember the texture. I remember the taste. I remember the smell.

My stomach lurched, and I took a steadying breath to control the bile bubbling in my throat.

I was suddenly distracted by the sounds of muffled voices coming from downstairs. Pulling the blanket around me, I climbed out of bed and quietly opened the bedroom door. The first thing I noticed was the spare bedroom. The door was open, and the bed was already made. Monica's suitcase was resting on top of the blanket.

Their voices became a little louder as I walked quietly toward the staircase, but there was no yelling. They were both calm and speaking in hushed tones. I didn't hear my name, but there was no doubt I was the topic of conversation.

"You hurt her."

"Lucas, you know that wasn't my intention."

Wrapping the blanket tighter around me, I sank down onto the top step.

"It doesn't matter if it was your intention. You were unnecessarily cruel last night."

"I was honest. You weren't there. You couldn't possibly understand . . ."

"This isn't Memphis, Monica."

"You're right, it's worse. This is a small town, and people in small towns don't handle change well. I pray this doesn't turn violent, but if it does, Sarah will get caught in the crossfire. Again."

"I won't let that happen."

Deciding I'd eavesdropped long enough, I left the blanket at the top of the stairs and slowly made my way down to the kitchen. The two of them were sitting around the table, and their heads snapped up when they heard me approach.

"Lucas, I'd like to speak with Monica alone."

He glanced between the two of us before finally nodding. Rising from his seat, he walked toward me and leaned down, kissing me softly on the forehead.

"I'll be outside."

I waited until he was out on the porch before taking a seat next to her. She was watching me closely, probably trying to determine if I was hurt or just simply pissed.

It was a little of both, actually.

Monica had been my best friend for nearly a decade. We'd been inseparable throughout college and she'd stood by my side when my grandmother passed away. She'd been my life raft during the most traumatic experience of my adult life, and I would always be grateful for her friendship.

Despite all of that, it was obvious Monica and I were two very different people now.

Maybe we always had been.

"Were you always this negative?"

Monica laughed. "Good morning to you, too. Am I negative?"

"I think so."

"I think I'm a realist. I don't have that sensitive maternal gene most women are born with. I don't have the ability to sugar coat. You've always known this about me. Nothing has changed, Sarah."

"I've changed."

Monica's eyes swept over my face.

"You're right," she agreed. "You're strong. You're happy. You're in love with a man who I'm pretty sure would take a bullet for you."

I laughed softly.

"You yelled at me last night." Her tone was quiet and proud.

"I'm not apologizing for that."

"I don't expect you to, but I need to apologize to you. I was out of line, but you have to know it came from a sincere place."

"I do know that."

"You love your students," Monica murmured gently, "and it's a wonderful thing. It's amazing your students feel so comfortable with you. When I was a kid, I never would've gone to a teacher's house for Halloween, and I certainly wouldn't have shared my darkest secrets with one. Your connection to your students is something I've always admired about you."

Monica sighed heavily and reached for my hand.

"I just know you so well, Sarah. If the shit hits the fan—and I really pray it doesn't—you're going to want to help this kid. That's who you are. Just promise me you'll be careful."

"I promise."

We shared a hug before she headed upstairs to grab her suitcase. I had no idea if Monica would ever come back to Sycamore Falls. Maybe it would be better if she didn't. I wasn't sure our friendship could survive another visit like this one.

Suddenly, Lucas opened the door and peeked inside.

"Everything okay?"

"Everything's fine. She just went to get her suitcase."

Lucas glanced over his shoulder. "Umm . . . you need to come outside, Sarah."

I was instantly suspicious. "Why?"

Monica reappeared then, and Lucas offered to carry her suitcase as he ushered us outside. The morning sun was blinding, but I barely noticed it.

"Holy crap," Monica whispered.

Billowy streams of white hung from the branches of every tree in my yard.

"Someone rolled my house!"

Rolling houses was a Halloween tradition in Sycamore Falls. In our early teens, Aubrey and I used to save our allowances all summer just to stock up on toilet paper for the fall. We only got caught once, and that was because Tommy's truck ran out of gas right in front of the preacher's house.

Sunday's church service had been awkward, to say the least.

"You're happy about this?" Monica asked in disbelief.

My eyes roamed my front yard. Nothing had avoided the toilet paper attack. My shrubs, my mailbox . . . even the porch swing was intricately woven with white.

"I'm ecstatic! Didn't they do a great job? They even wrapped the swing!"

Even Lucas was looking at me strangely.

"It's a Halloween tradition," I explained. "It's . . . acceptance."

Monica's eyes were wide. "It's a freaking mess."

I shrugged and smiled like a lunatic. Sighing, Monica asked for her camera.

"Sarah, you should go get yours, too," she said with a grin. "*This* is a Kodak moment."

Chapter Nineteen

"Where *is* it?"

Hundreds of cookbooks from a hundred different churches were tossed haphazardly around the room. On the table. Along the counters. In the floor. I think one had actually fallen into the sink.

I was dangerously close to tears.

To say Grandma Grace loved cookbooks was a colossal understatement. She especially loved church cookbooks, and every church within a fifty-mile radius was well aware of her obsession. They had always called once a year to ask if she'd like to purchase their latest edition.

She'd always said yes.

Baptist. Presbyterian. Methodist. Catholic. Episcopalian. Some I couldn't even pronounce. They were all represented, and Grandma had been proud of the fact that her cookbook shelf was so non-denominational.

The cookbook from Saint Michael's Catholic Church contained a recipe for cornbread stuffing she'd loved to make every Thanksgiving. I had no idea if the recipe differed from any others, but it was my grandma's favorite, and I wanted to make it for Lucas's parents.

Naturally, it was the one cookbook I couldn't find.

I would be meeting my boyfriend's parents in five days. I'd also be cooking Thanksgiving dinner and offering them my spare bedroom.

No pressure at all.

"This was your idea," I reminded myself as I dug deeper behind the shelf, praying the book had somehow fallen behind it.

It hadn't.

Defeated, I sat down in the middle of the cookbook chaos and buried my face in my hands.

"Sarah?"

Sighing softly, I lifted my head to find him standing in my doorway. The concern etched across his face only amplified when his eyes swept over my kitchen.

"What happened?"

"I can't find a cookbook," I answered timidly. Saying it aloud was a little embarrassing. It sounded ridiculous even to my own ears.

His brow furrowed in confusion as he examined the pile of books surrounding me.

"I can't find a *specific* cookbook."

Nodding slowly, he navigated through the maze of books and joined me on the floor. Sliding his arm around my shoulder, he pulled me close to his side as I leaned my head against his shoulder.

"You're stressing about this dinner, aren't you?"

I considered lying, but what was the point? One look at my kitchen proved I was close to having a nervous breakdown.

"It has to be perfect," I whispered.

Lucas laughed softly.

"It doesn't have to be perfect. My mother is terrible in the kitchen. You could serve ham sandwiches and it would be better than anything she could ever make."

He grabbed one of the nearby cookbooks and glanced at the cover.

"*Amish Cooking?*"

I shrugged. "Grandma loved cookbooks. It didn't matter the religion. It was all 'fruit for the spirit,' she used to say."

He chuckled quietly and tossed the cookbook back into the pile.

"So, what's so special about this particular cookbook you can't find?"

Sheepishly, I told him about my grandma's cornbread stuffing recipe. I didn't want him to think I was a complete lunatic, but this was important to me.

"Sarah, my parents won't know the difference between homemade stuffing and *Stove Top* straight out of the box."

"It's tradition. I can't serve boxed stuffing in my grandma's kitchen."

Lucas smiled softly and kissed my forehead.

"All right, what does this cookbook look like?"

We spent the next half-hour rummaging through the cookbooks and putting them back on the shelf. I'd completely given up hope when Lucas said my name. My head snapped up, and he triumphantly pulled the cookbook from Saint Michael's out of the sink.

Squealing, I raced toward him and leapt into his arms. We both laughed, and he gently placed me, and the cookbook, on top of the island. Stepping between my legs, he smiled up at me as I clutched his shoulders.

"Thank you, Lucas."

"You're welcome, baby." He nuzzled my neck before kissing me softly. My hands slid down his chest as a quiet moan escaped his throat.

"You should be rewarded," I whispered against his lips.

I'd barely gotten the words out of my mouth before he

lifted me off the island and rushed me up the stairs.

"She would've loved you."

Curled up in his arms, my back was pressed against his chest as he brushed kisses along my bare shoulder. We'd spent the entire afternoon in bed, which was becoming our favorite weekend activity.

"Who?"

"My grandma."

Lucas's arms tightened around me.

"And my *mother* . . . she and my dad had this fairytale marriage. He just adored her, and she'd always told me to never settle for anything less. You would have been my parents' dream come true."

Overcome with emotion and needing to see his handsome face, I twisted around in his arms. His expression was soft and sweet as he toyed with a strand of my hair.

"I really love you, Lucas."

Smiling, he pushed the tendril behind my ear. "I really love you, too."

I rested my head against his chest.

"I wish I could've met your family, Sarah."

"Me too."

He kissed the top of my head. "Are you nervous about meeting mine?"

"Nervous is a mild understatement."

"You shouldn't be." His fingers drifted through my hair, soothing my anxiety. "My mother already thinks you walk on water."

I looked up, surprised. "Why would she think that?"

"Because you make me happier than I've ever been," he said, brushing his knuckles along my cheek. "Don't stress, please. I want us to enjoy our first Thanksgiving together. And, maybe if it goes well, you won't mind inviting them back for Christmas."

"Or we could go to New York," I suggested, and I was surprised how excited I was by the idea. "I bet the city is really beautiful at Christmastime."

"Or New Year's Eve. We could brave Times Square."

It seemed so natural, the two of us making plans for the holidays. Plans for the future. I hadn't had the courage to make plans in so long, but somehow, it didn't feel strange.

It felt hopeful.

Was it okay to feel hopeful?

"Hey," Lucas whispered gently. "Come back to me."

He knew me so well. He could tell when I was overanalyzing and looking for trouble where there was none. It was a habit of a lifetime, and one I desperately wanted to break.

I wanted to enjoy these moments.

I wanted to trust these moments.

"I'm here," I promised him.

To prove it, I crawled into his lap, pressing my chest to his as my arms encircled his neck. I whimpered softly when his hands settled along my hips, tugging me closer. Nose to nose, his warm breath washed over my face.

"I love making plans with you."

His eyes brightened. "That's very good to hear, because I have so many plans for us."

"You do?"

"I do."

I was just about to ask him to enlighten me, but his lips were suddenly on mine, effectively ending any need for conversation.

At school, the days leading up to Thanksgiving break were a living nightmare. First semester final exams were coming up after the holiday and the basketball season was just getting underway. With our football season ending on a dismal note, everyone was eager to focus on another sport, and Aubrey was glad to have her husband home at night.

Thanks to the comments on the newspaper's website, Matt's private life was now a constant topic of conversation among the students, and to my great disappointment, the members of the faculty. There had been multiple reports of harassment several times each day, but the administration seemed unable, and simply unwilling, to get involved.

No one was surprised when Patrick denied posting the derogatory comment to the *Tribune's* website, but plenty of underclassmen were happy to take the credit. Patrick was considered a hero among many of the students, and his supporters were more than willing to take credit to keep him from having to defend himself. Of course, *so* many kids took the blame it was impossible for the real culprit to be punished.

Regardless, Matt came to school every day, and it was only in his creative writing assignments that I was able to get a true glimpse of the treatment he was receiving by his classmates. Writing was his way of keeping me informed— just as he'd promised—without having to snitch on anyone. Tattling would only make things harder on him, and he knew it.

I read his stories at night—when I was safe in Lucas's arms—so that I could cry in the privacy of my home. The instances of verbal and emotional abuse he described were worse than any of the physical.

So far.

By the time Wednesday arrived, my nerves were completely shot, which wasn't good at all considering I was meeting Lucas's parents the next day. I had to get it together, at least for the long weekend. Their approval was far too important to me, and I refused to embarrass Lucas by being my usual emotional mess.

With only one class left for the day, I thought I was

holding myself together pretty well. Then, during my planning period, I overheard Shellie gossiping at the copy machine, and my head nearly exploded.

"They say he has a boyfriend over in Bradley County," Shellie whispered loudly to a couple of science teachers.

"His poor parents must be horrified," Mr. Jennings said with a shake of his head.

"I hear they're going to ask him to leave the church," Mrs. Crosby muttered softly. "Can they do that?"

I'd heard enough.

"If the three of you are finished gossiping, please move aside so I can make copies for my next class."

Three heads pivoted in my direction—all of them looking a little too smug for my liking. Only Mrs. Crosby's eyes softened when she realized it was me.

"Oh, Sarah, this must be upsetting . . . what with everything that happened to you in Memphis."

"Well, we certainly wouldn't want a repeat of *that*," Mr. Jennings grunted. "Our little town is supposed to be immune from . . ."

Rage flooded me. "Hatred? No, Mr. Jennings, I'm sorry to say you can find it just about anywhere. Even at the copy machine!"

"Is there a problem?"

Tommy and Principal Mullins were both standing at the door, looking between the three of us with shocked expressions. I'm sure they were surprised. I wasn't normally a screamer.

Squaring my shoulders, I took a deep breath to control my voice.

"Yes, there is a problem," I replied stiffly, looking him straight in the eye. "Our faculty and staff are quite capable of standing around the copier and gossiping about Matt Stuart, but no one seems to want to do anything to protect him."

Principal Mullins glanced at Shellie and the other teachers who were standing there with their mouths agape.

"Miss Bray, why don't we discuss this in my office?"

I was fuming.

"Gladly."

The secretary watched us with wide eyes as we followed each other into the office. Tommy closed the door and the principal offered me a chair.

"Sarah, we're doing everything we can," Tommy said quietly.

I eyed him curiously. "Really? What are *we* doing?"

"Well, I've asked Howie to keep an eye on him while they're at school."

"It's not Howie's job to protect a student!"

"Miss Bray." Principal Mullins looked bored and fiddled with the pen in his hand. "We are truly doing everything possible, but I'm afraid our hands are tied."

That was such bullshit.

"Matt Stuart is being bullied every day in this school. Every single day! Either verbally or physically . . ."

"And how do you know this?"

"Because he tells me."

His smile was indulgent as he leaned back in his chair. "And you believe him?"

I narrowed my eyes.

"Why would he lie?"

He shrugged. "Attention?"

"Do you think he *asked* someone to slash his tires?" My voice harsher than it should be when talking to the boss. "Did he beg the defensive line to knock his books out of his hands on the way to class every single day this week?" My eyes shot to Tommy. "*Your* players, by the way."

"Sarah, we can't prove any of those things happened," Tommy said resignedly. "Until we have evidence . . ."

My blood ran cold.

"What kind of evidence do you want? Does someone have to get killed before anything gets done? Tommy Bryant, do you even *know* who you're talking to?"

"I know about Memphis . . ." he whispered.

"I know you do. Is that what you want to happen here?"

"You know I don't."

His voice was tired and hopeless, and it made my skin crawl.

"How many touchdowns has Matt Stuart scored for you?"

"Over the course of his career? One hundred twenty-five," he answered automatically.

"Did he attend every practice?"

"Yes."

"Do you love that kid?"

"You know I do, Sarah."

"Then why the hell aren't you doing more to protect him?"

Tommy bowed his head, and I knew he was ashamed. *Good.*

"Miss Bray," the principal said quietly, "Matthew Stuart is a gay, eighteen-year-old boy living in Sycamore Falls. If you expect this administration to protect him just because he wants to bring his boyfriend to the prom, then I'm afraid you and he are both going to be very disappointed."

And that's when I realized why the principal was doing nothing to protect this boy.

He simply didn't care.

Tommy raised his head, and his eyes were tortured.

"How he's living is wrong, Sarah," he whispered.

"So this is what he deserves?"

"I didn't say that!"

I closed my eyes and took a long, steadying breath.

"I am not debating whether being gay is right or wrong. That is not the issue here."

"Then what is the issue, Miss Bray?" The principal's voice was vaguely amused, as if there was anything about this situation even remotely funny. The fact I was a rookie teacher flashed through my mind, but I didn't care. I'd deal with the consequences.

"The issue is an eighteen-year-old boy—a young man who was this school's pride and joy—when he was scoring touchdowns. This is a *student*. It is this school's responsibility to protect the students within its walls."

The bell rang, signaling an end to my planning period. Both men watched with stunned expressions as I rose to my feet.

"With all due respect, Mr. Mullins, I believe how Matt is being treated by his classmates, faculty, and the administration is a far more urgent issue than who he may or may not bring to the prom."

I walked out, slamming the door behind me.

Without bothering to make my copies, I raced down the hallway, wiping away my tears. I was so pissed, and words couldn't describe how disappointed I was in Tommy, but I had to get a grip because I had a class waiting for me.

When I reached my door, Lucas was standing there. His eyes were half-crazed.

"Sarah, what's wrong?"

He reached for me, but I shook my head. We were at school, and I knew if he touched me, I'd completely fall apart. Not trusting myself to speak, I walked past him and headed straight to my desk. Grabbing a blue dry-erase marker, I shakily wrote FREE PERIOD across my whiteboard.

The cheers were immediate and loud.

I slumped in my chair and ignored the delighted faces of my seniors as they pulled their cell phones out of their pockets.

What did I care? I was getting fired anyway.

I was intently watching the clock and praying for the hands to move faster when a shrieking alarm sounded from the hallway.

"Fire drill!" Howie shouted.

I groaned.

Why couldn't this day just end already?

Somehow, I managed to get the kids organized into a single-file line and led them out onto the lawn. Electronic devices were sometimes wonderful things, and it didn't take long for word to spread that a freshman had pulled the alarm. I had just started to take roll when I realized two of my most notorious students were nowhere to be found.

"Where are Matt and Patrick?" I asked the class.

A few of the football players bowed their heads and shuffled their feet in the grass.

"WHERE ARE THEY?"

My class jumped, and Howie flew to my side.

"Matt went to the bathroom between classes," he said, his eyes full of fear. "I tried to go with him, like Coach asked, but Matt got all pissed . . . saying he didn't need a babysitter . . ."

Fear gripped me, nearly buckling my knees.

Suddenly, Lucas was there. His arms wrapped around my waist as he tried to hold me steady.

"Sarah, what is it?"

My sweater was suddenly too tight, and I couldn't breathe.

"I think Matt . . . and Patrick . . . are inside the building."

Why can't I breathe?

Horror flickered across his face. Lucas turned his attention to the frightened student at my side.

"Howie, I need you to go find Mrs. Bryant and bring her to me."

Howie nodded and ran across the grass. It didn't take long before Aubrey's class joined mine, and I felt her take my hand.

"A panic attack?" Aubrey whispered.

"Stay with her," Lucas said.

He'd just turned to go when I grabbed onto his arm.

"Where are you going?"

"I'm going inside."

Panic seized me. "I want to go with you!"

His gentle hands framed my face.

"I don't know what I'll find when I get inside," he murmured. "Please, sweetheart, stay here. Stay here for me. Promise me."

Tears filled my eyes, and I nodded as Aubrey helped me sit down on the grass. Fear threatened to suffocate me as he ran into the building.

If anything happens to him . . .

My entire body began to shake, and Aubrey squeezed my hand reassuringly. She was talking, but it was like white noise in my roaring ears.

The air was suddenly filled with the siren of a fire engine, which made the kids laugh since everyone knew it was a false alarm.

"Why aren't they letting us go back inside?" Carrie whined from her place in line. "It was just some stupid freshman pulling a prank."

My heart was beating frantically in my chest, and it only raced faster when, moments later, I saw Tommy sprinting toward the building.

"Why's Coach going inside?"

That got Aubrey's attention. Suddenly, she looked terrified.

"It's Matt, isn't it?" Aubrey whispered in my ear.

I could only nod.

Time passed. I had no idea how long we stood out there, but it was long enough that the kids finally dropped to the ground and made themselves comfortable. Most of them were texting and taking pictures of the completely unnecessary fire truck.

Suddenly, more sirens filled the air, and the kids got excited when the police cruisers rumbled onto the parking lot.

Sirens.

Screams.

Blood.

My vision began to blur.

"Sarah, stay with me," Aubrey coaxed, her hand now gripping mine. "You're safe. Lucas is safe. Everything is going to be fine."

More sirens, and this time, it was an ambulance. Finally understanding the situation was serious, a hush fell over the student body as the paramedics pulled up to the front entrance of the school.

I felt someone's arm brush mine. Through my tears, I could see Howie sitting by my side on the grass, and his face was ashen. I easily recognized the expression on his face.

Guilt.

I knew the feeling so well.

I prayed for words of optimism to flood my tongue. I wanted to tell him everything would be fine. I wanted to say everything was under control, and his friend was safe.

But I knew that would be a lie.

Chapter Twenty

Buses rolled out of the parking lot and the less interested students headed to their cars as the school day finally came to an end. The school had gone into full lockdown mode, but since everyone was outside anyway, the principal saw no reason not to dismiss the students to go home. Those of us who remained were instructed to stay outside. It was mostly seniors, I noticed, and many of them were members of the football team. The expressions on their faces were a mixture of confusion and grief, and I wondered how many of them had been directly involved.

Over time, my frantic anxiety had drifted into a numb bewilderment. Howie and Aubrey remained at my side, both texting furiously on their phones. There were plenty of rumors circulating, but none of them could be considered legitimate information.

The lack of news was horrible.

The waiting was worse.

Several students gasped when the front doors finally burst open, and everyone jumped to their feet as we watched the paramedics carry someone out on a gurney. It was impossible to see anything from a distance, and the students groaned with disappointment as the sirens blared and the paramedics raced off school grounds.

"There's Mr. Miller!"

Relief flowed through me as Lucas's eyes scanned the grass, his eyes locking with mine. Tommy and Mr. Mullins followed behind him, and seconds later, four policemen walked out onto the sidewalk with Mr. and Mrs. Stuart.

A student wearing a Panthers hoodie stood between two of the officers, and when the boy raised his head, a horrified gasp echoed from the students and teachers on the lawn.

Matt was bandaged and bruised, but he was standing. He was walking. He was talking.

Most importantly, he was alive.

Lucas's arms wrapped around me, and I sagged with relief against him while we watched the officers lead Matt to the cruiser.

"They're both okay, baby."

Both?

"I don't understand," Aubrey said, echoing all of our thoughts, "if that's Matt . . . who was in the ambulance?"

Lucas held me a little tighter.

"Patrick," he murmured.

"Drink this," Lucas said gently, offering me a mug. He'd insisted on following me home, and I'd been confined to the couch ever since.

Hopeful, I peered into the cup. "Is it alcohol?"

"No, it's hot chocolate."

Sipping slowly, I hummed in gratitude as the liquid

warmed me. Lucas adjusted the blanket around my shoulders before taking a seat next to me on the couch. I could feel his eyes on me while I quietly drank my cocoa.

"I'm okay."

Reaching for me, he wrapped both of his hands over mine, trying to warm me.

"Didn't you have a jacket?"

"Yeah, I just didn't bother grabbing it. I figured it was just a drill."

Lucas nodded.

I placed my mug on the end table. Needing to be closer, I climbed into his lap, tugging the blanket around us.

"This is my favorite place to sit," I whispered with a grin.

"I love it, too." Kissing my temple, he buried his nose in my hair. "How are you, really?"

"I'll be better once you give me all the details."

"I don't have all of them," Lucas reminded me. "I just know what I saw."

"What did you see?"

Lucas sighed softly and held me close.

"It was all pre-meditated. Apparently, Patrick had been waiting to get Matt alone. He saw Matt go into the restroom between classes, and Patrick convinced one of his friends to pay a freshman to pull the fire alarm. When I arrived, Matt was beaten and bloody, but he was the one holding the weapon as he stood over Patrick's body."

"What kind of weapon?"

"A metal pipe," Lucas replied. "I have no idea where it came from. Patrick's friends had apparently followed him into the bathroom, but they'd deserted him the moment he pulled the pipe out of his jacket. That's what Matt told the police, anyway."

"So there were no witnesses."

"Well, the police consider me a witness, since I was the person who saw Matt with the weapon."

"That's not helpful at all."

"I know."

"He was just defending himself!"

"I know, sweetheart. Unfortunately, just *knowing* isn't enough. They want physical evidence, and while Matt was obviously beaten, Patrick was the one taken to the emergency room, so . . ."

I closed my eyes. This was so bad.

"I *told* them something was going to happen. I told them!"

Lucas's forehead creased. "You told who?"

"Principal Mullins and Tommy." I then told him all about my confrontation with Shellie and the other teachers, which led to an even bigger confrontation with the principal.

"I'm not surprised," Lucas said after I told him about the principal's reaction. "I am a little disappointed in Tommy, though. *That's* why you were so upset when you returned to class."

I nodded and snuggled close to his chest.

"Will you still love me when I'm unemployed?"

He laughed lightly.

"I'm serious. I was definitely insubordinate. I'm a new hire. Even if I somehow survive this school year, I can't imagine Principal Mullins will recommend hiring me back."

"Don't worry about that now," he said, kissing my cheek softly.

He was right. We had much bigger issues to deal with at the moment.

"What will happen to Matt?"

"I don't know. He's eighteen, and Patrick could press charges."

"It was self-defense!"

"Can you prove it?" Lucas asked. "You can't, baby. And if they use me as a witness, I will have to admit I found Matt standing over Patrick's body with a pipe in his hands."

"Matt's arm was still in a cast. How much damage could he really do?"

His eyes looked haunted. "A metal pipe can do a lot of damage."

Lucas fell silent then, and I knew the discussion was over. Protecting me had become a religion to him, and there was no way I was going to get the gory details.

Trying to soothe him, I gently stroked his face.

"I'm sorry you had to see that."

"Sarah, it was terrible," he said, swallowing hard. "I don't particularly like Patrick—and I can't say he didn't deserve to have his ass kicked—but it was still hard to see him like that."

"Beating him with a metal pipe isn't an ass kicking. That's aggravated battery, and Matt could go to jail."

Lucas's cell phone rang, and I climbed off his lap and took my mug to the kitchen while he answered it. I was exhausted and emotional, and all I really wanted to do was crawl into bed with Lucas and ignore the rest of the world for the next four days.

Unfortunately, that was impossible, because I had a Thanksgiving dinner to prepare and parents to meet.

Opening the refrigerator, I made a quick note of some things I still needed to pick up from the store. What would they like for breakfast? Did they like coffee? I didn't even own a coffee maker.

"That was my mom," Lucas said as he walked into the kitchen. "They offered to postpone their trip until Christmas if we'd rather wait."

I spun around. "Why would we want to wait?"

"It's been a hell of a week, Sarah. Maybe it'd be nice to just have the holiday to ourselves."

It was so tempting, but I really did want to meet his parents. Besides, spending time with family was important. It was one of those lessons you didn't learn until your entire family was gone.

"What do you want to do?" They were his parents, after all, and he'd had a traumatic day, too.

He pressed his forehead against mine. "I want to do whatever will make you happy."

I rolled my eyes and grinned. "That's your answer for everything."

Smiling, he kissed me softly.

"We have a lot to be thankful for," I said. Despite the drama, and despite the fact I'm probably going to be flipping burgers at the diner next school year . . ."

Lucas laughed.

". . . the one thing that's perfect is *us*, and I want them to see how happy their son makes me. I want to be surrounded by family this Thanksgiving, even if it isn't my own."

Tilting my head up toward his, he kissed me tenderly. When he finally pulled away, his eyes were full of emotion.

Excitement. Happiness. Love.

So much love.

"*You* are my family," he whispered sincerely.

I smiled. "And you are mine."

"Breathe, baby."

Lucas's arms were around my waist and his chin was on my shoulder as we watched his dad climb out of the rented black SUV. Jonathan Miller walked around to his wife's door, and I smiled.

"Like father, like son."

Lucas kissed the side of my neck. It was his way of trying to relax me, but it was impossible. Wasn't it natural to be nervous? Not that I had any frame of reference, but I imagined meeting the parents for the first time was a big deal. Ryan had never introduced me to his folks, so this was completely new and totally nerve-wracking.

"There you are!" Olivia Miller squealed excitedly from

the bottom of the porch. She was dressed in a red blouse and jeans, and her hair was pulled back into a sleek ponytail. Smiling at me with her son's piercing blue eyes, she pulled me out of his arms and straight into hers, enveloping me in a bone-crushing hug.

"It's so nice to finally meet you, Mrs. Miller."

"Oh, I'm much too young to be called Mrs. Miller," she said with a bright smile. "I'm Olivia, and it's wonderful to meet you, too. My goodness, you are lovely."

"I have to be honest." Mr. Miller said after he and Lucas shared a hug. "I couldn't imagine anyone could be as pretty as my son described, but you certainly are."

My face was on fire. I wasn't used to so much attention.

"Thank you, Mr. Miller."

"Jonathan," he corrected, and I smiled.

Lucas and his mom shared a hug before he ushered us all inside.

"It smells so good in here!" Olivia smiled brightly at me. "Lucas says you're quite the cook."

"Lucas is very biased."

"With good reason," he said, kissing me on the cheek before helping his dad with the bags. "How was the flight?"

Jonathan complained about the turbulence while I dove headfirst into hostess mode. Everyone settled around the table while I poured lemonade.

"Your house is just beautiful." Olivia's eyes ghosted over the room. "It was your grandmother's?"

"Yes, it was."

Lucas tugged me by the hand and pulled me onto his lap. I could feel his parents' eyes on us, but he didn't seem to mind at all. He just held me close and told them all about the renovations we'd made over the summer.

"How many bedrooms?" Jonathan asked, his love for real estate kicking into high gear. I was sure my old house was nothing compared to the million dollar homes they sold in Manhattan.

"It has three. I use one for a guest room and the other is basically a place to keep my books."

"Three bedrooms are perfect." Olivia's eyes were shining and wistful, and I wondered what she was thinking. "And the location is just gorgeous. It's the perfect place to raise a—"

Jonathan loudly cleared his throat. "What Olivia means to say is you have a beautiful home."

His wife shot him an annoyed glare while Lucas buried his face in my hair to cover his chuckle. Obviously, I was missing some private joke.

"Thank you. Would you like to look around?"

"Oh, we'd love that!" Olivia said excitedly.

Lucas offered to show them the house while I stayed behind to check on dinner. I had just finished basting the turkey when my cell phone rang. Glancing at the screen, I took a deep breath before answering.

"Happy Thanksgiving, Aubrey."

"Happy Thanksgiving," she replied softly. "How are you feeling?"

"I'm good, thanks. I was just checking on dinner while Lucas showed his parents around the house. How are you? Are you with your folks?"

She sighed tiredly. "We decided to just stay home for Thanksgiving. Tommy was out late at the hospital and the police station. We just weren't in the mood to be sociable today."

"How are Matt and Patrick?"

"Patrick is resting comfortably for now. They'll have to do surgery on his jaw, so he has a long road ahead of him."

His jaw?

"Matt's home," she continued. "Tommy paid his bail, so at least he gets to spend Thanksgiving with his family."

I was stunned. "That was really nice of Tommy—of both of you, actually."

She grew quiet then. By now, I was sure Tommy had

told her about our argument in the principal's office.

"Tommy didn't want any of this to happen," she said softly.

"I know he didn't."

More silence, and it finally became so awkward that I faked a baking emergency and wished her a happy Thanksgiving before hanging up.

"Everything was delicious," Jonathan bragged, placing his fork on his now-empty plate.

"And the stuffing!" Olivia gushed. "I never would have thought to add apples and cranberries."

Taking my hand, Lucas and I shared a smile.

Thanks, Grandma.

Despite my initial nerves, it had truly turned out to be wonderful day. Lucas's parents were kind and soft-spoken (although his mother's voice did tend to raise an octave or two when something excited her, which was often). They obviously adored each other and were quietly affectionate.

It made me smile.

They reminded me so much of my parents.

Lucas leaned close, sliding his hand along the nape of my neck before softly kissing my cheek.

They reminded me so much of us.

Everyone offered to help with the dishes, but I insisted Lucas take his dad into the living room to watch whatever football game they could find.

"I'd like to help," Olivia said as she carried some plates over to the island. "Besides, they need some quality time together. Jonathan would never admit it, but he's missed his son."

I smiled. "I'm sure he has."

She handed me a bowl. "I've never understood the male fascination with football. It's a very confusing sport. So many positions and rules . . ."

I laughed while opening the dishwasher. "I always preferred basketball. I played in high school."

"Oh, did you?"

She seemed genuinely interested, so I told her a little about my very short career as a point guard, which had come to an abrupt end when I was sixteen.

"It sounds as if you loved it. Why did you stop playing?"

"My parents died. I stopped doing . . . pretty much everything."

Her eyes were full of sympathy for me. "I can't imagine how hard that must have been for you."

I nodded and focused on filling the dishwasher, desperately trying to ignore the melancholy that filled my heart. Sensing my need to change the subject, Olivia started talking about Lucas's teenage years, and her tone was warm and affectionate.

"He was so smart. Too smart for his age, really. Growing up in a city like Manhattan tends to make a child grow up a little quicker than they should. Despite your best efforts, you just can't shield your children from everything."

"I think that's true no matter where you live, though. It's impossible to protect them from everything."

We both grew quiet, and the roar of the dishwasher filled the silence. It wasn't uncomfortable or awkward, but the compassion radiating from her was making me a little teary-eyed.

"You miss your mom."

It wasn't a question.

"Every day."

Olivia pulled me by the hand and led me over to the kitchen table.

"I still find myself picking up the phone to call mine," she said quietly, squeezing my hand. "She passed away five years ago."

"I'm sorry."

"I'm sorry for you, too." Her eyes were shining with tears, too. "I didn't mean for things to get so heavy."

"It's okay," I replied, and I meant it. It was nice to talk about all of this with someone a little older . . . a little wiser.

With a mom.

She held my hand tightly in her own while I spilled my guts to this woman I'd met only hours earlier. Olivia listened patiently and intently, but it was when I told her about Memphis, that she finally dissolved into tears.

"You've endured so much," Olivia whispered through her sobs, "and yet you're still this wonderfully sweet young woman."

Embarrassed, I hastily jumped up from my chair to hunt for a box of tissues just as Lucas stuck his head inside the kitchen. Worriedly, he glanced between me and his mother.

"Is everything okay in here?"

"Oh, we're fine," his mother chuckled when I placed the box on the table. "Sarah and I were just getting to know each other."

Olivia dabbed at her eyes.

"You're okay?" he whispered, pulling me close.

Burying my face against his chest, I snuggled against him. "I'm fine."

Sighing heavily, he kissed the top of my hair before gazing down at me.

"I hate to see you cry," he murmured, brushing my wet cheeks with the back of his hand. "It kills me, every single time."

His sweet words made his mother weep even harder.

"This is a good cry, though. Just emotional girl talk, that's all."

Nodding, he kissed me softly before turning toward his mother. She offered him a watery smile when he leaned down to kiss her cheek. After taking one last glimpse at each of us, Lucas headed back toward the living room.

"He's a worrywart," I said, offering another tissue before sitting down with her once again.

Olivia looked proud. "He didn't used to be. You are so precious to him."

She was going to make me cry again. Bowing my head, I toyed with the tissue in my hand.

"We need tea," she announced, springing from her chair. "Do you have tea?"

I tried not to laugh as she swung open the doors of my pantry.

"I have sweet tea, and it's in the fridge."

Olivia made a face. "*Sweet* tea?"

Giggling, I rose from my chair and walked over to the cabinets. Without thinking twice, I wrapped my arms around her, hugging her tightly.

"He's precious to me, too."

It was very important she understood this.

Gazing down at me, her blue eyes welled with tears once again.

"I know, sweet girl. I know."

Chapter Twenty-one

Three weeks. I can do anything for three weeks.

Chanting my mantra in my head, I passed out the copies of the novel we'd be reading between now and Christmas vacation.

"Thank goodness it isn't Shakespeare," Carrie muttered, flipping through the pages of the book.

Amen.

With a heavy heart, my eyes settled onto Matt's empty chair. He'd been expelled, of course. Beating Patrick with a metal pipe had given Principal Mullins all the ammunition he needed to toss Matt out of school. Because he was a senior, the school board was allowing him to finish the year in alternative school, ensuring he'll still graduate in May.

It was something, at least.

Patrick was still recovering from his injuries and officially listed as a homebound student. His jaw was broken, and another surgery had already been scheduled to repair more of the damage. Lucas still refused to give me the gory details of that day, and a small part of me was thankful.

I'd witnessed enough disturbing images to last me a lifetime.

"Do you think it'll snow, Miss Bray?" Howie asked from his desk. Every head swiveled toward the windows, desperately seeking visual proof that December had indeed arrived.

"Snow is forecasted for this afternoon."

I couldn't deny it. I was a little excited to see my first mountain snow in years. I made a mental note to stop by the grocery store to stock up, just in case.

"Maybe we'll get a snow day tomorrow!" Carrie gushed excitedly.

This made me curious. "Did you get many snow days last year?"

Growing up, our community would sometimes come to a standstill with only a little snow. Small towns like Sycamore Falls rarely had the budget necessary to employ a large road crew to deal with the icy roads. A simple inch or two of snow usually resulted in a few days off from school.

"We had an entire week off last year," Howie explained. "A big storm hit in January."

Visions of being snowed-in for a week with Lucas danced in my head.

The bell sounded, breaking me out of my daydream. The class filed out and I turned toward my computer, quickly checking my school email. I was stunned to find a message from Matt's mom waiting for me in my inbox, asking if Lucas and I would consider tutoring Matt in the afternoons.

Was that even allowed? I had no idea, and I certainly couldn't ask Principal Mullins. His frosty glare had greeted me in the office this morning, pretty much reaffirming my belief I'd be looking for a new job next year.

Sighing heavily, I closed my eyes and rolled my head from side-to-side. It was my vain attempt to relieve the tension that always seemed to settle in my shoulders whenever I thought about Matt, the principal, or my future unemployment.

Suddenly, my hair was being pushed to one side, and I smiled when his gentle hands settled along my neck.

"How do you always know when I need your hands on me?"

Lucas laughed softly.

"Maybe I just always need my hands on you," he whispered, massaging my aching shoulders.

I hummed contently. "Maybe that's why we're so perfect for each other."

"Maybe so."

The tension of the day slipped away as his touch continued working its magic. Grabbing his hand, I kissed the back of his knuckles before twisting around in my seat. After glancing over my shoulder to make sure we were alone, I playfully tugged his tie and pulled his body toward mine. He took the hint and lowered his head, kissing me softly.

"Thank you."

"Anytime, sweetheart. Feel better?"

"Much."

He grabbed a nearby chair and pulled it closer to the computer. "Have you eaten lunch?"

"Not yet," I replied, glancing at my screen. "I was actually just checking my email."

"Did you get a message from Debbie Stuart?"

I nodded.

"Me too. What do you think?"

"I don't know," I admitted quietly. "I mean, I'd love to help Matt. I'm just not sure if it would even be allowed, and Principal Mullins hates me as it is."

Lucas shrugged. "I really don't know what he could

say. It's our personal time, and it wouldn't be on school grounds."

I grabbed his hand, squeezing it softly.

"I think you should talk to Principal Mullins. Make sure it's okay before you say yes."

"What about you?"

"I don't expect to be rehired, anyway. What more could he possibly do to me?"

Lucas carefully searched my face. "You're really worried about your job, aren't you?"

"I am non-tenured, and I was insubordinate. If he wants rid of me, he has the perfect excuse to do so."

"But you're a good teacher, Sarah."

"Good teachers get fired all the time."

He considered this before sighing softly.

"What would we do?" Lucas suddenly asked, his voice low and gentle.

"What do you mean?"

"If you don't get rehired." His eyes fixated on my left hand. I watched, fascinated, as his pinky gently stroked my bare ring finger. "Where would we go?"

Where would we go?

There was no question about it. I'd have to leave Sycamore Falls. I didn't have a mortgage, but I'd still need to work, and there were zero jobs in our little town. Besides, I wanted to teach, and if the only high school in town refused to rehire me, I was out of luck.

"You wouldn't have to go anywhere. You'll be rehired, Lucas. Your evaluations have been great and the principal loves you."

He looked up at me with his big blue eyes and shook his head.

"How is it possible you still completely underestimate my feelings for you?"

I blinked rapidly.

"I don't. I know how much you love me."

"Do you really?"

"Of course I do," I replied, squeezing his hand. "I just don't expect you to quit your job and follow me wherever I go."

"Would you do it for me?"

"Absolutely," I answered without hesitation.

He smiled and tugged my hand, pulling me out of my chair and into his lap. I looked nervously toward the door and wrapped my arms around his neck.

"Wherever you are is where I want to be," Lucas whispered. "I'd follow you anywhere, Sarah."

"But you love it here."

"I love you more."

He made it sound so simple.

I gently cupped his cheek, and without giving one glance toward the door, I brushed my lips against his.

Maybe it *was* just that simple.

The next morning, I was awakened by warm lips brushing across my cold shoulder, causing me to shiver and reach blindly for my blanket.

"Wake up, baby," Lucas whispered against my skin. "There's something you have to see."

Groaning, I opened my eyes, expecting to have to shield my eyes from the sunlight. Instead, a pale, wintry light streamed through the windows. I shuddered again, and Lucas's body covered mine.

"Am I dreaming?" I murmured as his lips nuzzled my neck.

"You're wide awake, Sarah."

"But you didn't spend the night."

"I know. I used my key," he said softly, gliding his nose along mine. "I really want to show you something."

I grinned and tilted my pelvis toward his.

He smirked. "Not *that*."

I pouted.

"Okay, maybe *that*, but first things first." Lucas crawled off the bed and pulled me upright.

"What time is it? Are we late for school?"

Grinning widely, he tugged me by the hand until I was standing on the floor. Following him over to the window, I couldn't contain my excited gasp when I looked outside.

A blanket of beautiful snow covered the earth, and it was still falling.

"No school today," he murmured against my ear.

"Oh!"

Mountain snow was just as pretty as I remembered it. Everything shimmered, and I had to blink rapidly so my eyes could adjust to the glistening white.

"The roads are terrible," Lucas said. "I'd never driven in snow before. It was definitely an experience."

I peered through the frosty glass. "How much is out there?"

"About four inches. We're supposed to get another three by tonight."

"That means no school tomorrow, either."

"Wow, schools rarely close in New York." His lips brushed against my ear. "Are you smiling, Miss Bray?"

"I am, Mr. Miller." Slowly, I turned around in his arms. "You braved the icy roads just to be snowed-in with me?"

"Of course. It's our first snow day."

I smiled. "We just had our first Thanksgiving. Pretty soon it'll be our first Christmas."

"That's a lot of *firsts*." His eyes then flickered with emotion as his voice became a whisper. "The first of many, I hope."

Gently, I pulled him toward the bed. Lucas fell back against the mattress as I crawled over his body, my hair falling around us when I teased his lips with mine. His quiet groan vibrated through me as we slowly undressed each other. Goosebumps erupted on my flesh, but I hardly noticed. All I could feel was the warmth of his body against mine as we made love in the early morning light.

It was only later, after he'd drifted off to sleep in my arms, did the enormity of his words weave their way into my heart.

The first of many.

His words were thrilling because I knew, deep in my soul, they weren't *just* words. It was also terrifying, for that very same reason.

Lucas was ready for more.

Was I ready to give it to him?

As if he sensed my anxiety, his arm tightened around my waist. I closed my eyes and forced myself to focus on the man whose head was snuggled against my chest. I concentrated on the warmth of his breath against my skin and the quiet peacefulness of his snores, and I desperately tried to ignore the nagging voice in my head that was trying to convince me I was far too wounded and not at all worthy of this wonderful man.

"I love you, baby." His soft voice was like a beacon, and it was exactly what I needed to hear.

A quiet reminder.

A tender promise.

Lucas snuggled deeper into my arms. Pulling the blanket around us, I closed my eyes and prayed when the day finally arrived, I would be ready.

"Something smells good."

After sleeping until noon, we'd finally showered and spent the rest of the afternoon downstairs. He'd spent a few hours on his laptop while I'd finished grading some papers.

"Beef stew." I smiled as he wrapped his arms around my waist, resting his chin on my shoulder. "Grandma always made it whenever it snowed."

"And it's still falling," he said. I continued stirring as we gazed out the window. "I think the meteorologist missed his prediction."

"That sometimes happens in the mountains. We might be snowed in the rest of the week."

Lucas kissed along my neck. "I could think of worse ways to spend the rest of the week. You might get sick of me, though."

"Never," I whispered, shivering as his nose inched along my skin.

Luckily, his cell rang, saving the stew from a definite scorching. I quickly removed it from the heat while he took the call.

"No school tomorrow," I heard him say. I could only assume he was talking to Tommy. "Yeah, we're just going to stay in, unless I can convince her to make a snowman."

I laughed and gathered bowls and silverware, taking everything to the table. They talked for a few more minutes before Lucas finally slipped his phone back into his pocket.

"Tommy says most of the roads are impassable," he said as he took a seat next to me. "Daniel had a fever, so Tommy had to slip and slide his way to the pharmacy."

"Did his fever break?"

"Yeah, about an hour ago." Lucas lifted the spoon to his lips, humming appreciatively. "So good."

"Thanks."

"He did mention Aubrey was missing you. How long has it been since you talked?"

My spoon stilled.

"We talked at Thanksgiving," I answered lamely. *For an entire five minutes.*

"Sweetheart, don't let this situation with Matt ruin your friendship with Aubrey. Tommy is trying to make amends. He really does love the kid."

I was still so disappointed in Tommy, but it was true. Paying for Matt's bail was definitely a step in the right direction.

"I don't have a problem with Aubrey."

"No, but you have a problem with her husband, and they are fiercely loyal to each other. It would be the same way with us."

"What do you mean?"

Lucas shrugged as he reached for a roll. "I'll always be on your side, no matter what. If someone asked me to choose, I'd stand by you."

"I didn't ask her to choose sides," I replied, my voice a little harsher than it should've been. "There isn't a *side*. It's just common decency. We're the teachers. We are supposed to protect those kids."

He took my hand. "I know, but you've told me time and time again how conservative this town can be. Tommy was born and raised here. He's having to question everything he's ever been taught. We need to have a little patience with him."

Lucas squeezed my hand and finished his stew.

Frustrated, I leaned back in my chair and thought about Tommy. Even growing up, he'd been vehemently against homosexuality. When we were fifteen, a transfer student from Charlotte had arrived at Sycamore High. I couldn't even remember his name, but he dressed a little nicer than the rest of the guys, and Tommy and his friends had bullied him mercilessly. He survived a week before his family moved back to the city. Now, Tommy was being faced with the reality one of his players was gay.

"I just want Tommy to be a little more tolerant—for Matt's sake," I finally whispered. "Is that wrong?"

"No, but Tommy has to come to terms with the fact that being kind to Matt doesn't mean he agrees with the kid's lifestyle. It's a very fine line, but he's trying, Sarah. He really is."

I nodded thoughtfully. "I do miss Aubrey."

"I know. Just talk to her, Sarah."

I glanced out the window. "I will, if we ever get back to school." I decided a change in subject was in order while we continued to eat. "So, you want to make a snowman?"

His eyes danced with excitement.

"Maybe. It would be my first."

"Your first snowman?"

I couldn't believe it.

He grinned shyly and pushed his empty bowl away. "There just aren't a lot of places in Manhattan to build a snowman."

Another first.

The first of many.

"Hey," Lucas whispered gently. "We don't have to go out, Sarah. I'm perfectly content to stay inside and cuddle with you on the couch."

"I'd love to build a snowman with you, Lucas."

"Then what's wrong?"

"Nothing," I said, smiling at him.

He didn't press the issue, but I could feel his eyes on me while I finished my stew. After clearing the table and loading the dishwasher, he finally gathered me in his arms and pulled me close.

"Please tell me what's wrong." His voice was a soft plea. "Am I suffocating you? Is it too much? Because I can go home—"

"No!" I whispered emphatically, framing his face with my hands. "I want you here. I always want you here."

He sighed with relief.

"It's not you, Lucas. It's me. I have this tendency of letting my insecurities get the best of me at times."

His forehead creased with confusion. "Why are you feeling insecure?"

I wasn't explaining this very well.

"Maybe insecure is the wrong word," I muttered. "I feel unworthy. Undeserving."

Lucas pushed a strand of hair behind my ear. "Undeserving of what?"

"Of you."

Suddenly, I was being lifted into the air. Lucas settled me on top of the island, stepping between my legs as his

220

arms encircled me. His eyes were brimming with adoration and devotion and a thousand other emotions that all resulted in the same sentiment.

"It's overwhelming, being loved this much."

Lucas smiled. "I'm sorry, sweetheart. I'll try to love you a little less if that will make you feel better."

Giggling, I gripped his shoulders, pulling him closer. "Don't you dare."

He tenderly kissed the tip of my nose. "If it's any consolation, I'm overwhelmed sometimes, too."

"You are?"

He nodded. "I've never been in love, so I have absolutely nothing to compare this to. I just know you invade my every thought. I want to be with you every second of every day, and when I think about the future . . ."

I watched as his throat bobbed nervously.

"You think about the future?" It was such a silly question to ask. Of course he did.

Very gently, his fingertips traced my cheek. "All the time. Is that scary to hear?"

"Yes," I admitted, "but it's not a bad thing. I think about the future, too."

"A future with me?"

He sounded so unsure, and the last thing I wanted was for *him* to feel insecure.

"With you," I said softly.

He kissed me, and it was sweet and tender as Lucas's hands wove in my hair. With a quiet moan, my lips parted, and his answering groan vibrated through me. We were panting when he finally pulled away, burying his face against my neck, and holding me tight against him.

"I love you so much, Lucas."

He pressed his forehead to mine. "I love you, too. I know it's overwhelming. I know it's scary. But don't be afraid. Don't be afraid of this."

I nodded, and it was my solemn promise to try.

"Now," I said, smiling at him, "come build a snowman with me?"

His entire face lit up with happiness.

*C*hapter *T*wenty-two

"He needs . . . something," I said, appraising our third and final attempt at building the perfect Frosty.

Lucas couldn't stop smiling. We'd spent the afternoon rolling snowballs, trying to get them the right size before piling them on top of each other. It had been a slow process, mostly because I kept falling in the snow, which would then lead to kisses in the snow. We were absolutely freezing, but we didn't care.

It was the perfect snow day.

"Maybe a hat?" Lucas suggested. "I have a Sycamore Panthers cap in my back seat."

I giggled. "If you can get to your car."

He patted Frosty's head. "Sorry, buddy. Your hat may have to wait until I can find a shovel."

The snow had stopped for now, but Lucas estimated we had about ten inches in the front yard.

"So," Lucas whispered against my ear as he settled his

hands on my waist. "Are you frozen yet?"

"Almost."

Twisting around in his arms, I tried to wrap my arms around his neck, which was no easy feat thanks to the multiple layers between us. We were both in heavy coats, scarves, hats, and gloves, making any sort of embrace a little awkward.

"Your nose is red, baby."

I laughed. "Like your cheeks."

Lucas chuckled and pressed his cold lips to mine. "Thank you, Sarah."

"For what?"

"My first snowman."

"We can make another one tomorrow, if you like," I offered. It wasn't like the snow would be melting anytime soon.

"I'd love to, but right now, I think we both could use a hot shower."

I pretended to ponder this. "How about a bath instead?"

Excitement flickered in his eyes, and he grasped my gloved hand, practically dragging me into the house.

Over the next two days, we fell into a routine. Sleeping in, having late breakfasts, playing in the snow, bubble baths . . . it was all very domestic and comfortable, and I found myself hoping the snow would never melt.

By Sunday, the crews had cleared most of the main roads leading into town. I was content to stay in the house until spring, but Aubrey called on Saturday night, inviting us to sit with them at church on Sunday morning. Lucas convinced me it was her version of a peace offering, and I decided to accept it.

"The place is nearly empty," Lucas said as we walked toward the pew. Aubrey and Tommy had yet to arrive. I did see Matt sitting with his parents, and I offered him a smile when he waved.

We took our seats and grabbed a hymnal to share. We'd only slid a few times on the curvy two-lane road, but it was enough for Lucas to announce we would own an SUV before next winter.

We.

"Why are you smiling like that?" Lucas whispered over the strains of the piano.

"Am I smiling?"

He lifted my hand and pressed a soft kiss along my knuckles. "Something is making you very happy this morning."

All I could do was nod in agreement, but, honestly, my happiness wasn't limited to just this morning. It was every single day. Granted, life wasn't perfect, and I was facing unemployment, but even that didn't ruin these moments with Lucas.

For the first time in my life, I was able to find happiness in spite of the misery.

"Did you guys have any trouble?" Tommy asked as they settled into the pew on each side of us. Aubrey brushed my shoulder and we shared a smile while Lucas began pumping Tommy for information about the best makes and models of four-wheel drives.

"Where's Daniel?"

"Mom offered to keep him," Aubrey explained as she unzipped her coat. "He was still running a low-grade fever this morning. That's why we're late. He's so clingy when he's sick. It broke my heart to leave him, but Tommy really wanted to come. Apparently, Matt asked to speak to the congregation today."

My eyes widened as Pastor Martin welcomed us. We did the obligatory singing of hymns and offered prayer requests before the pastor began his sermon. It was a short one, and after the choir's quiet rendition of "How Great Thou Art," the pastor brought Matt to the altar.

"Matthew Stuart has asked to speak to the congregation this morning," the preacher announced. Dressed in his black suit, Matt looked nervous as he fiddled with the paper in his hand. "Matthew has been a member of our congregation since the day he was born but officially joined our church when he was eight years old. I had the privilege of baptizing this young man in the waters of the Sycamore River . . ."

As the preacher continued introducing Matt, I glanced around at the congregation. Neither Patrick nor his parents were in their usual pew, and snow had kept several regular attendees away. The members who had braved the snow and ice were looking everywhere but at the eighteen-year-old boy who bravely stood before them this morning

"Good morning," Matt said, his voice trembling as he stepped closer to the microphone. "I stand humbly before my church family today to seek your forgiveness. I have already spoken with Patrick and his family, and while he is willing to share the blame for our fight at school, I cannot ignore the fact he is the one with the broken jaw. He was the one who was carted out in an ambulance, and for that, I am very sorry."

There were a few murmurs among the congregation before he continued.

"I love my hometown. I love my school, and I love my church. I have spent my life trying to be a good Christian . . . a role model to these young kids who watched me play football every Friday night. I know I have failed them, and I apologize."

"Is he going to apologize for being gay?" A voice sounded behind me. My breath caught in my throat, and I looked over my shoulder to find myself staring into the bitter eyes of Principal Mullins.

Why isn't he sitting in his usual spot with the other deacons?

I turned my attention back to a nervous Matt who was fidgeting with his tie. He took a deep breath and lifted his eyes toward the congregation.

"I cannot stand before you today and not address the rumors about me," Matt whispered to the crowd. "That would be dishonest, and if there's one place you can't be dishonest, well . . . this would be it."

Matt squared his shoulders and stared straight ahead.

"I am gay."

There were a few gasps. I could hear someone crying, and I looked over to find Debbie Stuart sobbing into her tissue. Her husband looked stoic, but his arm was wrapped around her shoulder. I chanced a glance at the pastor who was intently watching his congregation. He was doing exactly what I was doing—trying to gauge their reaction. Gossip was a way of life and could sometimes be ignored, but to have the rumors confirmed right inside the church walls was an entirely different situation.

You could see it immediately. Lines were being drawn in the sand. Sides were being chosen. An older couple in the front row actually stood up and walked down the aisle and right out the front door.

Matt didn't notice. His eyes were now planted firmly on his mother whose weeping had quieted. She was now smiling at her son, trying to offer him encouragement from the confines of her seat.

"I understand my being gay goes against our beliefs," Matt said softly. "That's why I'm here. Not only did I want to apologize for hurting Patrick, but I also wanted respectfully to ask your permission to remain a member of this church. It's the only church I've ever known. It would break my heart to have to leave, but I would understand, and I would leave without a fuss. The last thing I want to do is bring more shame to my family or to my church."

He thanked us for listening and Pastor Martin rose from his seat, placing a supportive hand on Matt's shoulder. The two men nodded at each other before Matt walked toward his mother. She met him halfway, wrapping her arms around him and hugging him close. Matt's dad remained in his pew, and his face was a blank mask as he stared at the wall.

An eerie silence filled the sanctuary until the pastor cleared his throat to say a final prayer. Organ music filled the air, and we were dismissed.

"Can they ask him to leave?" Lucas whispered to me.

I glanced at Tommy whose eyes were watching the scene between Matt and his mother. "Can they?"

He sighed loudly. "I don't think the deacons or pastor can *force* him to leave . . ."

"No, but we can certainly make him miserable enough to want to go," Principal Mullins replied behind me. All of us watched as our principal placed his hat under his arm and walked straight toward the rest of the deacons.

Tommy shook his head sadly before rising to his feet. "We should get going. We need to stop by the drugstore again."

"Call me?" Aubrey asked.

I promised I would and she gave my hand a squeeze before she and Tommy followed the crowd out the door.

Lucas and I were frozen in our seats. My eyes darted between Matt and his parents, and then across the aisle, where the deacons were huddled in a discussion with the pastor.

"They can make him miserable? At church?" Lucas whispered. "I thought church was supposed to be a safe haven . . . a place to worship . . ."

I watched with a heavy heart as Principal Mullins led the pastor and deacons through the doors behind the pulpit—the doors that led directly to the tiny meeting room.

"He's just a kid," Lucas murmured. "Why can't they just love him, no matter what?"

I wished I had an answer. I prayed for an answer.

It never came.

Lucas was quiet as we drove back to the house. He did offer to stop by the store, but I assured him I'd stocked up on enough supplies to get us to spring, if necessary. He'd smiled at that before turning his attention back to the road. He was obviously upset about Matt, but I couldn't help but wonder if something else was on his mind.

My suspicions were confirmed later that night. I was lying in bed, reading an ebook on my laptop, when he finally made his way into the bedroom. He'd been quiet all throughout dinner, and after we'd finished the dishes, he'd taken his cell into the living room to call his parents. I wasn't offended in the least. There'd been many times in the past I'd wished I could pick up the phone and hear my mom's voice. I would gladly give him privacy and not feel the least bit insulted that he wanted to be alone.

Lucas crawled into bed, and I powered down my laptop, placing it on the nightstand before turning off the lamp. His arms immediately reached for me, and I went willingly, placing my head against his chest as we snuggled close.

"I think we should tutor Matt," Lucas whispered in the darkness.

I smiled. "So do I."

Suddenly, Lucas pulled away, resting his head on his fist as he gazed down at me. The moonlight was pale, but it was bright enough I could see his face. Lifting my hand, I gently stroked his cheek.

"Do you want to live here forever?"

The question surprised me.

"Forever is a long time."

"It is," he agreed, "but if you could? Is this where you'd live the rest of your life?"

"I don't know. There's a very good chance I won't get a choice."

"Maybe it's a blessing in disguise," Lucas said, rolling onto his back. His face was tortured.

"Lucas, please talk to me. What are you thinking

about?"

My fingertip traced his lips, and he kissed it softly.

"I'm thinking about this town. I'm thinking about Matt . . . our jobs . . . our future."

"Of that list, all we can control is our future."

He nodded. "I know. I told my mom about the situation with Matt, and she asked me a very important question."

"What did she ask?"

He laced his fingers with mine. "Do I really want to raise my children in a town like Sycamore Falls?"

My entire body froze. *Children?*

"I don't want to freak you out, Sarah. We don't have to talk about this at all."

"No, it's okay. We should talk about it. What did you say?"

"I told her Sycamore Falls was so . . . sheltered. Which is good and bad, you know? But do we really want our kids to be *this* sheltered? Do we want them to grow up thinking anything or anyone different is wrong? Do I want them to feel pressured to conform just so they can fit in?"

"But those pressures exist everywhere," I reminded him.

"But to this extent?" Lucas asked, his voice laced with misery. "To the point a young man has to stand before his church and beg them not to toss him out?"

"I'm not defending Sycamore Falls," I assured him, "but I'm not sure we're all that different from any other small town."

"I know, which is why I'm not sure living in a small town is the answer."

"Living in a large city isn't the answer, either," I whispered grimly. "There's prejudice everywhere. There's hatred everywhere."

Growing quiet, Lucas held me close. His fingers gently slid through my hair, and I'd almost drifted off when I heard his quiet whisper.

"Are you happy?"

"You make me happy," I said, pressing a kiss to his chest.

"I have to warn you. My mother is already planning our wedding."

I laughed. "Does she know something we don't?"

"No," Lucas replied sleepily. "I think she just knows her son is very much in love with you, and he'd marry you today if you'd let him."

It didn't take long until his soft snores filled the air, which was ironic, because after that little declaration, I was suddenly wide-awake.

By Tuesday, the roads were decent enough for school to resume. The students were excited to be back and were talkative most of the day, but overall, the return to work was blissfully uneventful.

That is, until the end of the day, when I walked into the office to check my mail.

"Miss Bray, the principal would like to see you in his office if you have a moment," the secretary said, offering me a sympathetic smile.

I glanced down at my watch. Today was my first tutoring session with Matt.

Sighing, I thanked her and made my way over to the principal's door. It was open, and he was sitting behind his desk, tapping away on his computer. I knocked lightly, and he didn't even bother looking up as he invited me inside.

"Close the door, please," he instructed. He then offered me a chair, which I accepted. After a few minutes, Principal Mullins finally lifted his head, gazing at me with some unreadable expression.

As fun as it was to sit and stare at my boss, I had more important things to do this afternoon.

"You wanted to see me?"

His smile was cold. "Am I keeping you from something, Miss Bray?

At my persistence, Lucas had finally spoken to the principal about his tutoring for Matt. Principal Mullins agreed he had no control over our personal time, and while he didn't approve, he admitted it was Lucas's decision to make. I didn't bother asking permission. I knew it would only lead to another confrontation, which was something I was desperately trying to avoid. Principal Mullins apparently had other plans, so I decided to be honest.

"Yes, actually, but I have a few minutes. I have a tutoring session at four."

"With Matthew Stuart, I presume."

I nodded and braced myself for attack.

Principal Mullins stood up slowly from his desk and walked around to the front. He leaned against it, watching me closely.

"Miss Bray, I'm not sure you're a good . . . fit here at Sycamore High. You don't share our vision."

You mean I don't share your vision.

"Of course, as a non-tenured teacher, that will be up for the school board to decide, but they do seek the principal's recommendation in the matter of rehires, and I am very honest when it comes to my recommendations."

"My evaluations have been top-notch," I reminded him calmly.

"Yes, but your attitude stinks."

Only with you, I wanted to say. Instead, I bit my tongue. Anything I might say would just add fuel to the fire. Obviously, it was time to look for another job. He was making it quite clear I wouldn't be coming back to Sycamore High. I was actually glad to have the confirmation. Most non-tenured teachers didn't find out until spring. He was giving me plenty of notice, which, in a strange way, I appreciated.

"I understand you and Mr. Miller have become quite

close."

"I'm not sure that's any of your concern, Mr. Mullins."

"Oh, but it is. I expect my teachers to be role models. Shacking up with his girlfriend is not what I would consider a positive influence on our students."

I stiffened. So far, we'd avoided gossip considering our sleeping arrangements.

"Lucas has his own apartment."

"Which he rarely occupies," Principal Mullins said with a sneer. "It's a small town, Miss Bray. Word gets around." Walking around his desk, he dropped back into his leather chair, his fingers steepled in front of him. "Mr. Miller is a fine instructor. Very few know about his unfortunate situation in New York, and that is in thanks to me. But now . . ."

Rage flooded my veins. "He was innocent of those charges."

"So they say, but you know small towns, Miss Bray. All it takes is a little rumor to ruin someone's reputation. I'd hate to see that happen to Mr. Miller."

Is he threatening me?

"What is it exactly you want from me, Mr. Mullins?"

His smile was sinister. "Your support. Unbelievably, I am being met with much resistance from the pastor and the deacons of the church. They are supportive of Matthew—as are you and Mr. Miller. I feel—and many agree with me—Matthew is no longer welcome in our congregation. He is violent, and he is a homosexual. He is a sinner, and has no rightful place in our church."

"I fail to see what any of that has to do with me or Lucas."

"I'm merely seeking your support," Mr. Mullins said slowly. "And in exchange, Mr. Miller's past scandal will remain buried and both of your jobs will remain intact."

I furiously jumped to my feet. "Are you blackmailing me?"

"Such an unpleasant word," he murmured as his eyes

searched mine. "Consider it a peace offering. You scratch my back . . ."

My blood was boiling with fury. This man was a school administrator. A deacon of the church. A pillar of our community.

"You're out of your mind. It will be a cold day in hell—and that's exactly where you're going—before I support you in anything. There is absolutely nothing keeping me from calling every member of the school board and telling them about this conversation."

He laughed darkly. "If you do, please say hello to Phil Randall for me. He's the chairman of the school board, as you know, considering he signs your paychecks. He's also been my best friend for thirty years. A fine man."

That's when I was reminded small towns can be great places to live—if you know the right people.

Unfortunately for me, all of my people were dead and gone.

Once I was in the car, I called Debbie Stuart, asking to reschedule today's tutoring session. I broke every speed limit on the way to my house, but I needed the sanctuary of home.

I needed him.

I was visibly upset, and he would panic. What would I say to him? Could I tell him I'd just been blackmailed? Could I tell him his job and his professional reputation rested in the hands of the most evil man I'd ever known?

Could I protect him?

By the time I walked into the kitchen, I still had no idea what to say to him. All I knew was I needed to feel his arms around me. I slammed the door, and he immediately jumped up from his place at the kitchen table.

"What's wrong?"

I dropped my bag onto the floor and rushed toward

him, leaping into his arms. Winding my legs around his waist, I crushed myself against him as I finally let the tears flow.

"Baby, what's wrong? What's happened?"

Lucas carried me toward the table, sitting me gently in his lap.

"Everything," I whispered through my sobs. "Everything is wrong."

But as I said the words, I knew they weren't true. Not *everything* was wrong.

Lucas was here, and he loved me.

And I knew I couldn't keep this from him.

*C*hapter *T*wenty-three

I was exhausted, but I wasn't tired.

It was the strangest feeling, but truthfully, it wasn't the first time in my life I'd felt this way. Just painfully fatigued, and yet, unable to close my eyes because my nerves were absolute live wires.

To say Lucas was pissed was an understatement. I'd never seen him so angry, but he wasn't upset with me. After my confession, he'd immediately called his lawyer who was ready to take the first flight out of New York. He was now on the phone with his parents, and while I had no idea what that conversation consisted of, I wondered what they thought of me. After all, I'd had the power to protect their son. Would they despise me if he lost his job?

Without his arms around me, it was so easy to doubt myself. Principal Mullins could ruin our careers, and not only in Sycamore Falls. I didn't care so much about mine, but to know Lucas's troubles could haunt him, and I had the power to keep that from happening . . .

Correction—I'd *had* the power.

"Well, my parents are livid," Lucas announced as he walked into the kitchen. I was standing at the counter, angrily chopping vegetables for a salad we were much too upset to eat. "They want us to resign immediately and move to Manhattan."

"That doesn't sound so bad to me."

Lucas's eyes snapped to mine. "Really? Because I can book us a flight tonight. We'll go anywhere you want and we'll never look back."

The determined look on his face assured me he was serious.

"Maybe you should go without me," I whispered softly.

His face darkened as he dropped his cell phone onto the table. Slowly, he made his way over to me, and I dropped the knife against the cutting board.

"Why would you say something like that?"

His voice was soft and sad, and it only broke my heart even more. I blinked back my tears and he whispered my name, gently lifting my face toward his.

"He could ruin you, Lucas."

"I don't care."

His inability to see just how much Mullins could destroy him infuriated me. "You should care! You need to listen to your parents and go back to Manhattan."

"Without you?"

"Yes."

"Not a chance."

His eyes flashed with anger. Exhaling a shaky breath, I leaned on the counter for support as he stepped closer. The only sound in the room was our labored breaths and the chime of the grandfather clock.

"Stop this," he whispered, smoothing my hair out of my face and gently stroking my tear-stained cheek. "Don't you dare do this. Don't even think about trying to push me away because it won't work. You will never convince me

I'd be better off without you, so don't waste your energy."

"I should have kept my mouth shut."

"You think it would have been better if you'd just kept this to yourself? Dealt with it alone?"

"Yes."

His fingertips stroked my cheek. "Aren't you tired of dealing with everything without someone by your side? Haven't you done that long enough?"

I bowed my head.

"And now you're trying to push me away. But that's how you deal with every crisis, isn't it? You push away the people you love."

I gasped. "That's not fair, Lucas."

"You're right. It's not fair at all," he agreed quietly. "But you did it to Aubrey when your parents died. And in some twisted way, you did it to Monica by leaving her in Memphis and moving back home. Life gets rough, and you push away anyone who has ever meant anything to you."

I couldn't deny it. Ending my friendship with Aubrey had been completely selfish on my part. I'd been a sixteen-year-old girl who'd just buried her parents. In my mind, if I closed myself off to everyone, then maybe it wouldn't hurt so much if they left me. I'd grown up, but my philosophy hadn't changed.

But this time, it was different. I wasn't trying to protect myself.

"I just want to take care of you." Tears finally trickled down my cheeks. For the first time in my life, I was trying to be selfless, and he wouldn't let me.

Lucas's face softened.

"And I want to take care of you." His hands gently framed my face. "That's how it's supposed to work, Sarah. We're supposed to protect each other. I don't need you playing the martyr. I just need *you*."

I closed my eyes as his lips brushed across my wet cheeks.

"I love you. I want to spend the rest of my life with

you," he whispered forcefully. "You're not alone anymore, and I will not let you push me away."

As he lifted me into his arms, I encircled his waist with my legs and buried my face against his neck while he carried me upstairs.

Kicking the bedroom door shut and lifting me against it, Lucas pressed his body into mine. His lips blazed a trail along my throat, causing me to moan and tense my legs, pulling him tighter against me. With a groan, his mouth crashed against mine, and I could do nothing but cling to him when he lifted me away from the door and carried me toward the bed, laying me gently against the mattress. Crawling over my body, Lucas slid his hand up my leg and along my thigh before finding the buttons of my blouse. His eyes never left my face while he gradually unfastened each one. I reached for the zipper of his jeans, and we undressed each other slowly, our earlier frenzy settling into something familiar and real . . . and just as passionate as being pinned against the door.

"I love you, baby."

Whimpering, I repeated his words and drew him closer. All of the fear and desperation mingled with the absolute certainty of the words we were whispering to each other came crashing over me.

He wouldn't leave me.

I wouldn't leave him.

Simple promises made with adoring whispers and quiet passion, and just as binding as if we were reciting them at the altar.

From that day on, there was no more talk of leaving.

There was, however, much talk about Christmas vacation, which was only two weeks away. It was the favorite topic of conversation at both home and school.

It snowed a little every day, blanketing the mountains

and adding to the excitement of the season. I couldn't deny I was excited, even though Lucas was becoming more secretive as the holiday crept closer. I'd catch him on his laptop or on his phone at the weirdest times, and he'd just shrug it off and distract me with Christmas trees, sugar cookies, and hot kisses under the forest of mistletoe he'd hung throughout the house. There was really no rhyme or reason to it. Sprigs hung in the usual places—like the archway leading into the living room, and to my amusement, above the bed—but it was when he hung mistletoe from the ceiling above the shower that I'd finally drawn the line.

As if he needed an excuse to kiss me.

Thanks to a weeklong bout with the flu, Principal Mullins had been blissfully absent from school, postponing the inevitable conversation. He'd want to know what I'd decided, and Lucas had already demanded to stand by my side when the day arrived.

We were united, and there was no more talk of leaving.

"Miss Bray, are you listening?"

I smiled apologetically at Matt, and he laughed.

"Thinking about Mr. Miller, aren't you."

I flipped through the pages of his textbook and pretended to play dumb.

"Why would you assume that?"

"Because I catch him daydreaming, too," Matt replied with a grin. "It's cool, though. I get it."

Lucas and I were tutoring Matt twice a week. He didn't really need our help; Matt was an intelligent young man. What he did need, however, was motivation and some positive influences. He was surrounded by thugs at the alternative school, which made his mom understandably nervous, but the isolation from his friends had sent Matt spiraling into a depression that kept him locked in his room all day long. His father had been less than supportive, which only added to Matt's stress. Debbie admitted he was happiest when Lucas or I were there, which made the fact that I wasn't paying attention to him an absolute shame.

"I'm sorry, Matt. So what do you think of Poe?"

"So much better than Shakespeare."

I couldn't agree more.

"He *is* a little morbid," Matt continued, "but life is morbid sometimes, so I think it's pretty realistic. Death is a part of life, right?"

"It is. Do you have a favorite?"

"*It was many and many a year ago, in a kingdom by the sea . . .*"

Closing his eyes, he quietly recited the first stanza of "Annabel Lee."

I smiled. "That's my favorite, too. How are you, Matt? Really?"

It was a stupid question, really. I could tell by the dark circles under his eyes he wasn't doing well at all.

He shrugged. "I'm just trying to get to graduation, Miss Bray. No matter how much I love this town, I've seen enough in the past few weeks to know I'll never truly be happy here. I want to live in a place where I can get lost in the crowd and still live my life."

"Are you still thinking about college?"

"Florida State is still interested in me," he said excitedly, and it was the first time today he'd shown any enthusiasm about anything. "Not for football, obviously, but if I can keep my grades up and stay out of trouble . . ."

I wondered if the university knew about his fight with Patrick, but I decided not to ask. Matt was a smart kid, and I was sure it was something he'd already considered. We discussed possible majors, and he surprised me by admitting he was considering teaching.

"I've had some good teachers," Matt said, "but you're the first one who made me realize there could be more to life than just what Sycamore Falls has to offer. You left this place—"

"But I also came back," I reminded him.

"Doesn't matter. You're happy here, right?"

While driving home, I was still pondering the answer to Matt's question.

Am I happy here?

In so many ways, I was happier than I'd ever been, but did my happiness have anything to do with Sycamore Falls?

Pulling into my driveway, I turned off the ignition and took a long look at my grandma's beautiful house. After Josh's death, I'd needed the quiet refuge of home. I'd needed the security and familiarity that came from the faded wallpaper in her kitchen and the chime of the grandfather clock. I'd needed this time to refocus. Regroup. Recharge.

I'd never planned on falling in love.

Never even dreamed it was a possibility.

Suddenly, the screen door flew open, and out he walked, carrying a string of lights. Lucas had been hanging Christmas lights for days. He hadn't spotted me, so I watched closely while he carefully wound the lights around the wooden beams.

Lucas loved this house, which had been obvious this summer when he'd spent every spare moment renovating it. I could never sell it—the house was far too important to me—but if we moved, we'd have to find someone to take care of it.

I shook my head and took a long, cleansing breath. I couldn't worry about these things. Not right now. I wanted to enjoy our first Christmas together.

For the first time in my life, I was willing to let the future take care of itself, and I knew that was because of the handsome man who was painstakingly stringing lights around my porch.

Chapter Twenty-four

It was Christmas Eve, and Lucas and I were spending the evening with Aubrey and her family. Her little boy was curled up in my lap, watching Rudolph on the plasma screen, while the grown boys were sprawled across the living room floor, carefully assembling the train set we'd bought Daniel for Christmas.

"It was the perfect gift for Tommy," Aubrey said with a grin.

I smirked. "For Lucas, too."

The two men had been arguing over the directions for nearly an hour now, but the tracks were finally beginning to take shape as they wound around the Christmas tree.

The night had been full of presents, food, and classic Christmas cartoons. It was as if the adults had secretly decided to ignore our unresolved tension and focus on the little boy's happiness. We hadn't even had to force smiles while we baked cookies and played with the presents

Daniel had been allowed to open early. There were still plenty of gifts, and I had a feeling Santa would bring more before morning arrived. We'd made a big production of putting milk and cookies under the tree and hanging stockings along the fireplace, happily putting aside our differences to make sure one little boy had a wonderful Christmas Eve.

As I stared at the twinkling lights of the tree, I thought about another boy and how his life would be happier if our differences could be set aside for him, too.

It was late when Daniel finally fell asleep in my lap. Aubrey offered to take him to his bedroom, leaving me on the couch, watching the guys assemble the final pieces. Lucas's eyes brightened with excitement when a gleeful Tommy reached for the remote.

"I wouldn't do that," I warned him. "Your wife might just murder you in your sleep if you wake the baby."

Their faces fell with disappointment, but Tommy nodded and flipped off the switch on the remote.

"That's okay," he said, rising from his place on the floor. "I wanted to talk to you guys, anyway."

Lucas sat down with me on the couch, wrapping his arm around my shoulder and pulling me close. Tommy sat down in his recliner just as Aubrey returned. She settled herself against the arm of his chair, and I smiled at the irony. There had been time when the three of us would have stood beside each other no matter what.

Those days were gone.

It wasn't uncomfortable, necessarily, and it wasn't sad. It was just as it should be. A husband and wife are supposed to support each other and present a united front. I wouldn't expect anything less from either of them.

Lucas reached for my hand, and I offered him a smile. We might not be wearing wedding rings, but I knew our bond was just as strong.

"Sarah, I owe you an apology."

Tommy's voice was soft, and I couldn't hide my

surprise. "An apology?"

"When we were in the principal's office, I should have defended you . . . not that you needed it. You're so strong, Sarah. You always were, but I still should've stuck up for you."

"You think I'm upset because you didn't defend me?"

He shrugged. "We've been friends a long time."

"I didn't need a friend, Tommy. Your quarterback could have used one, though."

Lucas squeezed my hand—a silent, subtle reminder to keep my temper in check. I took a deep breath.

"Tommy, I appreciate your apology, but I was never upset with you because you didn't defend me. Just because we're friends doesn't mean you have to agree with everything I say. I don't expect that. I just wish you could have been a little more sympathetic to a young man who had played his heart out for you."

"We both love Matt," Aubrey whispered. "But, Sarah, surely you don't agree with the way Matt's living his life. The Bible says . . ."

"I don't need a Bible lesson, Aubrey. I know what it says."

"And she never said she agreed with the way he was living his life," Lucas offered quietly. "Neither of us can stand to watch Matt be bullied and completely alienated from the town he loves so much."

"We don't want that either," Aubrey said.

Her husband nodded in agreement. "And you're right. I should have done more to protect him."

"I'm not asking either of you to ignore your beliefs. I'd just like to think that it's okay to disagree with him, but still treat him like a human being."

"His mom told me his depression is getting worse," Lucas said. "He doesn't leave the house—except to go to alternative school. Howie is his only friend. He doesn't even know if he'll be welcome in church for the Christmas service."

"No one can keep him out of church," Tommy reminded us.

"No, but you heard Mullins. They can make him feel so unwelcome he'll never want to go back."

"Well, we'll just have to make sure that doesn't happen," Tommy sounded determined, and it warmed my heart. "I'll call in the morning and invite him and his family to church tomorrow."

"They could even sit with us," Aubrey offered.

Lucas and I smiled.

Daniel whimpered from his bedroom, causing Aubrey to bolt off the chair and dash down the hall.

"We should go," Lucas said.

Tommy walked us to the door, and I'd just stepped out onto the porch when he pulled me in for a hug.

"I really am sorry," Tommy whispered against my ear.

I hugged him tightly.

"Me too."

Soft, feathery kisses lingered along my spine, waking me and causing me to tremble. The room was chilly, but that was to be expected when you were naked and the sun had yet to rise.

"Merry Christmas," Lucas whispered against my skin.

I hummed contently and rolled onto my side. Smiling down at me, he gently stroked my cheek.

"Merry Christmas, Lucas."

Leaning down, he kissed me softly.

I giggled. "How is it possible you already taste like toothpaste?"

"I've been awake for a while," he said with an excited grin. Suddenly, he was out of bed, and I immediately reached for the blanket, missing the warmth of his body. He quickly tossed me a robe. "Get up. It's Christmas morning, and there are presents to be opened."

He thought he was being so stealthy. What he didn't know was I'd seen him through the school office window, signing for a package from our delivery guy, just three days ago. I'd wondered why he hadn't had the package shipped to the house, but then I understood when I spotted a tiny red and silver box with a pretty bow resting under our Christmas tree later that night.

The curiosity had driven me insane.

"You're worse than a kid," I mumbled as he took me by the hand and led me downstairs. We passed the grandfather clock, and I groaned. "Five o'clock? Really? I bet even Daniel is still sleeping."

Grinning, he swiftly pulled me toward the living room. The Christmas tree lights were already aglow, casting a peaceful light around the otherwise darkened room.

"I couldn't wait," he whispered, gently tugging me toward the tree.

I sighed when I noticed the extra presents under the tree that hadn't been there the night before.

"I thought we'd agreed just one present."

He dragged me down to the floor. "These are from Santa."

I rolled my eyes, but his happiness was infectious, so I bit my tongue and took the first present he offered me.

"Lucas, I only bought you one . . ."

Granted, it was an expensive one, but still.

"Doesn't matter," he said. "These are just little things, I promise."

Sighing, I carefully pulled the bow and lifted the top of the box. Buried inside was a beautiful leather photo album.

"For all of those pictures you took back in the fall."

"I love it," I replied, smiling as I flipped through the blank pages. The album was huge. "I didn't take *that* many pictures, though."

"You will someday."

The rest of the gifts were just as thoughtful. An ornament for our tree with our names engraved, a new cookbook, and a collection of short stories written by Poe.

"Your gift is really for both of us," I said, offering him the envelope with the plane tickets inside. "I thought we could do what you suggested and visit your parents for New Year's."

He smiled down at the tickets in his hand.

"That's . . . perfect, actually. They'll be so excited. Thank you."

I leaned over to kiss his cheek. "Thank you, too."

"You're welcome," Lucas said quietly as he reached for the last tiny box. I heard him take a deep breath when he placed it in my palm.

"This has been driving me crazy," I admitted with a grin, quickly tugging on the silver bow.

"Wait." He placed his hand over mine, and I noticed his trembling fingers. Curiously, I watched his face as he swallowed nervously and took another deep breath. He closed his eyes, and when he reopened them, they looked determined.

That's when I realized this was important—far more important than I'd ever imagined.

And now, my anxiety was a perfect match to his.

"I love you," Lucas whispered, his fingers skimming along mine. "I want you to know I meant what I said. I truly want to spend the rest of my life with you."

My heart hammered in my chest as he lifted the tiny lid. Nestled inside the tissue was a black, velvet box.

"What's in this box, is . . . very special. It belonged to my grandmother. My dad's mom. She died before I was born, but she'd passed this down to him."

He didn't even have to lift the lid; I knew what was inside. He'd been so secretive the past few months—always online and whispering on the phone. I'd dismissed it all, never once considering the very real possibility he was considering *this*. He'd dropped so many hints, and I'd ignored them, assuming he was talking about some time in the distant future.

I had no idea my future would arrive on Christmas morning.

With unsteady fingers, he finally lifted the lid.

Growing up, I'd never really imagined what my engagement ring would look like, but as I gazed down at the silver band and its shimmering diamonds, I knew this was it.

It was simple and undeniably pretty, with a square diamond in the center of a platinum band.

"Do you like it?" His voice was laced with hope.

Tears filled my eyes. "I love it."

His relief was evident.

"My mom wanted her own ring," Lucas said, laughing nervously as he lifted it from its case, "so they saved this one for me." He took my left hand and slipped it on my finger. "I've been saving it for you."

My tears were uncontrollable now, and he gently pulled me into his lap.

"Please marry me," he whispered, pressing his forehead against mine.

All I could do was nod, but for him, that was enough.

"Joy to the World" was floating in the air in the little country church. It was the perfect song, because I'd never felt more joyous. Lucas was by my side, holding my left hand and running his finger along the band of his grandmother's ring.

His smile was endless.

My smile was endless, and it only brightened when I saw Tommy had kept his word. Matt and his mother were sitting with us, and it didn't matter that some of the longtime members of the church were pointedly ignoring their presence. There were many, many more who stopped by our pew just to say hello and to welcome him back, and the effect it had on Matt was obvious.

Matt's smile was endless, too.

My hand was wrapped in Lucas's palm, but the shimmering band on my finger was impossible to hide. During the prayer, I heard Aubrey's quiet gasp, and I lifted my eyes to find hers gazing at our joined hands. She smiled brightly and elbowed Tommy, and Lucas and I tried to contain our laughter.

The entire service was filled with Christmas hymns, and I sang louder than ever. Perhaps my happiness could be blamed on the Christmas spirit. It might even be blamed on the Holy Spirit.

Today, maybe it was a little of both.

*C*hapter *T*wenty-five

Life always has a way of reminding that you can make all the plans you like, but Mother Nature is always in control.

"It's a blizzard!" I groaned loudly as scenes from the Northeast flashed across the television screen. Manhattan had received nearly a foot of snow.

"Sixty mile per hour winds, according to my dad." Lucas handed me a bottle of water before sitting down next to me on the couch. "I've already contacted the airline and changed our reservations. Our flight would have been cancelled, anyway."

I couldn't hide my disappointment. We'd been so excited to see his parents. On Christmas day, we'd called and told them about our engagement, and his mother had sobbed like a baby.

"You'll love New York in the springtime."

"We could have used some time away from this place," I muttered.

Spring Break was just too far away, although you wouldn't know it by the weather outside our window. While his parents were braving a blizzard, our temperatures were now hovering in the fifties.

"Mountain weather is so strange," Lucas said as we watched our local forecast. The rest of the week was much of the same—scattered rain showers and above normal temperatures.

"We had a white Christmas," I reminded him.

He was actually pouting, and I giggled at the wounded expression on his face. I grabbed the remote and turned off the depressing weather forecast before climbing into his lap. His pout turned into a sexy smirk when I wiggled against him.

"Marry me," he said softly, nuzzling my cheek.

"I already said yes."

"Actually, you didn't," Lucas muttered, trying so hard to sound serious. "You just *nodded*."

He was right. A nod was all I'd been capable of in the moment. Smiling, I wrapped my arms around his neck and pulled myself closer to his chest.

"Yes," I whispered against his lips.

"Yes, what?"

"Yes, I'll marry you."

A soft, contented smile crept across his face. "Today?"

"Now, you're pushing it. Your mother would kill us both."

"That's true," he admitted with a sigh. "Do you have a date in mind?"

"Eager, Mr. Miller?"

"Slightly."

"Hmm." I really hadn't thought much about setting a date. Of course, we'd only been engaged a few days. I couldn't be sure, but I didn't think Lucas would want a long engagement. "Maybe June?"

He smiled. "I like June. Do you want a church wedding?"

I shook my head. "Not unless you do. I think I want it outdoors."

"We could get married here," Lucas suggested, his arms tightening around me. "Right in the front yard."

Suddenly, I had an idea. "What about at the falls?"

His face brightened, and we spent the next hour discussing wedding plans. We just wanted a small ceremony, overlooking the falls, surrounded by our closest family and friends.

I had a brief pang of sadness when I thought of my parents and grandma, but Lucas reminded me his family was now mine, and I'd never be alone again.

The New Year came and went, and before I could blink, school was back in session. The news of our engagement was thankfully overshadowed by talk of college acceptance letters, and the entire month of January was filled with excited seniors announcing which schools they'd been admitted, and which colleges were offering the best scholarships. The local community college in Winslow always offered scholarships to the top ten percent of our graduating class, but seniors with big dreams and unrealistic expectations rarely gave the little college a second glance.

I could relate, because once upon a time, I'd been one of those students.

"Community college is for people who can't get accepted to a real school," Carrie said as she breezed into the room. "Or for people who can't afford to go anywhere else."

Howie turned to me. "How many schools did you get accepted to, Miss Bray?"

"Three," I replied, leaning against my desk. My answer caused a few raised eyebrows and a lot of hushed whispers.

"How many did you *apply* to?" Carrie wondered.

"Three."

My reply began a discussion about how many schools everyone had applied to, and that's when I realized college acceptance was a competition to these kids. *How many schools did you get accepted to?* I'd heard the question all week, not realizing our kids were in serious competition with each other over something ridiculous.

Didn't they have enough pressure? Did they really need to add more stress to their lives?

"I applied to Memphis, North Carolina, and Winslow Community College."

A few of the students rolled their eyes at the mention of the little school.

"What a lot of you need to understand is it doesn't matter how many schools you're accepted to. You need to find one that's a good fit for you, not to mention, the one you can afford. I was just like you. I wanted as far away from Sycamore Falls as I could possibly get, so when Memphis offered me a full scholarship, I jumped at the chance. However, don't discount Winslow just because it's a community college. You can always transfer later, and sometimes, a smaller school is a better option for you. It just depends on what you need."

Needless to say, we didn't write in creative writing that day.

I was still thinking about my seniors when I arrived at Matt's later in the afternoon. As I walked toward the porch, I noticed his mother sitting on her porch swing. Her eyes were tortured and hard, and my stomach dropped.

"Debbie, what's wrong?"

Suddenly, I could hear screams coming from inside the house.

"Matt wasn't accepted to Florida State," she whispered weakly. "His . . . *altercation* with Patrick caused the admissions office to take another look at his application. We've been on the phone with them all afternoon, but now Patrick's father wants to press charges . . ."

"Oh, Debbie, I hadn't heard."

"Neither had we, until yesterday."

The shouting was getting louder, and I could hear Mr. Stuart telling his son he was a miserable excuse for a human being.

Hot, angry tears filled my eyes.

"You should go, Sarah."

Nodding numbly, I slowly walked back to my car.

Florida State had been Matt's opportunity to get out of this town. To get away from his father. To begin a new life. His chance was now gone, and my heart broke for the young man. He deserved a clean slate, but—in pressing charges—Patrick's father was going to ensure that never happened.

I cried all the way home.

A few days later, I was searching for wedding dresses online when Lucas walked into the kitchen.

"How'd it go?" Today had been Lucas's scheduled session with Matt.

"It didn't," he said quietly as he closed the door behind him. "Our tutoring services are no longer needed."

I wasn't surprised, but it still hurt a little.

"Did you at least get to see him?"

"I didn't make it past the front door," Lucas explained, sitting down next to me and kissing me on the cheek. "Debbie did say Matt isn't doing very well. He absolutely refuses to come out of his room, and he hasn't eaten in days."

I closed my eyes and tried to keep my tears at bay. Lucas wrapped his arm around my shoulder and pulled me close.

"Sweetheart, we can't save them all."

"I want to try."

"I know you do," he said, nuzzling my cheek with his nose. "It's just one of the reasons why I love you so much."

"I love you, too," I whispered.

He kissed my cheek again before turning his attention to the computer screen.

"Still looking at dresses?"

I sighed. "I just want to try to focus on something positive, you know?"

Smiling, he pointed to a particularly short wedding dress with lots of lace and very little fabric. "I like this one."

I smirked. "Of course you do. Now go away. You know it's bad luck for the groom to see the dress."

He laughed and kissed me softly before making his way into the living room. I had been spending most of my evenings online, making notes, and looking at bridal websites. I was surprised how excited I was about planning the wedding. I'd never been a fan of ceremonies, but this was different. It was the one bright spot in my otherwise chaotic life, and I was determined to enjoy every moment of it.

I had just emailed a few dress pictures to Lucas's mom when he walked back into the kitchen. His face was ashen, and he was holding his cell phone.

"Tommy just called," he announced quietly. "Matt's been taken to the hospital in Winslow."

My blood ran cold.

"What happened?"

"Debbie found him unresponsive in his bedroom," Lucas explained. "We probably won't be welcome at the hospital, but if you want to go—"

I jumped out of my chair. "I want to go."

Lucas nodded and grabbed his keys off the counter.

The waiting room was filled with people—or maybe it just seemed that way—because the room was so small. Tommy and Aubrey were in one corner, sitting next to a pale-faced Howie. My stomach somersaulted, and I clutched Lucas's arm as Aubrey rushed from her seat.

"He's okay," she whispered to us. "We don't know a lot of details. Debbie's in the chapel. The pastor is on his way . . ."

I looked up at Lucas.

"I'd like to go see Debbie."

"Okay."

The chapel was easy to find. It was small, too, with a few pews and candlelight dancing at the altar. Debbie was sitting up front, and we quietly made our way to her side. Her tearful eyes didn't seem at all surprised to see us. She just gave us a sad smile when we sat down next to her. I took her hand in mine and gave it a gentle squeeze. Minutes passed, until finally, she squeezed my hand in return.

"The doctor says he's going to be fine—physically," Debbie whispered weakly. Her voice was hollow and haunted. "It's funny. I could hardly get him to take one pain pill when he was in that cast. I told the doctor it had to be accidental—my son would never intentionally try to hurt himself—but nobody accidentally takes that many pills. Not all at once."

I didn't ask how many. The number was irrelevant.

"The past few weeks have been terrible," Debbie continued. "It's been one thing right after another. First, there was the news about college. Then Patrick pressed charges. Yesterday, Matt got a call from one of the deacons of the church, telling him it might be best if he didn't help the youth with the Spring Carnival this year. He always volunteers . . ."

Determined to stay strong, I blinked back my tears. Lucas wrapped his arm protectively around my shoulder.

"And his *father*," Debbie laughed hoarsely. "It's hard to

remember why I ever loved that man. If I'd known what a hateful, stubborn father he'd turn out to be, I never would have married him."

We sat with her until Pastor Martin arrived. He offered us a quiet hello and a sad smile as he took his place at Debbie's side. We stood to leave, and Debbie grabbed my hand once again.

"He loves you both so much. Thank you for loving him."

We simply nodded before making our way out of the chapel.

Chapter Twenty-six

"We're going to be late," Lucas said as he straightened his tie.

I said nothing. I just continued staring at my laptop screen, clicking through the images. I was so frustrated. Everything was too small, too big, or too expensive.

"Sweetheart, the dresses will still be online after we get out of church."

"I'm not looking at dresses."

Lucas sat down next to me at the kitchen table before glancing at my monitor.

"You're looking at houses?"

I nodded and continued clicking the mouse.

He didn't ask any questions. He didn't have to.

I'd been unforgivably moody since Matt's trip to the hospital nearly two weeks ago, and it had nothing to do with us. That was just another reason why we had to move as far away from Sycamore Falls as possible. I refused to let this town taint the one good thing I had in my life.

"The only reason I'm even stepping foot in church is

because Debbie asked us to be there today."

"I know, baby," Lucas replied softly. His patience was endless, and I didn't deserve him. "After today, we'll never go back if that's what you want."

It was the perfect thing to say, and it was the only thing that convinced me to leave the house.

The congregation was visibly nervous as Debbie Stuart headed to the pulpit. She'd asked the pastor if she could address the church today, and while some assumed this would be an update of sorts related to Matt's health, others feared she was here to hold the deacon responsible for finally pushing Matt over the edge.

What they weren't expecting was Mama Bear.

"This is the last day I will stand in Sycamore Baptist Church," Debbie announced, her voice strong as it echoed through the sanctuary. "I am not doing this in an attempt to separate myself from the Lord, because I believe the Lord will love me no matter where I choose to worship. This is me, separating myself from the hypocrisy my son and I have encountered over the past few months. We will be moving away from Sycamore Falls when he graduates, and we will join another church in another town."

Quiet murmurs flowed through the church.

"My son is gay. Does this make me happy? Of course not. Does it make me love him any less? Of course not. And it shouldn't have made you love him any less, but it did. But that's why a mother's love is perfect and unconditional. My son did not need your judgment. He needed your prayers. He needed your counsel. This is my child, and until recently, he was *your* child, and you loved him. When he was scoring touchdowns for your school, you loved him. When he was bagging your groceries, you loved him. When he was volunteering with the youth of this church, you loved him. But he's learned a lesson. He's learned some love *is* conditional and judgmental."

Aubrey was crying quietly, and I watched her sweet son pat her face, promising her with an innocent whisper everything was going to be okay. I wiped away my own tears and turned my attention back to the altar.

"Not once did my son ask you to accept his beliefs. All he wanted was to be allowed to remain a member of this church where he could worship the Lord as he's done since he was a little boy, but we see that's impossible. Not here. This town has turned its back on him. Many members of this congregation have done the same, not to mention the school administration."

"What I think hurts most of all is his own father won't even look at him. Aren't you supposed to love your child unconditionally? Even if you don't agree with him? Even if he breaks your heart? Even if he's not at all what you expected him to be?"

Overcome with tears and emotion, Debbie closed her eyes and leaned against the podium for support. Lucas was out of his seat in flash, rushing to her side and taking her by the hand. She was pointing to her Bible and whispering furiously. Lucas then nodded and cleared his throat before facing the congregation.

"Debbie would like to leave you with this scripture from the book of Exodus. Chapter thirty-four, verses six and seven," Lucas said. "*And the Lord passed by before him, and proclaimed, The Lord, The Lord God, merciful and gracious, longsuffering, and abundant in goodness and truth, keeping mercy for thousands, forgiving iniquity and transgression and sin.*"

"Amen," I said through my tears.

"Amen," Tommy and Aubrey echoed.

Debbie hugged him before placing her hand in his, and I watched with pride as my fiancé—and the future father of my children—escorted a Mama Bear straight down the aisle and right out the double doors of Sycamore Baptist Church.

Debbie's courage made me brave, and that's why on

Monday afternoon, I decided to face my very own Goliath, all by myself.

"Miss Bray, I've been expecting you."

Principal Mullins took a seat behind his desk as I closed the door behind me.

"This will just take a moment. I just wanted to let you know I will not be seeking a renewal of my contract next school year."

He couldn't hide his surprise. "Is that so?"

I nodded.

"You have a job offer elsewhere?"

"No, I don't. Not yet."

He smiled. "I hope you don't assume I will be offering you a glowing recommendation."

"Actually, it's my hope you won't offer any recommendation—glowing or otherwise. You want me to leave, and I wish to go. We both get what we want."

"And what about Mr. Miller?"

"That's between you and Mr. Miller," I said calmly. "He's right outside. I'm sure he's eager to speak to you, as well."

Mullins leaned back in his chair.

"So, the two of you are leaving Sycamore Falls."

I remained quiet. It wasn't any of his business what we were doing.

"I heard about your engagement. I haven't had the chance to congratulate you."

"I don't need your congratulations," I said. "You were right. Sycamore High isn't a good fit for me. I will be tendering my resignation, effective July 1."

Principal Mullins sighed loudly.

"Sarah, I hate that it has come to this. This was never about *you*."

I quickly rose from my chair. "No, but you made it about me, and about Lucas, and I refuse to work for someone so manipulative. You've gotten what you wanted. Matt's gone, and now, so am I."

"Miss Bray . . ."

I didn't even look back as I walked out, slamming the door behind me. Lucas was out of his seat in an instant, taking my hand and pulling me close.

"I'm okay." My hands were shaking and my vision was a little blurry, but I'd never felt stronger.

"Go on home," Lucas whispered.

"I want to wait for you."

"It's a beautiful day," he said, smiling down at me. "I'll deal with Mullins, and then I need to make some copies for tomorrow. Why don't you meet me at the falls?"

It'd been so long since we'd visited the falls, and I felt a rush of excitement. A trip to the falls was exactly what we needed.

It might have been February, but spring was coming, which was evident by the flowers already trying to bloom along the trail. Despite my aggravation with the people in our town and my desire to leave it all behind, I knew I'd never find another place as beautiful as the falls.

I would miss it.

We would visit, of course. The house would still be here, and we'd want to see Aubrey and Tommy, but I needed a clean slate. A true, fresh, start without the memories and negativity that surrounded my hometown.

Lucas had already called to let me know he was on his way. His meeting with Mr. Mullins had been heated, but in the end, the principal had apologized for dragging us into the middle of his personal vendetta against Matt. He even tried to convince Lucas to rethink his resignation, but his plea fell on deaf ears.

We were moving on to our new lives in our new hometown.

Wherever that may be.

The wind was chilly against my skin as I made my way

toward the falls. I'd just stepped onto the sand when I noticed someone sitting against our rock.

He was wearing a Panther Green hoodie and gazing out at the water.

Matt.

He was skinnier than I remembered. And pale. So pale.

His head pivoted toward me, and he sighed.

"Of all the people who might have found me, why did it have to be you?"

His words ripped through me, piercing my soul, and shattering my heart.

"I can't do this with you here," he whispered gravely. His left hand dangled at his side, but his right hand remained his pocket. "I'm already going to hell, but I won't do that to you. I won't. Not to you."

I had no idea what he was talking about.

"What are you doing out here, Matt?"

"Escaping," he said softly. "I'm just trying to escape, Miss Bray."

I cautiously took a step forward and sat down on the rock.

"That's why I come here, too. It's peaceful here."

"Peaceful," he murmured.

Matt stood and walked along the sandy shoreline, stopping just short of the river.

"Do you think it's true, Miss Bray?"

"Is what true?"

"What they say about washing your sins away?" Matt said as he toed the murky water. "Do you think there's enough water in his river to wash away my wickedness? To make me the son my father wants me to be? To be the man this town wants me to be?"

"Matt, you're wonderful just as you are."

He laughed darkly. "I'm probably going to jail. I'm a disgrace to my father. My mother is filing for divorce and looking for a job in Winslow. My mom hasn't worked a day in her life, but because of me, she's going to be flipping burgers at some fast food place just because her son is evil."

He finally removed his right hand from his pocket, and that's when I saw it. He'd been holding it all this time, and my body began to shake.

And it was silver.

"Matt, why do you have a gun?"

I heard a rustle on the path, and suddenly, Lucas was there. His eyes widened as they flickered between me, and an oblivious Matt. With his back turned to us, he gazed across the water with the gun at his side.

"They say God works in mysterious ways," he whispered over the rushing water. "They're right. He sent you here, because He knew I wouldn't hurt myself. Not in front of you. You've seen enough death to last a lifetime. I won't do that to you. I won't make you live with my weakness. I won't."

Relief flowed through me as Lucas inched closer. His trembling hands found mine and pulled me close to his side.

"I want you to go home, Miss Bray."

I forced my voice to remain strong. "I'm not going anywhere."

He shook his head and lifted the gun close to his temple. My feet itched to move closer, but Lucas held me tight.

"You know that kid in Memphis?" Matt asked, his voice dripping with despair. "I wonder if he felt like this. I wonder if he felt the hatred that I feel from almost everyone in this town. I wonder if he was relieved when that basketball player walked into the cafeteria and shot him right there in front of the rest of the students. I think I'd be relieved . . . to have it over. Done. No more guilt. No more hatred. No more pressure to be something I'm just . . . not."

"Matt, I couldn't save him," I whispered tearfully.

"Maybe he wasn't worth saving," he said, his voice void

of emotion. "I'm not."

Finally, he turned around. He didn't seem surprised to see Lucas standing there. I tried to take a step closer, but Lucas's arms tightened around me, holding me in place.

"I have to help him."

Lucas closed his eyes in defeat, but he didn't let me go. Instead, he took my hand and led me closer to the water.

"Matt, please throw the gun in the water," Lucas said softly.

The boy tilted his head to the side.

"You really love her, don't you, Mr. Miller."

"Yes, I do."

"Then, I'm begging you. Please take her home."

"I can't do that. She loves you, Matt. She'd never forgive me if I left you out here all alone."

"She can't see this," he whispered.

"You're right. She can't."

Matt's eyes flickered to mine, and for a few heart-stopping moments, I was back in that Memphis cafeteria. But this time, I wasn't staring into the dead eyes of a high school senior. I was looking into the sweet eyes of a lost and desperate child.

My child, just like this mother had said.

"Matt, you are a kind and compassionate young man who is going to find his place in the world," I murmured softly. "It's so easy to believe the negativity, but you are a *good* person. You're so good, and you are going to go to college, and do something really wonderful with your life. And you are going to invite me to your college graduation, and I'm going to sit with your mom, and we're going to scream so loudly when they call your name."

At the mention of his mom, Matt's haunted eyes flickered to life.

"You are not weak. You are strong. So much stronger than this. *This* is not the answer." My voice was just a whisper as I raised my hand. I felt Lucas stiffen next to me, but he stayed quiet while Matt gazed at my outstretched hand. "Please give me the gun."

Matt shook his head.

"Tell me it'll get better," he begged softly, tears rolling down his cheeks.

"It will get better," I promised. "The only way it could get worse is if you pull that trigger. Please give me the gun, Matt."

Seconds. Minutes. Hours.

I had no idea how much time passed as we stared at each other, until finally, he removed the gun from his temple.

"I won't give it to you, Miss Bray. I won't let you touch it."

Turning around, Matt raised the gun into the air and swiftly tossed it into the muddy waters of the Sycamore River.

Chapter Twenty-seven

"That was Lucas on the phone," Aubrey said, handing me a cup of tea. "He's on his way home."

I nodded, pulling my grandma's blanket tighter around my shoulders and taking the mug in my hand. I couldn't seem to get warm, no matter how many blankets I had wrapped around me.

"Where's Matt?"

"At the hospital," Aubrey replied. "He's been admitted, but his mom is right by his side. Tommy and Lucas made sure she was allowed to stay."

"How is she?" It was such a stupid question. No doubt, the woman was a basket case.

"She's hopeful and very grateful to you."

I leaned my head back against the couch and closed my eyes, waiting impatiently for Lucas to get home. I needed his arms around me, but I'd insisted he take Matt to his mother and then follow them to the hospital. I'd begged to go, but Lucas had vehemently refused. Instead, he'd called our best friends, and Aubrey had driven me home.

Now, she was driving me crazy.

"We could look at some wedding dresses," she offered, pointing toward the laptop on the coffee table. "Or invitations? Or maybe flowers? Have you thought about what kind of flowers you want? I assume wildflowers since you're getting married at Sycamore Falls."

She was just trying to distract me. I knew this, and I appreciated it, but getting married at the falls was not an option anymore. It was no longer the most beautiful place on earth to me.

We heard the kitchen door slam, and every muscle in my body relaxed when Lucas walked into the living room.

"Hi," I whispered.

"Hey," he replied tiredly, sitting down on the couch and instantly pulling me against his side. "Are you cold?"

I nodded and snuggled close.

"Is Tommy home?" Aubrey asked, and he nodded. "Then I should probably go. You're okay?"

"I'm okay. Thanks, Aubrey."

"Call me tomorrow?"

I promised I would.

After she left, Lucas and I stayed on the couch for what seemed like hours. I was finally warm and relaxed, and no matter how many times he asked if I was ready for bed, I just couldn't make myself move.

"How is he?"

Lucas sighed softly and kissed my forehead.

"He's under seventy-two hour observation. It's standard procedure, the doctor said."

I nodded. "What about Debbie?"

"She's very shaken up, but Bill arrived not long after Matt was admitted."

"Bill?"

"Matt's dad."

I stiffened.

"I think it was the first time I'd ever seen a grown man cry. Finding out your son was that close to ending his life apparently put some things in perspective for Bill Stuart. I'm not sure Debbie will be able to forgive him, but she didn't ask him to leave. When Tommy and I left, they were talking and holding hands," Lucas said.

I buried my face against his chest as he held me tighter.

"When I saw Matt with the gun in his hand . . ." Lucas whispered, his voice aching. "All I could think about was getting you out of there."

"He never would have hurt me."

"I didn't know that. *You* didn't know that."

"I had to help him, Lucas."

"I know, and you did. You saved his life, Sarah."

Lucas pulled me into his lap and held me close, rocking me, and whispering the sweetest words against my ear. Overwhelmed with all of the emotion I'd been holding in for hours, I finally dissolved into tears.

"We have company."

I finished flipping the pancakes before joining Lucas at the kitchen door. I squealed when I saw Matt and Debbie were making their way up the sidewalk.

"I'll finish breakfast," Lucas said with a grin. "Go say hello."

I kissed his cheek and quickly rushed out the door, letting it slam behind me.

It had been three weeks since that day at Sycamore Falls. Debbie had called with daily updates, but we hadn't been allowed to visit. Matt needed time to concentrate on his recovery, his doctor had said. Taking one look at him as he walked up the steps, it was obvious the treatment was working. Matt's eyes were bright and alive, and he looked healthier than he'd appeared in months.

I didn't even say hello. I simply rushed toward him,

wrapping my arms around him, and hugging him tightly.

He laughed. "Hey, Miss Bray."

"Hey," I said, wiping the tears from my eyes. I couldn't stop smiling. "Are you hungry? We were just making pancakes."

Lucas appeared in the doorway, grinning at each of them.

"We can't stay," Debbie replied softly. She nodded toward the car, and I saw Mr. Stuart sitting behind the steering wheel. He nodded, offering me a timid smile. "I just wanted to say goodbye, Miss Bray."

"Goodbye?"

He nodded, and Lucas invited Debbie inside while Matt and I sat on the porch swing.

"This is a cool swing."

"Thanks. It was a gift from Lucas."

Sighing softly, he leaned back against the swing and began to push us gently.

"We're moving to Winslow. The doctor thinks it's a good idea to distance myself from Sycamore Falls, at least for a while. Dad found a house close to the hospital, so I can continue seeing my therapist. He's trying really hard, Miss Bray. He still isn't happy with me, but I don't expect him to be. I don't need his acceptance. I just need my dad, you know?"

I nodded.

"Patrick dropped all the charges, so I don't have to worry about that anymore."

"He did?"

"Yeah. He admitted to his attorney he'd been the one to bring the pipe, and I was just defending myself. He just wants to move on with his life, too. His dad is pissed, but Patrick's eighteen. There's nothing he can do."

It was the best news I'd heard in weeks.

"What about high school?"

"It's all worked out. I'll finish school there, and I'll still graduate in May." Matt smiled sheepishly. "I've been accepted to Winslow Community College."

I grinned. "That's great!"

"It's just two years," he explained, "then I'll transfer to finish my teaching degree."

"You still want to teach?"

He shrugged. "You've inspired me, Miss Bray, what can I say?"

I couldn't hide my smile.

"You're the best teacher I've ever had," he said sincerely. "You made us think. You told us it was *okay* to think. To ask questions. To not settle. And you told us the world isn't really much different from Sycamore Falls, which is something I never would have believed." He paused and took a deep breath. "And you didn't judge me. Even though I know you don't approve of the way I'm living my life. You love me anyway. I'll never forget that for as long as I live."

He grew quiet then, and I knew he was trying to find the words to say what was really on his mind. He wanted to apologize, and while it wasn't necessary, I knew it was probably something he felt compelled to do.

"That day at the river," Matt whispered. "I want to apologize. I really think God brought you there to save me. He knew you and my mom would be the only two people who could talk me out of it, and she couldn't have handled it. Thankfully, He knew you could. You're the strongest person I know, Miss Bray."

I swallowed down the emotion that was bubbling in my throat.

"There's a little church in Winslow," Matt continued. "It's a really nice place. They don't care if you're black, white, gay, or straight. They're just glad you're there."

"It sounds like a great place."

"It is. You and Mr. Miller should visit sometime."

"I'm not sure where we'll be after the school year ends," I said. "We're not coming back to Sycamore High next year."

He looked surprised. "Because of me?"

"No, it has nothing to do with you." I patted his hand reassuringly. "Sycamore Falls just isn't the place for us."

Matt studied my face carefully. "What about your house?"

"We'll keep the house, and we'll visit from time to time. We just want a fresh start for our new life."

"I understand." Matt gazed out across the yard at the mountains in the distance. "You know, there are a lot of good things about Sycamore Falls."

"Like what?"

"Well," he said quietly, "in August, I always loved riding the merry-go-round at the county fair even though I'm way too old for it. Despite everything, I love the people in this town. I love that they smile and wave even if they don't know your name. I love that I can sit on anybody's porch and look across their yard, and all I can see are mountains. For seventeen years, I was happy here. I wasn't content, but I was happy. It's just not the place for me, either. Not right now."

It amazed me this young man could find something positive to say about a town that had treated him so harshly.

"Come on, Miss Bray." He grinned, nudging me with my shoulder. "There has to be something you like about Sycamore Falls."

I started with the obvious and easiest answer.

"I love this house. It's big and filled with memories, and it's mine. I love that my grandma knew me better than I knew myself, because somehow, she realized I would want to come home someday . . . that I'd *need* to come home. She could have sold this house, but she gave it to me. She knew . . ."

Suddenly, I remembered something Catherine Thomas had told me during my first trip to the grocery store. *"Grace always said a young girl needs to spread her wings, but a young woman needs roots, as well."*

"Roots and wings," I whispered with a smile.

"So we're both flying away," Matt said with a bright grin. "We'll be back, though. Those Sycamore roots run deep, Miss Bray."

He hugged me tightly just as Debbie and Lucas walked back out onto the porch. Matt and I rose from the swing, and Lucas wrapped his arms around me.

"That's some rock on your left hand," Matt announced, making us all laugh. "I want an invitation to your wedding."

"And we want an invitation to your college graduation."

"You got it."

I stepped away from Lucas, and was immediately enveloped in Debbie's arms.

"I can't thank you enough," she whispered against my ear. "Your mother would be so proud of the woman you've become. So proud."

Not trusting myself to speak, I smiled through my tears.

Lucas's arms found me once again, and he stood behind me, pulling me close to his chest, while we watched Matt and his mom walk hand-in-hand toward their car.

"Don't be nervous," Lucas whispered, squeezing my hand as we pulled into the parking lot of Riverdale High School.

"I'm not nervous."

I was such a liar. I was a complete wreck because I wanted this so badly.

We wanted this so badly.

Riverdale was a two-hour drive from Sycamore Falls. It was a college town with a population of nearly twenty thousand people. It was thriving, which was evident by the beautiful new high school that had just been built, which would be opening in August.

It wasn't a small town, but it wasn't a large city, either. For us, it was perfect.

Finding it had been a complete accident. While I was handling the wedding planning, Lucas had glued himself to his laptop, checking out real estate websites and searching for houses in our price range. We'd found the beautiful white house in Riverdale, complete with a wrap-around porch and a lovely view of the mountains.

It was hard to escape the mountains.

The house was perfect, with four bedrooms and stainless steel appliances in the kitchen. I was in love, but neither of us was eager to make an offer with unemployment looming. The realtor, sensing she was losing a sale, immediately told us about the new high school. We drove straight home and applied online. The very next day, we each received phone calls, requesting interviews.

The stars were aligning.

As long as I didn't blow this interview.

We walked hand-in-hand into the lobby of the high school. It still smelled of fresh paint, and construction workers were still milling around, putting last-minute touches along the baseboards and hanging pictures along the walls. It was only early May, but it looked very close to completion.

The office was brightly lit and painted with a soft, mint green. The secretary smiled brightly at us, and then we both jumped when we heard our names.

"You must be Lucas and Sarah."

We looked toward the principal's office to see a woman standing in the doorway. She looked around my age, dressed casually with her hair in a ponytail.

"Come in," she said, smiling and waving us inside. Surprised, Lucas and I looked at each other. "I figure you're a package deal, right? So, I might as well interview you both at the same time."

Relief flowed through me and we followed her into her

office.

"Please excuse the mess." She picked up a stack of files, making a place for us to sit in the two chairs facing her cluttered desk. "We're still trying to get things organized. I hear power drills in my sleep, I swear."

We laughed nervously and took our seats.

Smiling brightly, she introduced herself. "I'm Phoebe Hamilton. I've lived in Riverdale all my life. I actually went to high school in the old building. That place has been around since my father had been a kid, if you can imagine. We needed a new school so badly."

"It's a beautiful building," Lucas said.

"We're very proud of it. The current principal is retiring at the end of this school year. He was *my* principal when I was in school, and I've been his assistant for a couple of years. Many people say I'm too young to lead my own school, but I'm ready to prove them wrong."

Phoebe took a deep breath and smiled widely.

"This is probably the most unprofessional interview ever, but I don't believe in intimidation. If you work here, we're a team. I am on your side—always—as long as you love your kids and do your job." She shuffled some papers on her desk. "This is why I was so excited to see your application, Sarah. Your reputation precedes you."

"Great," I mumbled.

Lucas reached for my hand and gave it a squeeze.

"It *is* great," Phoebe said with a nod. "I knew your name sounded familiar, so I did some digging. The fact you're still in the profession after what you encountered in Memphis proves to me you are exactly the kind of teacher I want in my school."

I sighed with relief. "Thank you."

"And Lucas," she said with a laugh. "How a Yankee ended up in a place like Sycamore Falls is a story I *really* want to hear someday, but your evaluations are flawless and you come highly recommended from your previous placements. I'd be honored to have you, as well."

We offered her our resumes, which she examined closely. She asked each of us questions, listening intently and making notes in our files. Throwing caution to the wind, Lucas explained why he left New York, and I told her all about Matt and the circumstances surrounding our decision to leave Sycamore High School.

It was the only time throughout the entire interview when Phoebe Hamilton was speechless.

"You see it on television all the time," she said quietly. "Kids being bullied to the point they see no possible way out. We are a profession ruled by test scores, and sometimes, we forget there are bigger lessons that need to be learned. Sometimes, teaching tolerance and love is far more important than teaching them about chemical equations and Robert Frost."

Lucas and I shared a smile—a smile that plainly said we would gladly beg this woman for a job.

Luckily, the stars aligned, and we didn't have to.

$\mathscr{C}$hapter $\mathcal{T}$wenty-eight

"Graduation is a bittersweet time, when we take the time to remember our past while looking forward to our future."

Howie had practiced his Valedictorian speech for nearly a month. He'd written it, revised it, and written it again. I'd helped him with the grammatical errors, but the words were all his.

It was probably a hundred degrees inside the gym, which was filled to capacity. Once the bleachers were full, people had begun to line the walls. High school graduation was as important a tradition as Friday night football games, and the town had practically shut down in anticipation of the ceremony.

"We have the opportunity to make new friends, and we have the chance to remain close to the friends we love. It's strange, thinking there are faces in this crowd I may never see again. We'll go to different schools. Some of us won't go to school at all. Some of us will move far away, and many of us will stay right here in Sycamore Falls. I will be attending Winslow Community College before transferring to finish my Bachelor's degree. I don't plan to return to Sycamore Falls to live, but a very wise teacher taught me you never know when life might bring you home, even if it just brings you home for a little while."

Lucas brushed his lips against my temple, and I smiled.

The students, dressed proudly in green gowns, made their way to the stage, and I couldn't help but think about Matt. He wouldn't be walking across any graduation stage; his high school diploma would be mailed to his home.

I couldn't be disappointed, though. Matt wasn't. He was healthy and strong and sharing an apartment with Howie in the fall. Howie had proven himself to be a true friend, and I couldn't have been prouder of him.

A sea of emerald caps were tossed into the air, and with a deafening cheer, the senior class of Sycamore High School went out to face the world.

And so did two of their teachers.

The June skies were beautiful and blue, and the flowers we'd planted last year were finally blooming.

"It's a beautiful day for a wedding," Olivia whispered in my ear.

I giggled and closed the curtain.

"It certainly is."

"Nervous?"

I shook my head. "Not at all. I don't think I've ever felt more content."

She smiled wistfully and adjusted the veil on my head. I'd threatened to forego the veil entirely, but Lucas's mom had found this one in a vintage shop in Manhattan. It was simple and pretty, and complemented my dress perfectly.

"Are you disappointed we aren't having a bigger

wedding?"

Our guest list contained a grand total of twenty people. The wedding cake had two tiers, and we'd only agreed on two because the baker insisted we freeze the top tier for our first anniversary.

"I could never be disappointed," Olivia said softly. "My son is marrying the girl of his dreams. The girl of his *mother's* dreams. You make him happier than he's ever been. If this is the wedding you want, then this is the wedding you should have. And to have it in your grandmother's front yard, where it all began—"

"Technically, it all began in Mr. Johnson's hardware store."

She laughed. "You know what I mean."

"I do."

Turning back toward the mirror, I was adjusting my veil when someone gently rapped on my bedroom door. Lucas's dad peeked inside, smiling brightly when his eyes settled on me.

"I have a very impatient son who wants to see his beautiful bride."

Olivia and I laughed.

"Are you ready?" she asked gently.

I took one last look at myself in my grandmother's full-length mirror.

I'd never been more ready for anything in my entire life.

"Dearly beloved . . ."

Pastor Martin was speaking. I was sure of it. He was offering words of hope and wisdom and gratitude, but I was oblivious to all of it.

All I could see was him, and his crystal-blue eyes, standing in front of my grandmother's house. All I could feel was his hand as he slipped my wedding band against my finger, and all I could hear was his soft voice as he promised to love me until the day we died.

We'd barely finished kissing before our family and friends surrounded us. Aubrey held a sleeping Daniel in her arms while Tommy kissed my cheek and shook Lucas's hand. Mr. Johnson and his friends from the hardware store congratulated us and gave us a toolset for the new house. Howie arrived with his girlfriend, a pretty girl named Mia, who he'd met in Winslow. Catherine Thomas brought a fruit basket from the grocery store and made me cry when she told me how proud my grandmother would be of me. Even Monica had accepted our invitation, and we had the chance to meet her professor boyfriend.

And of course, looking happier and healthier than ever, was Matt Stuart, with his mother by his side.

It was the perfect day, full of smiling faces and happy tears.

"You look so sad, baby," Lucas said has he placed the box of books next to the door.

It has been an emotional morning. Over breakfast, we'd said our goodbyes to Aubrey and her family. Nearly everything we owned was packed into boxes and loaded into the moving van. I had saved the kitchen for last, knowing it would affect me the most.

"I'm not sad, really." Dropping onto the floor, I grabbed a couple of cookbooks. They were all making the trip with us to Riverdale. "I'm just emotional, I guess."

Lucas nodded before bending down and kissing my forehead.

"Are you okay? I've got two more boxes to bring downstairs."

"I'm okay," I said, smiling up at him. He kissed me softly before making his way back upstairs.

"I'm going to need a bigger box," I muttered. I really

didn't need all of the cookbooks, but I just couldn't bear to leave them behind.

We were still undecided on what to do with Grandma's house. Mr. Johnson had offered to oversee it for now, but I knew someday, I'd have to make a decision. For now, it would sit here, collecting dust, just as it had before I'd returned to Sycamore Falls.

I'd just reached for the last cookbook when I noticed an envelope sticking out of the back page. Opening it up, I gasped when I noticed my name on the front. The penmanship was shaky, but I instantly recognized my grandma's handwriting.

Carefully, I placed the book into the cardboard box before lifting the seal on the faded white envelope. With trembling fingers, I unfolded the letter.

The first thing I noticed was the date.

My grandmother had written this letter one week before her death.

Tears swam in my eyes as I began to read.

Dear Sarah,

If you're finding this letter, that means you've come home, just as I knew you always would.

My time in this world is coming to an end. I know this. I feel this. And I have to say it's the most peaceful thing—knowing the end is near. You wouldn't think so, would you? You might expect someone to be scared of the unknown, but I'm not afraid.

I'm tired. I'm sick. I've been sick for a while. You knew a little about that, but not enough. I didn't tell you everything because I knew you'd give up on your dreams just to come home and be with me. And for what? To watch me wither away? Why put you through that when there was nothing you could possibly do to save me? I apologize for keeping you in the dark, but we both know it's for the best. These days, my happiness comes from knowing you're happy.

I've realized I've neglected to tell you some important things about life. Lessons I've learned that, I hope, will help you during your journey through your own life. You were always such a good student, but these aren't lessons you'll learn from your textbooks. These are life lessons, and I want to share some of them with you.

People—and not just those who live in small towns—can be narrow-minded and set in their ways. You will meet these people, and you will have to deal with them on a daily basis. There are two subjects that will always cause a fight, so avoid them. Never discuss politics. Never discuss religion.

It's nobody's business who you vote for, and it's nobody's business how you pray.

As you know by now, I've left the house to you. It's filled with memories, but do not feel you have to make your own memories within these walls. It's okay to build your own walls. Build your own life, even if it isn't in Sycamore Falls. You can make memories anywhere. You can be happy anywhere.

Friends come and go. It's a sad fact of life. Sometimes, it's not so sad. Some friendships aren't meant to last forever. Catherine Thomas still visits me every day. There are neighbors I've known for fifty years who haven't darkened my door. You learn who your true friends are when you need them the most. Those are the friendships to treasure.

And finally, when it comes to love, do not settle for anything less than a man who absolutely adores you. This doesn't mean you agree with everything he says, or with everything he does. It means he treats you with respect, and he shows you every day you are loved.

And that works both ways. Men don't admit it, but they need to be adored, too.

Show him every day.

I hope you've found him by now. But if not, you will.

I know you will.

You are a strong woman in a long line of strong women. I don't know where you are in your life right now, but I know you are making me proud. And maybe, someday, you'll make a list of your lessons learned, and you'll share them with your own granddaughter.

I love you, baby girl.

Love,
Grandma

Tears flowed down my cheeks as I carefully folded the letter and gently placed it back into its envelope.

"That's the last of it," Lucas announced. He stopped abruptly on the landing when he noticed my tears. Dropping the boxes onto the floor, he was at my side in an instant, lifting me off the ground and pulling me into his arms.

"What's wrong?" Lucas whispered, placing me on the counter. He brushed the hair away from my eyes and tenderly kissed my wet cheeks.

"I found this letter."

He looked confused as he opened it, but his face flickered with understanding when his eyes roamed the page.

"She'd be so proud of you, baby," he said, pressing a kiss to my forehead.

"Do I show you every day how much I love you?"

"Every single day," he murmured sweetly. "Do I show you how much I absolutely adore you?"

"Since the very first day we met."

Lucas kissed me softly before lowering me down onto the floor. He grabbed the last of the boxes while I took one last look around my grandmother's kitchen.

"I really do hope you're proud," I whispered into the air, before flipping off the lights and locking the door behind me.

Lucas was waiting for me on the porch swing.

"That's coming with us, right?"

He grinned. "I was hoping you'd say that."

Fifteen minutes later, the porch swing was packed away in the moving van, and I was standing in front of the house I'd loved for so long. In many ways, this would always be my home—my little sanctuary nestled in the mountains of Sycamore Falls.

Strong arms encircled my waist, reminding me that my real sanctuary was right here, and it had nothing to do with geography.

Lucas was my sanctuary.

Lucas was my home.

And I was his.

"Any regrets?" Lucas asked.

I had asked myself that question for weeks now. Would I regret leaving Sycamore Falls? Was I the same old Sarah—packing my bags and avoiding my problems?

"Lucas, do you think we're running away?"

He sighed softly and kissed my hair. "No, sweetheart. I think we're moving on to a new life. Just like Matt. He's happier now. Most importantly, he's alive, and that's because of you. Maybe that's what brought you back to Sycamore Falls."

Smiling, I twisted around in his arms. "What about you? What do you think brought you to Sycamore Falls?"

His beautiful blue eyes gazed into mine.

"You."

It was the perfect answer.

Rising on my toes, I kissed him softly.

"Are you ready to go, Mrs. Miller?"

I was still getting used to the name, but I couldn't deny how happy it made me.

Sarah Miller.

A new name for my new life.

"I'm ready."

And I knew it was true.

Epilogue

There was just something about "Pomp and Circumstance" that made me sentimental. The song signified an ending . . . and a beginning, and I always found it bittersweet.

This graduation was far different from the one we'd attended in Sycamore Falls over four years ago. Instead of a sea of green, today's graduates were wearing black robes, and the gymnasium was on the campus of the University of Tennessee.

Today, Matt Stuart was graduating *summa cum laude*, and in the fall, he would be teaching English literature in a high school just outside of Knoxville. During his time at UT, he'd volunteered with local youth groups, giving presentations on coping with bullies and embracing diversity. He'd kept in touch with us through emails and

Skype, and he and Howie were still the best of friends.

"How are you feeling?" Lucas asked.

Sighing, I placed my hand along my stomach. Morning sickness had never been this brutal with our first baby. Gracie had arrived just after our one-year anniversary. She was beautiful, with her father's sweet eyes and calm demeanor. I was just four months along, but I could already see this second child was going to be the death of me.

"Apparently, your son wasn't happy with his breakfast."

He grinned. "He's a boy?"

"Must be. My daughter never made me this queasy."

Lucas knew better than to laugh. Instead, he kissed my temple and pulled a small packet of crackers out of his blazer pocket. He kept a supply of them on hand at all times, which only solidified his status as the perfect man.

Thousands of graduates filled the seats. There was really no way to spot Matt in the crowd, so we sat in the bleachers, hot and uncomfortable, as the president of the university called name after name. Finally, the graduates from the College of Education were asked to rise, and that's when I saw him—standing tall in his cap and gown—walking toward the stage.

"Matthew Stuart," the president announced.

His smile was just as I remembered—big, bright, and full of life. Matt shook the man's hand and accepted his degree, pausing at the end of the stage to wave toward the crowd. I gasped, realizing his parents had been sitting just five rows below us. Debbie was crying uncontrollably with her husband by her side, both looking unbelievably proud of their son.

"Matt!" Lucas yelled over the roar of the crowd, and his head jerked up, scanning the crowd, and our eyes locked.

With a smile as bright as the sun, he mouthed my name and offered me a wave.

I was so proud of myself. I managed to wait until he returned to his seat before I dissolved into tears.

Knowing the crowd would be crazy and we'd have zero chance of finding each other, the five of us had made plans to meet at a nearby restaurant for lunch. The place was busy, so Lucas had gone inside to reserve a table while I waited outside on the bench. I'd just finished calling the babysitter to check on Gracie when I heard my name being called from the parking lot. Glancing up, I saw Matt running toward me, and I started to rise.

"No, don't get up!"

"Matt, I'm just pregnant. I'm not dead."

"Still," he muttered as he sat down on the bench next to me. "You need to rest, Miss Bray . . . sorry, Mrs. Miller."

I smirked. "I keep telling you it's time you called me Sarah."

"Nah, too weird."

I shook my head. We'd had this discussion so many times over the past four years.

"You look good in that hat," I said, grinning at his graduation cap perched on his head.

"You think?"

I nodded. "Very smart."

Smiling, he lifted the hat off his head and placed it on top of mine.

"I want you to have it, Miss Bray." He grinned at the use of my maiden name. "You're still the smartest and strongest person I've ever met."

Tears flooded my eyes.

"Matt, I can't accept—"

"Yes you can," he said softly. "You taught me how to be a good teacher, Miss Bray. You deserve it, and I want you to take it home with you. I want you to show it your little girl, and when she asks what it is, tell her it's not just some stupid graduation cap. Tell her it's a symbol of love, and that love saved the life of your favorite English student."

My husband returned to find me a sobbing mess.

Matt looked horrified. "I didn't mean to make her cry, Mr. Miller."

Lucas chuckled and kissed my hair. By now, he was used to my hormonal crying jags.

Moments later, Matt's parents arrived and we shared hugs before the happy graduate led us all inside. As the hostess led us to our table, Lucas gently pulled me aside. Grinning down at me, he kissed me tenderly.

"Your smile is beautiful, Mrs. Miller."

I sighed contently and wrapped my arms around his neck.

"So is theirs," I whispered, kissing him softly, "and so is yours."

Book Club Discussion Questions

1. Sarah struggled with religion, especially after the death of her parents. Can you relate to Sarah's shaken faith? If so, did you find your peace?

2. While Lucas and Sarah may have had grounds to sue Principal Mullins for his blackmail, do you think that was a viable option for either of them?

3. Do you think Lucas, Sarah, and Matt "ran" away from their problems by leaving Sycamore Falls?

4. Have you ever been bullied or been witness to it? How did you handle the situation?

5. If you were Matt's mother or father, how would you have reacted to the news that your son is gay?

6. Did your perception of the people of Sycamore Falls change throughout the course of the book?

7. Sarah and Monica's friendship changed dramatically once Sarah returned to Sycamore Falls. Do you think they ever reconnected?

8. How realistic was the characterization? Would you want to meet any of the characters?

9. If you could write an alternate ending for the book, how would you write it?

10. If you were asked to choose your favorite scene from the book, which would you choose and why?

About the Author

USA Today Bestselling Author Sydney Logan writes heartfelt stories that feature strong women and the men who love them. In addition to her novels, she has penned several short stories and is a contributor to Chicken Soup for the Soul. She is a Netflix junkie, music lover, and a Vol for Life. Sydney and her husband make their home in beautiful East Tennessee.

To learn more about Sydney and her books, visit her online at sydneylogan.com.